LIFE'S PALIMPSEST:

LIFE CANNOT BE REWRITTEN WITHOUT SCARRING THE SOUL

Saúl Balagura

D1377948

Life's Palimpsest

Saúl Balagura

ISBN: 978-0-578-87192-9

For Robin & Miles
generous patrons
of the Arts.

Saul

Mar. 30. 2021

DEDICATION

To my wife, Ursula, who made my life possible.

TABLE OF CONTENTS

ACKNOWLEDGMENTS

When I sat down to write this novel, I had it all in my mind. But from brain to paper there is quite a road to travel and this one took many years. Throughout every sentence and paragraph my wife, Ursula, served as a loving, but severe critic. When all the words were finally in place, it was up to Irene Zion, a dear friend, to read the manuscript for content and to make suggestions that were of immense value. In addition, I wish to thank Doctor Samuel Mowerman and his wife, Charlotte Tomic for their encouragement and suggestions.

I wish I could also thank my agent, my editor(s) and publisher for their dedication to the project, but alas, they were not willing. It appears to me, that looking for them was akin to going fishing on a pond brimming with dead fish: No matter how many times I reeled that baited hook, there were no fish willing to bite. This is a sad metaphor for to world of contemporary publishing.

Saúl Balagura March 2021

PROLOGUE

Life cannot be rewritten without scarring the soul.

(A   poet   I know)

Perhaps you may ask, why such a title? The easy answer would be, "read the book and you'll find out." Writing a book, even a novel, is no easy task. Surely the author would want to give his book an attention calling title; something that will catch the eye —candy for the eyes— and hook the reader, making it impossible not to acquire. But it would not be fair with the readers, to make up a great title that has nothing to do with the book's contents. In ancient times, humans began painting or writing over stones. Eventually, writing was done over soft clay tablets that were then allowed to harden under the baking sun. One can imagine that such writing would not permit lengthy documents, for their weight would have been prohibitive. Human ingenuity came up with a better and lighter base for writing: the skin of animals, mostly sheep, cow, or goat. Of course, it had to be prepared before anyone could write on it. Animal skins had many uses and becoming writing scrolls was just one of them. Once the skins were selected, they had to be scraped smooth, stretched and dried. It was an elaborate process making these scrolls very expensive. This form of recording information has been used for at least 4,500 years. In order to economize, old manuscripts were erased and reused to write new documents. The word palimpsest comes from the old Greek word *palimpsestos* that means, "something rubbed smooth again." The major problem when rewriting on previously used skins is that the ghosts of previous writings can be seen as well. Hopefully, this metaphor illuminates this novel's title.

It is said that although a cloud is just water vapor, its shape is rigidly determined by an almost infinite set of physical conditions such that at any given moment it cannot look like any other cloud but itself. Each one of us at any given time is the result of an infinite number of factors and happenings that determine exactly what we are, who we are, with whom we interact. No story is isolated. No one person is an island. My mother used to tell me "nothing is new under the sun". The concept had not been an invention of hers. It turns out these words were said by King Solomon as part of a beautiful poem and written about 2,400 years ago as part of the Old Testament in Ecclesiastes, (*Kohelet* in Hebrew) 1:9. Indeed, the complete phrase is majestic: "What has been will be again, what has been done will be done

again, there is nothing new under the sun". When I was a child, the meaning of this phrase escaped me. As a grown man, I still am not able to fully comprehend its full meaning. The butterfly effect, that a flapping of its wings influences history —so interconnected are all things— may be another way of looking at it. In any event, sometimes, poems become reality.

Saúl Balagura May 2021

PART ONE

THE BEGINNING
IS THE END

1

It is late. The first rays of sun, squeezing through the branches of the pine tree forest on the eastern horizon, begin to shine through the lace curtains of the window in my study. I hope to have done justice to Moses Benjamin. Writing this book has taken many years, and I had to visit many places and interview countless number of people, for you see, Moses never bothered to put his thoughts in writing. He kept many inside his head. And although he touched a good number of persons, no one knew him wholly and even less of his story. Yet, the imagery that populated his mind was the most prodigious I ever encountered.

It has been decades ago, when I first had the privilege of meeting him. Many years had come and gone in that jetsam and flotsam we call living, when I finally was permitted and able to retire. I had not forgotten him, but he was not at the frontage of daily thoughts either. Rather, one morning, taking my breakfast on the back porch of my country house, I read a brief notice in the obituaries page of The Star-Ledger. Curiously, there was a photo of the man, but no name was given. He had died in a nursing home the previous week. I was shocked. The face in the photo reminded me of Benjamin's, but I was not completely sure. My memories were reawakened. The face staring at me had written on it so much suffering and so much soundlessness, that even after so many years had passed, it could only be his. I decided to look into it and prepared a small daytrip bag and left the following day for the city. My search would start at the nursing home. That was six years ago.

After digging in my own notes and interviewing a countless number of people, I began writing a novel. A book dealing with the most remarkable mind and life of my ex-patient. Of course, I had to change names, but all in all, I hope that I was able to bring to life, to you the reader, the person and peripatetic life of Moses Benjamin. It could happen to any one of us. Legit Cave, reader beware. What follows is the story.

Sincerely,

Jane McKensie, M.D., F.A.P.A.,

Retired Psychiatrist

It is not that I complain all the time, nor for that matter that I am silent most of the time. When it comes to life, and I mean life as it should be lived, with cloudy and sunny days, with children's cries and little hands sticky with melted chocolate, with adult eyes deep and sexy, and breasts calling upon you like mountains taunting to be escalated, that kind of life I am talking about, I like to say that I am a failure. But most people are failures in this respect too. I mean, how many people do you know can say without rationalizing that they are living, or have lived, a full and satisfying life? And coming to think about it, I am not sure that there are too many people that even think this way when it comes to assessing their own lives. I mean looking in the mirror and saying: am I happy and who am I, can I be better, could I have been something else? Yes, I know, you think this is a matter of "the grass is greener on the other side of the fence" kind of thing but believe me it is not. Not at all. It is a deadly serious matter.

I sit alone watching the day dying, for in spite all that sun and all that splendor it could not win the battle with the queen of the night and now it is time to submit to the daily blanketing of darkness. Darkness, mind you, that can be brightened by luminary planets and stars and constellations, making all as splendorous sometimes as the very day can be when the Sun is not too harsh and burning, and shade trees caressed by a mild wind, in turn cover with shady gentleness whomever stands beneath their canopy.

It is during moments like these when I miss my friends the most. Oh sure, I have plenty of friends: Look around. Wherever I turn to there be someone potential friend or a foe. But I am not talking about these kinds of friends. I am referring to friends with whom you feel fulfilled, with whom you feel there is no need to talk to fill the blank spaces of time, with whom a single interchange of a look can communicate that all is well, or not, at a level so deep within oneself that there are no words as of yet invented to convey all that is conveyed with by that simple glance, friends with whom you feel alone even if they are so close you can touch them, but not the kind of alone of loneliness, of a figure casting a single, painful shadow along a forgotten path, rather the kind of alone that one may feel if one is complete, whole, one with oneself, that kind of friend is what I am talking about. Coming to think about it, how many people –and I am counting you in this as well– can say they have had a friend like that?

So I am not perfect, they say. I have flaws, yes. I admit it. I am very aware of myself. When I look in the mirror, I see the person who is looking into the mirror, not some other image of who knows who. I have flaws, but who doesn't? And how many have had friends like the ones I am talking about? I have one such friend. Or at least, I had one such friend. No, I did not kill him. He died one day all of a sudden. One second he was alive and the next he was dead. There was nothing that could have been done. This kind of death comes unannounced. It strikes like lightening on a clear day. One is walking on a field covered with grasses and flowers bending to the gentle breeze and all of a sudden, from nowhere –or what appears to be nowhere– here descends, or ascends depending on what scientific basis you may be using to define a lightning strike, a million volts of power that pass through you from head to toe or toe to head and there is no functioning anymore. Every neuron and glial cell in the brain stops working within a nanosecond, the heart contracts no more, there is no breathing, no sensing, all of a sudden there is no more. Before, you were you and were thinking that this may be a good place and time to fart given the fact that there is no one around and then, all of a sudden: nothing. Before you were you, by whatever means you would like to think of yourself as you and a nanosecond later, there is no you. So, it was with my friend. He was laughing at a comment one of his patients had made, with that honest, open laugh he used to have, opening his mouth fully, so fully that one saw his uvula hanging there half contracted, solitary in the middle of his palate, perhaps moving to the rhythm of the laughter, almost like an opera singer singing a sustained note somewhere around the upper-middle range, and then, all of a sudden, he bent down and rested his head on his patient's clinical notes, the very notes he had been taking all those months, session after session, kind of an explorer's diary, but lacking description of mountain passes and rivers, instead describing unknown paths leading to self-discovery and the healing of past and ancient psychological wounds where the footprints carve entire personalities, and he stopped laughing and he who had been my friend just a second before ceased to be anything at that very moment. So I, who was alone when I was with my friend, now remain solitary, like a leafless tree: not even insects inhabiting its rotting bark.

Days come and go; sometimes the nights do the same. Mostly, when I look through the window hoping to see birds flying, I find nothing to see, often it is too hot or too windy or too lonely. Sure, I could talk to my other friends, the ones that call themselves my friends just because when they met me, they decided to call me by my first name. Who are they to sneer at all that I have gone through in my life, to desecrate my past, to swipe it clear of all that I was or knew, just because they assume that I am like one of them? Perhaps I am like one of them, perhaps they have smelled the odor of rotten flesh –human flesh– or have witnessed tears running down the haggard cheeks of someone that is about to lose a loved one, the very reason for them to exist, the very reason why they are who they are, the very reason why days seemed shorter and nights felt cool and safe, or perhaps they have seen eyes wide opened and tearless, too tired to blink, breathing shallow through ribs barely covered with skin.   Have they seen those little arms extending, rising away as if to reach something that no one but them can see? How many times have they seen what moments before were proud heads, bend their necks and rock back and forth at the tempo of their shallow sobs? Perhaps some have, but please don't think you are my friend just because you call me by my first name and I did not protest!

I remember the time when I was walking down this path, the grass kept short by the traffic that had compacted the earth beyond what any possible growth could sustain, roots hugged by fertile earth too tight around them, like parents that care so much for their children that don't permit them to develop. Walking this path, winding around shady trees and climbing and descending along gentle hills in a landscape that extended from where I walked to as far as the tallest mountains one can imagine, blue and pale bending upwards at the distant horizon with the white brush strokes of snow capping them under the hot and distant sun.   I had just recently lost my pony, my little horse friend, too fragile to live without me bottle-feeding him every day. Still can hear his footsteps as he trotted happily towards me searching with his soft muzzle my hand –poor replacement for his mother's love– avid for my touch. Yes, this is the way we are: we conform and content with second best after having lost best. Can you imagine walking on a street so muddy that you sink up to your knees in the stuff? My parents did so, many, many years ago when they were still not my parents and I their son: Winters as cold as freezing steel and wet as the bottom of a dark lake, blanketing all in crepitant shivers. That is the kind of parents I have; well, I had before they died and after they conceived of me; walking with freezing mud up to their knees across the Atlantic sea, running away from a world more murderous than the cold itself, running as far as they could go and still have feet, as far as they could be without feeling that stopping would permit their memories to bring them back to where they had run away from, like a giant rubber band. That is the stock I come from: parents that cared where they would have their children run, that cared who would teach them and who would guide them and be their friend. So, when I tell you that I was walking on that country path winding around gentle hills I am talking about God, yes God, in the shape of rolling hills covered with grass as green as green can be and still be grass and cows with their calves ruminating and roaming without fear under that same gentle breeze that made the trees bow in accordance with the laws of nature and that beckoned me to rest while they extended their shade unto the soft ground. It is so easy to say calves and to read the same word and think one caught the meaning of what the author meant when he wrote the word calf. But believe me, that when I think calf, I don't get the meaning of the offspring of a cow. What I get is that absolute serenity that nature can sometimes show you, and that if you were wise enough, perhaps you would soak it in and grow to a new level of understanding, or confusion, as the case may be. A calf is not just the offspring of a cow, it is also absolute tenderness, it is infinite dependency, it is innocence. Do you see? We do look at the world through different eyes. In any event, I kept walking and walking as far as I could walk and now, I forget where is it that I was trying to reach. And as I was walking, I remembered a passage from the Torah, referring to the first day of the month of *Sivan*:

"In the third month of the Children of Israel's exodus from the land of Egypt, on that day, they arrived in the Sinai desert. They journeyed from Rephidim and came to the Sinai desert, and camped in the desert; and Israel camped there, before the mountain."

I was not in the desert as the passage refers to, but

I could not help to feel that the distant mountain peaks were my Sinai; that if I could just reach them I too could receive the word of God; that I had a purpose in this world beyond consuming energy and occupying space. The Talmud teaches that God created man so that no two are physically alike and no two are of equal mind. But then I started thinking, and what about identical twins, are they not physically alike? And you can see that this really pulled me away from my mountain and back onto my dirt-packed path, way before I had the chance to receive any divine word, even if not at Sinai at least by the foothills of the mountain that beckoned me across air as clear as ethereal angel whispers and even though my ancestors might have gotten the law amidst thunder and cloud, I now, so far away from them, walked aimlessly on packed dirt. And on top of it all, I had forgotten where it was that I was going to begin with.

2

Sometimes I think I hear the quiet flutter of wings outside my window and look in vain for a sign of life. They say that the birds and the butterflies were the first to die in the concentration camps where all the friends of my parents died: First the birds, then the butterflies, then the honor, then the pride, then the hope. I keep looking for them, I know all of them could not possibly have died, but sometimes it is not the fact but the gesture that counts and not even my screams have brought them back, so I look at an empty park void of life, of insects, of birds, of nannies pushing carts with chubby babies, of children running in their wobbly legs and smiling faces towards mothers watching them with concern, nothing, just nothing.

We live in terrible times. It is said that at the beginning all was chaos and then God put order and created the universe. But I think that we are back where we started. Liberal thinkers have become leftist fanatics and have joined fanatics from the right; they are all obsessed with pushing their own agenda onto others, even if in doing so – or in order to accomplish this– they forbid opposing voices to speak, to be heard, to be counted among those that matter. There was a time when it was intellectually criminal to think that the end justifies the means. In fact, the concept that no evil act was justified, the concept of turning the other cheek, that one had to yield to pacifism, that no bad means could ever be justified by altruistic goals, that concept is now completely obsolete, even though in principle, it is held dearly in the pantheon of the gods. Isn't it curious that society always worships the very thing that they are soiling? We have become intransigent in our intolerance of any voice that may question the principles of free speech. Freedom fighters turn into murderers and when night comes, instead of spending a sleepless night, instead of vomiting at the very sight of their faces reflected in the mirror, instead of feeling shame as they prepare in the morning for another day of slaughter, sleep like drugged babies not even aware of the wrong they have committed on the prior day. Teachers, that for thousands of years have been in charge of passing knowledge from one generation to the next, have by and large, become passive, while generations of students

wash onto our societal shores carried by waves of
ignorance, ready to take on life's demands. We
have grown so inure to our collective arrogance
that we don't find fault when a totally biased person
is referred to as an analyst, forgetting that an
analyst should be a person that capable of
analyzing without introducing biases to the task.
We now listen to actors, in commercials, acting in
roles as if they were medical doctors, telling us
what to eat, how to diet, what to do that is best for
our own health, and we believe them, even though
they tell us that they are actors. The process
begun many years ago, I was just a child then, but
even so, I noticed. Politicians were not judged by
what they said or did, but by what the radio or
television expert analysts reported the politicians
had said or done. And now, of course, we have
gone several steps further, basically to be
controlled by what famous personalities advise us
to do or think. And if this were not enough, we
have injected hate into the whole process. Mind
you, that when two animals fight, there is no hate
involved, it is a confrontational fight. But when we
fight, we often fight with hate.

Yes, we live in terrible times. After the Holocaust
passed, the phrase about those that don't learn
from history are apt to relive it became popular.
But time has its way of eroding, filing away the
rugosity that the suffering of individuals provides to

the surface of our planet Earth. Now, a billion people deny the Holocaust ever existed, and at least two billion do not even know what the Holocaust was. And yet, when I stand still, I can hear those cries of agony, I can hear parents calling their children with ever more desperate shouts, I can see the distant columns of smoke carrying within them the ashes of hundreds of thousands of people, I can smell the absolute putrid air that filled the concentration camps' barracks, I can see into the sunken eyes that had lost all luster, that had no shine and no tears, no blink; I can see the shallow breathing of those that were close to death, perhaps just a few seconds or minutes away. And when I want to talk about these vivid, tender visions of mine, others, they turn their faces away.

We have become a hypocritical society too. We could not accomplish the duality of loving freedom and forbidding its realization without having a solid hypocritical core. I give you an example: We say we love pets but tolerate those that torture them. We love pets, but exclude them from hotel rooms and restaurants under the banner of being a health hazard and at the same time permit that mothers let their sickened mucus-dripping-coughing children walk on the tables and touch with their saliva impregnated short fatty little fingers the tablecloth, the china and the utensils in the very establishments where our pets are not allowed in. And of course, we care for our children, the very same children that are permitted to be born in homes that don't care about them; the same children that are supposed to learn so that they can grow-up to be free in the pursuit of happiness; the very same children that return home to find that not only no one helps them with their homework, but are actively discouraged to study, to learn; the very same society that underpays teachers and demand less of them than of a hair dresser in terms of accomplishing their task; the society that demands that its teachers should teach and discipline their students but forbids them to do so; the same society that in order to keep its children in school, forces into the same classroom bad and good, bright and slow-minded, evil and pure under the pretext that this variety will bring tides of good learning to the fragile minds –a concept as important as this has less research dedicated to it than the effort given to a single winter Olympics. A hypocritical society that values life above all things –that is why some object to the death penalty as punishment– and that is why we punish severely a pharmaceutical company that markets a product that may kill one of every one hundred thousand consumers helped by its drugs, but barely slap the hand of the drunken driver that terminates the existence –with a single turn of the wheel of his car– of a family on their way to church. So I ask you: is it not as it was in the beginning, before God said, "let there be light"? Do you expect that I see butterflies and flowers?

At night all is dark. Sometimes, during the day all is dark too. I am not talking of the darkness described by the color black, such a color only implies the absence of the reflection of light, I am talking of the darkness that may describe the absence of light, the absence of warmth, of a friendly hand, of puppy love, of grass bent by the breeze in afternoons of skies covered with puffs of clouds and birds flying high, it is that kind of darkness that sometimes comes over me in the middle of the day or even in the night. I can see then my grandfather with his curved back, walking slowly with a slight limp, holding me by his hand, walking towards the south end of town, or so I thought until not too long ago when I saw a map and stood corrected after noticing –after all this time– that we had been walking north: So is the legacy of carrying the memories of a small child. But it is those memories that make the very foundation of the pier from where we will eventually launch the boats of our lives. So, after I don't know how many years, it turns out that my grandfather and I had been walking in a northerly direction, perhaps as far as five or even ten city blocks, stopping under a large shady tree on the right side of the road, which would make it the east side of the road, and we would stand there, surrounded by green grass, with the horse racing track to our backs, looking at the distant mountains, under that tree. I am not sure we talked about anything in particular or anything at all; I am not sure that we spoke at all given that my grandfather did not speak the same language I was learning to speak and that, as of then, he had not been able to learn at all. Perhaps we talked using symbolic language, even emotional language, to communicate. After all, if we can use it with a dog, it certainly could be used between a child and his strange looking grandfather. Whatever we spoke about, I do remember that it was quieting, that I had an inner peace that filled me with content, even if all we did was just to stand there, under the shade of the large tree, and watched the mountain as it rose lazily in a series of ridges until it finally took off high into the horizon, where greens become pastel violets and time has no meaning. I might not have launched my boat from that pier of satisfying silence, and I will never know if it all had not turned differently had I done so. And now I am embedded in this mantle of darkness. I can see the lights of people trying to reach me, but I wonder if they are trying to reach me to sink me or to pull me up towards them. All is too confusing by now; one may even say it is too late. As my nanny used to say, "one sleeps according to the bed one makes" and I have made my bed the way I made it and that is that. Of course, it would be good if I could sleep on it, but it has been a long time since I could sleep.

Sleep is good. Sleep helps restore the wounds suffered during the day. Sleep brings resolution to the conflicts of the soul. Sleep is necessary for the body to dispose and metabolize the byproducts of a defective machine. It is a thing to behold, this sleep. I mean, how do you know that sleep is good if not because you wake up and realize that you were sleeping and then you fall asleep once more? In those nights when one sleeps through and through, there is no satisfaction of having slept, because there is no experience of having slept, there is only a feeling that you were awake and then that you woke up. But on those nights when you wake up in the middle of the night and feel cozy and not too cold and not too warm, and you coil within the cover sheets and fluff the pillow and begin to feel drowsy and then somnolent and then you wake up a few hours later and go through the same comforting experience, then, when you finally wake up in the morning and it is time to get up, you feel wonderful, you feel that you had a wonderful sleep even if you do not remember if you had a dream or not or if it was pleasant or not. So, when little by little, relentlessly, night after night, you begin waking up and surface to the point of becoming aware that you are not asleep but fully awake and you begin noticing the folds on the sheets of the bed, and the noises brought up by the silence of the night become more and more noticeable, when you can hear the wrist-watch left on the table fifteen feet away ticking and tacking, interrupted only by the rhythmic thumping of your heartbeat as you accommodate your head against the pillow that suddenly has become too hard or lumpy to remain in one position for too long, and when those moments of wakefulness become minutes and those minutes become halves of one hour and then hour after hour assaulted by thoughts that you cannot even finish having because just for a moment you go back into a sleep trance just to come back to full wakefulness and realize that just two minutes have elapsed since you last saw the fluorescent digital dial on the night table clock. And little by little, day after day, one becomes afraid of the coming night anticipating that it will bring eight or six hours of stretched time when in spite of being awake one is not capable of cogent thinking and simply becomes a victim, like in a torture chamber, incapable of controlling destiny, not knowing if one finally will be allowed to rest, and the experience repeats day after night after day, over and over until finally, one day, while you are sitting watching some program on the television, or reading a magazine article, without realizing it, you fall asleep and wake up four hours later feeling as if you had been drugged, and then realize that although the nap has brought some equilibrium into your life, now, having slept during the day, you will for sure not fall asleep during the night, and that the realization of this simple fact of life, wakes you up, out of your stupor, and then all that remains is to wait for the cycle to begin all over again. So, I vacillate from my chair as I look through my window at a park void of life. It is during these long nights that, out of nowhere, the memory of your first flannel blanket comes back to you to hunt you with the childhood feelings of pleasure that clinging to a soft flannel blanket in the middle of the night, when you awoke, if only momentarily, can truly fill a child's basket with utter delight. And it is upsetting, more so because it has happened to all of us, or almost all of us, that we lost our childhood flannel blanket. That somewhere, perhaps as we were becoming teenagers, one night we went to bed and did not notice that mother had replaced the blanket with a new one, and it would not be but many years later, when it was too late, that we would recall, in the middle of a sleepless night, that soft childhood blanket that gave us so much comfort and love.

The other day I was thinking about eating, I mean what we eat and why we eat it and clearly there is no clear answer for this complex issue. The amazing thing about eating is that once you have finished, it is a sure thing that you will start eating again in a few hours. Or, once one starts eating, no matter how hungry one was at the start, satiety will overcome hunger and one will stop eating. It is a law that can be stated as a cycle of hunger or a cycle of satiety, perhaps of both. It is not like breathing. The need for breathing is self-explanatory and highly convincing. One needs to breathe in and breathe out. The interesting thing is that although most people think that the need for oxygen is what triggers breathing, the truth could not be farthest from it: one breathes because of a craving to get rid of the carbon dioxide accumulated in the blood. That horrible need to take a deep breath after one holds breathing is not due to the depletion of oxygen from our system, but from the accumulation of toxic carbon dioxide. And yet, this apparent reversed imperative assures our survival from one moment to the next throughout our lives. Eating on the other hand does not follow the same rules. Very likely the mechanical and chemical signals that trigger the desire for food are not intrinsically life savers –one can certainly skip a meal without any consequences– rather, the physiological need for food is more subtle, it kind of reminds the organism that eating is desirable, not to say that the consequences of not eating are not dramatic and even lethal to the body, the problem is that it takes a rather long time to show its effects. Which brings me to the problem that came to me the last time I was looking at the ceiling one night, that is, the problem of hunger in our midst –and don't think that I didn't notice the two insipient crevices extending all the way across the ceiling from the window. During those few moments when the news media have nothing negative to report about the government, when the diplomatic core is in sync with our friends –allies and enemies– and when reporters find themselves close to reporting time and there is nothing to report about, when one more time, they consider that reporting the accomplishments of our scientist and artists has no value, during those moments they think of hunger in America. I don't mean hunger like it is twelve noon and I want a hamburger; rather, hunger like I have not eaten in several days. Of course, when time comes to document this horrible situation, to write about it, then truly the fan is hit by who knows what, because the pictures that the media come forth with are those of rather obese children and cigarette-smoking parents being interviewed by the decaying wood steps of their porch. I don't need to dream to see how starving children look like, their faces gaunt, caving in to the sinking skin that pulls at their eye-sockets, opening them wide and giving them that characteristic appearance that respects no boundaries of country, race, religion or upbringing; I don't need to imagine the dried up bodies of hungry children with their ribs pushing their way out from under their skins while their limbs, curved like parentheses, barely hold them up as they, unknowingly are being photographed by well-fed photographers and reporters secretly praying that more flies should land on the dried up mucus that now replaces the tears in their starving children's eyes; I have seen them all, by the hundreds in real life and by the thousands in photographs of war and persecution. Hence when the media tries to raise hell because we have starvation in America and all that they come up with is a couple of obese children, it makes me feel nauseous. Of course, all is relative:

we have re-defined poverty. For us, poverty means to have only one car (uninsured of course), and one refrigerator, and perhaps no dishwasher, and only one-color television, even if those are shared in a common room by seven people, while at the same time, a few clicks away in all other societies, the middle class is defined by wanting to have all those things that the American poor have. The system has gotten so rotten and distorted that our distinguished media cannot comprehend what real poverty means and is: people that are constantly feeling there are at the edge of a grave and that at any moment they may fall in, people that do not receive any subsidy from any government, that when sick have no place to go, that when dead have no tombstone to live under, but often a common grave, or a hole nearby. I am talking poverty, anything else is psychobabble for credits or television stations or newspapers pushing personal political agendas and perhaps hoping to win a Pulitzer for their great insight into a problem created by their own people so that they can report on it to get increase viewers and with it more advertisement moneys to coming in.

What I get is a picture of our poor being obese. Mind you that I do believe that we have poor people in our midst. Not so much in absolute terms, but in relative scales. Because, being rich or poor is just a measure of where one stands on the riches relative scale. I go to the buffet-all-you-can-eat chain restaurants lining up America's Main Streets. I see the triple servings of deep-fried chicken wings and the plates bursting with mashed potatoes brimming with brown sauce. I see them seating on chairs that barely support a third of their very generous anatomical seats. I see them going for seconds and thirds. I see them lovingly looking at their three children, already covered in four inches of lard underneath their ballooning skin, condemned to a life of stares and medical problems. It is funny how we, such a developed nation, explain away in that pseudoscience we call sociology or social psychiatry, or social studies our obesity problems. We say it is the uncertainty and feeling of inadequacy of the poor that make it a status symbol to be obese. I say hogwash! There are plenty of societies with plenty of poor that wish they had the money or resources to feed themselves enough not to die of starvation and diseases brought about by under nutrition, where parents feel plenty of insecurity, where their children are skin and bones. No, we happen to be a perverted society, self-centered as the very center of the planet Earth, we are the very measuring standard for any conceivable adjective or condition, and so we define poverty as we like and starving children as whatever we wish they look like. And if one tries to open the eyes of those that care not to look, then one is called a bigot or a right-wing extremist, or as in my case, one is left with no other recourse but to look at an egg-shell white ceiling caressed by the darkness of the night.

3

I am not above the law of the land or the laws of an evolving society. I, no different than you, was initially bothered by the uncut grass along the highways of our nation. Then, I don't know exactly when it stopped bothering us, perhaps when we noticed the garbage along the roads, the soda cans and the beer bottles. And if as by miracle, we stopped caring about highway dirt when the crime rate began to surge. When we could not ride those same highways without being shot at, that's when we stopped noticing the broken bottles as we sped by. Of course, the occasional highway shooting became inconsequential when the kidnappings started, it was at that moment when we stopped caring about the abandoned buildings and the lack of education and the lack of tenderness and the fact that most of us came from broken homes. And why should we bother with all that when the value of a human life became close to nothing, when most of our cities became the "murder capital" of the world. Of course, we are now bothered mostly by that, but the problem is that I am still bothered by the uncut grass in the public spaces and the broken bottles on the side of roads, and the lack of education and our continuous lack of realization that we have failed in regard to our young.

I, of course have been unable to awake the voice of reason in those that surround me. But in sleepless nights when I can hear the force of my own blood thumping against my eardrums, when I count in vain the thousands of stars on the dark infinity of a cloudless firmament, when, assaulted by a thousand different thoughts try to fix my sight on some passed memory of me as a human being, like a dancer fixing his sight to avoid the ensuing dizziness after a series of spins, it is then that I keep wondering if all was worth it. What a price, what a price!

We all have dreams. Sure, that's what is said. I don't have any reason to doubt it. It is just that I have not dreamed for a long, long time. I had a dream once. Once I was a child and I did have dreams, or rather, I had two dreams and that's it. Or was it three dreams. Yes, that's it, three dreams. Now I have no dreams. The darkness of my universe is perhaps too brutal to even dream about. But there was a time when I had three dreams. The one that gives me some pleasure is the one about flying. It was I flying, and not you, so don't tell me that you have also had such a dream. It was I flying the way only I could fly –I should be able to fly like that now, but that is just a dream: It is my hometown. There are gigantic trees on each side of the avenue. The time may be twilight, but I don't know if the sun is setting or rising. It does not matter to me and it should not matter to you either. All that counts is the fact that I am floating, soaring in the air with my arms extended and that I am above the canopy and falling little by little, like an airplane on ground effect. You know, ground effect? When the air currents generated by the low flying wings bounce against the ground and make the plane float over the landing strip even though you have cut the engine power off. It is the most peaceful moment during a flight: floating soundlessly. I am falling, a controlled fall and then I turn and flap my arms a few times and I am again soaring, distancing from the ground. This is pure pleasure, absolute peace. I am not talking of the times when I am flying and suddenly find myself rapidly approaching a series of high voltage electrical towers with dozens of wires hanging with their bellies down from tower to tower, like tired guitar strings, and I have to negotiate flying in between those wires! No, that is not the kind of dream I want to remember. It is the one where I am soaring above the canopy, effortlessly. Yes, I am alone; I am flying alone, without friends. It is a lonely dream, full of peace and yet there is a sense of foreboding because, after all, we were not made to fly. Oh, sure, we can fly in an airplane, but I am talking flying on arm power. That is the kind of flying I am talking about, and that kind of flying cannot be accomplished with a friend tagging along. Those trees, the big, gigantic trees with their extended canopies, they are beautiful. On the other hand, big black vultures often rest on the branches of those same trees. Have you smelled the vultures when you are walking under one of those trees? Difficult to describe. It is as if odors and language where not designed for each other, not meant for each other. Like lost lovers searching in vain for each other inside a dark miasma. No one can describe a complex odor. Well, when I tell you that there is a specific odor detectable when one passes under the extended branches of these gigantic trees, I am making a statement that only I know the true reality of. Nonetheless, there is such an odor. Once, when I was a child and was walking under one of those trees, from high above, a piece of something fell right just a few steps from me. It clearly was a piece of some dead animal, perhaps even a person, but I was not able to tell where it had come from and the vulture that lost it was not about to tell me. That is the kind of experience that is more oneiric than a dream, the kind of experience that makes you realize that in this life, nothing can be taken on its face value and everything is as it is.

Take parents, for example. If we are lucky, we have them for years and years, nurturing us and annoying us to no avail. We love them, we live with them, and we share a dinner table with them. And then, one day, if we are lucky, and I mean lucky in the sense of survival and nothing else, they are gone. They die. We find ourselves alone. No more protective wings over us. It is at that moment that we truly complete our growth. We stopped being known as their son or daughter and become ourselves. And then little by little, we begin to ask the questions that only they, our parents, could have answered. Now, no matter how much we want them or need them, no matter how good or bad are the questions or our love for them, they are silent. All those years of having them around and talking about trivialities and now they are gone and you want to ask them questions! And just as sure as night follows day, the very fact that you have questions for your dead parents augurs that you are getting old, that the roots of your life are becoming more important than the branches of your living. And it is at that moment that one realizes that trees need their roots as much as they need their beautiful greening branches.

Did I tell you I had a little fawn once? Yes, I think I

did. But no matter, because it is too tender a memory to not tell it again. How many people have had a little horse? I bet not too many. I don't mean a horse on a farm, or a horse on a stable, or a horse that is a horse. I mean a little young horse, totally uninhibited, giving himself totally to you. He did not know he was a horse and I did not know I was just a child. I felt his soft snout against the palm of my hand and his lips tickling me. That is what I am talking about: having a little horse for a friend. Who cares!

There is a dark blue empty space. It is a vast space; it has no temperature, no sound, and no shape. Can it be that blue can be so distinct and yet so infinite? This is a real blue, dark; almost awesome in the way I perceive it. I am discussing my dream. Not the dream I had yesterday, because I do not seem to be dreaming as of lately, but a dream I had when I was a child, perhaps as young as two or three years and going on until I was about ten. Dreams are also the desires people have for their future, for their loved ones, but I am not talking of that kind of dream, but of the type of dream that once you experience, it is not forgotten, never, never in your entire life.

All is blue and yet it has volume, it is not a flat blue, rather a space occupying blue. I am tranquil, even though as I dream the dream again, I may know what is coming, although I am not sure if this is correct. As I was saying, all is quiet, I feel at ease. Then, little by little, smooth waves enter into the blue space. These are not water waves, not sea waves like the ones we are familiar with, the infinite number of different and yet almost identical waves, masses of rising and falling water crowned with the length of foam and rushing from who knows where to who cares where. These are not the waves I am experiencing in the dream. Rather, they are orderly undulating waves of letters. Yes, letters like a, b, c, etc. but in any order, this is to say that they are apparently random in their presentation. The only characteristic that I can remember is that they are orderly, waves gliding inside the blue space. Have you seen a kayak gliding on water early in the morning when the wind has not yet picked up and the surface is as smooth as a mirror, sleek as oil? That is the kind of peaceful environment into which I often long for being, where every swing of the paddle pushes forward the vessel in a silent glide, almost as if it were a plane or a bird advancing soundlessly in space. It is this kind of orderly wave that I am thinking of, but not occupying one plain, but three-dimensional. Waves of silent letters gliding in waves within a three-dimensional space and I am just a silent witness, almost not participating in the event; or perhaps I am that blue space. Order, I say, is that state in which nothing occurs, but from which anything can spring forward. Then, suddenly, without any specific precipitating cause, the letters begin to bounce against each other and the orderly waves cease to be and all of a sudden there is no further peace within that dark blue space that now is assuming the shape of the walls of my childhood bedroom with little images repeating themselves about ten inches from the ceiling, just before the wall becomes a solid white color. And there I am contemplating, even though not participating, this apparent chaos of space and abecedary fighting with each other within the dark blue. Not much of a dream, or nightmare. And it is possibly a nightmare in that I do not feel well when the smoothness ceases and randomness begins. That is the kind of dream that I do not have any longer, but that I used to have, or at least I think I don't have any longer, because I have not remembered a dream for many years. And what do you do when you do not remember your current dreams if you have them? You conjure up your old dreams. It is funny that in this case old does not refer to many years but to few years, to the years you had when you were young, which happens to be many years ago. Interesting that in this case "old" becomes almost a physics' conceptualization of a relativity theory. But I was dealing with my childhood dreams and physics is not even part of my adulthood, unless one wants to consider the effects of physics on one's life, in which case there are very few instances in which physics does not play some role.

It is precisely having had a little fawn for a friend

that catapults a person into a world of tenderness difficult to enter into if you have not had such a friend. One becomes at that moment an alien among other children and later on, when you grow up, you still remain an alien.   No one can experience the tenderness of a baby horse and remain unaffected by it. Oh, I am sure that there must be some people that remain unchanged, but I am sure that those people will grow up to become the kind of people that can attack others and not feel they are doing anything wrong because they are on the right side of some unethical law, or because there is no law forbidding whatever is that they are doing, even though by any standard it is amoral.   And some will say that morality is conventional, that all is relative. But I am proposing that such an elaboration is poppycock, that there can be certain actions that are universally amoral or unethical or unlawful because when you were a child you had the privilege of befriending a young little horse that fanned its tail in happiness upon seeing you approaching.

I sit on a chair, lulled by the sound of water. I am stating that if there is a paradise somewhere, be it here on earth or down in hell or up in heaven, if there is such a thing called paradise, then, there is water there as well. Still water does not make a sound. If you agree with this you are probably wrong. Still water can caress you with the sound of silence, or if there are other sources of noise or sound around, then, it can modify these sound waves so that they are perceived differently than if there was no still water close by. Still water not only has a beautiful crown of sound, but it looks equally beautiful. Just think of a small pond somewhere inside a landscape of rolling hills. There is no brook feeding it with its gurgling disturbing the silence, rather, water sips from the surrounding ground feeding with its filtered transparency and coolness, the silent pond. I was thinking more on the line of running water, active water, water with life, falling water, trickling water, cascading water. In fact, I was thinking of a fountain, like the Romans used to have, or like the little fountain that is occupying the space just a few feet from me at this very moment. Between my fountain and the Roman's there are two thousand years. What can one say to two thousand years? All that happened in that space of time! History was being made so that in later years it could be written and rewritten by dedicated people expert in the fields of restoration and fiction. And now I sit close to my fountain and can almost hear the people of Rome hailing their emperor, I can feel the heat in the middle of the Colosseum, or the soft and tender hand dipping into the fresh water, still cool like the mountain brook from where it originated before it was forced into the stony canal miles away from where now that hand is dipping into. So much has happened between my water fountain and Rome that it would be impossible to know it, even if there was a way of learning about it, even if you were to study it for a thousand years. Of course, we know that we barely live seventy years, so that there is no point in going there. Seventy years! That is all that we may live and perhaps be productive in one lifetime, and I sit in front of my fountain, listening to the water cascading down from the upper platform to the lower basin, falling twenty-six inches in not more than one second and as it splatters and joints the rest of its rippled body, it makes a splattering sound that has been mesmerizing people for thousands of years. I close my eyes and listen to the water falling gently and the next time I open them fifteen minutes have passed. Where did all this time go? I cannot tell you; it is not for me to tell. All that I know is that it was not wasted time, it was time lived and that is what we came to earth to do, to live each one of those seventy or so years that we have been allotted here. And when I open my eyes and look at the little fountain, it is right there where I left it sometime before, just before I closed my eyes. All looks exactly as I left it, all is the same around with the exception that I am now fifteen minutes older and perhaps wiser –Wiser, wiser for having closed my eyes? Ridiculous, some may say. But not the way I look at it. During those fifteen minutes, I did not learn any misinformation that could thwart whatever I might have known before; I was able to let myself go, relax if you will, and perhaps during that time, previously learned material was finally permitted to integrate and strengthened itself in my brain; if I was tired, then I had the luxury of relaxing and replenish my muscles with energy, and finally, when I opened my eyes, I felt good, good like when a child touches the warm pelt of his little horse, or when as an adult, he remembers having done so.

4

There is no going around about certain topics. Like the saying goes, one has to grab the bull by the horns. It might have been a Tuesday when the car headed south, expecting to reach the next city in just about fifty-five minutes. It was a bright and sunny morning. Inside, the driver, a scientist from a nearby laboratory, was thinking that upon returning home, he would like to take his wife and two daughters for dinner to the Mexican restaurant that they had spotted during their last Sunday drive along the Jemez Mountains. Of course, his mind was loaded with formulas and propositions and derivatives, but must importantly, he had conceived of a clear path to reach his team's goals. Oh, it was a big project, but he was used to big projects. Big projects had almost gotten him the Nobel Price the year before; perhaps the next year, or the year thereafter he would, after all he was on the short list for it. These are the things that occupied the mind of the driver as he headed south. But in physics, there is always a counter mass or energy, and if some matter is headed south, then some other matter must head north: all for the sake of equilibrium. Physics is a vast science, often very precise, and often so imprecise that when things don't add up, they just make believe that something must exist somewhere, just to complement whatever is not adding up –the solution is to add another Greek letter to the formula. But this time, physics was very precise. Midway between his workplace and his home, at the widest portion of the highway, the north driven car crossed the extensive terrain dividing the south and north bound lanes, perhaps fifty yards of dusty ground, and headed straight on towards the southbound car, its physical end point being to annul the oncoming car thus bringing to equilibrium two opposing forces within the confines of our physical universe. The following day the papers reported that a scientist from the Lab had been killed in a head on collision with another car. Police were testing if alcohol or drugs had played any role. When I read the news that morning, seated just a few feet from my fountain, watching little birds come and drink and dance by the water, taking their morning baths, I stopped listening to the water cascading down, not because I wanted to, but because, water has no sound when death strikes the innocent. I knew immediately that on following days the investigation would reveal that the driver of the north-bound car was a drunkard with ten previous arrests, no license and no insurance. I also knew deep inside in my mind that person's reason of being –his *raison d'être*– had been to murder the driver of the southbound car; if you believe in destiny, he had achieved his purpose. I was sure that the drunkard would survive with minimal injuries, and that his family and friends and his lawyer, along with those caring hearts that so often clutter our urban environment, would argue in future issues of the newspaper that the homicidal driver was basically a good person, who just happened to be a victim of a terrible addiction against which society had not made any serious efforts to intervene. Each of his previous traffic accidents, they would claim, where calls for help. And as I was thinking, nay, recalling these arguments, I became seriously aware that before that driver started his car on that faithful morning, there was an entire family of relatives and friends that could have stopped him but did not, because they ignored or did not care for the consequences of letting him drive. And they did not care, because they themselves would experience no consequences for letting him drive. And even worst, because their mind set was such that whatever this man did, in terms of his driving intoxicated, was inconsequential to them. Life and quality of life for them was a matter of love, hate and revenge –classical opera with ugly music. In a way, a parallel universe to the extreme collegiate thinking mind, that would have interpreted the entire episode as a matter of well-balanced retribution within the universe of the existential soup upon which they fed daily. And of course, it set off a series of observations that came cascading into my consciousness, all at once.

Have you ever stopped to think about the miracle of reading? Here you have an individual, looking at a piece of paper on which a series of symbols have been printed. From the page, the reflected light stimulates the retina, after passing through a series of conductive crystalline media, perfectly designed for the purpose, i.e., the cornea, the lens, the vitreous and even the eyeglasses or contacts. On the retinal surface, they would stimulate a series of photoreceptors that would in turn transmit their converted light signals to electricity, and in turn via a series of conducting fibers to various intermediary groups of specialized cells, would reach the occipital cortex of the brain. On their path to their final destination, they would have given offshoots to other sites containing stored information, what we may call memory, which in turn would send their output into the cerebral cortex. By a series of matches, each symbol would be identified with a pre-existing one, so that at a given point, via associations based in part to previously recorded experiences, the original symbols on that sheet of paper the eye was looking at, suddenly acquired a meaning. But if you think things stop here, you are wrong, because even though the symbols on the page may have a universal meaning, the meaning to the individual would vary depending on a specific set of personal experiences. So that the phrase "the sky grew darker" will be read by all those who can read it as such, but it would have a slightly different meaning to each person, according to their own set of previous experiences about a dark sky. I just described the simple process of reading. Now, to it, you must add all the hundreds of thousands of pages that a studious person has read up to a given point in his or her life. And add all the decisions and choices that needed to be made to read all those pages, and to complicate things even more, add to it the emotions experienced when instead of going for a swim or to a dance, that person decided to read those pages. But the magic does not stop here. Because once all those pages have been read, as they enter the brain and they are encoded, they also begin to interact with each other, reinforcing existing information, or modifying it in what we call a creative process. And this latter portion of the brain's operation is what really makes the human brain what it is. In fact, it is so complex, that all the computers of this world put together cannot match the brain of a simple person, let along that of a learned mind. And that was the brain that was smashed that Tuesday morning by a man who had chosen to pickle his own brain in alcohol. And our illuminated society still was rooting for the survivor, surely there was a way to rehabilitate him. So, you see why I do feel that I am plowing a field of stones?

After a day of hard thinking, there is nothing like listening to the sound of water running. It is then, that with the soul exposed naked, the defenses dropped, one can receive nature as a child might. Sure, one can ask how you know how a child would receive nature. And therein lies the answer, or the lack of comprehension of an answer. For we all have been children at one point in our lives. The problem is, often, we forget to be children. This does not imply that one has to stop developing at age six, but it does imply that for a full development, one must retain the child. It cannot be put in a dark drawer and be forgotten. The child in us must be allowed to sit with us during those times when we lower our guard and quietly let the sound of a water fountain serenade the wind. It is then, sitting side by side with the child in you, that ideas merge and music occurs and paintings draw themselves and scientific facts are seen from a slightly different angle. It is then, during these moments when the breeze pushes the droplets to one side like the silky hairs from a lovely woman, that the fountain starts to sing. It is then, one realizes that the fountain is alive and it is only then, at that moment, that birds lose their timidity and approach the waters, flirting with their wings and rejoicing in the cool comfort of the shallow pond, themselves playing new music with the falling waters, and it is at that very instant when we, if only for a moment, are invaded or perhaps surrounded by absolute peace.

This is the inner beauty of falling water, that it can define peace. How often have you thought about peace: "peace is the absence of war" or one such variation? But I am telling you that peace is not the absence of war. The absence of war may define that period between two wars. But peace can only be felt for short moments, when the clouds blunt the heat from the sun's rays and the wind dies down to a mere breeze and suddenly one realizes that for the last few seconds, one was a part of this fantastic concert of nature, when instead of musical instruments like violins or trumpets or cymbals playing, there is innocence and smiles and softness and tenderness letting their sounds reach us, as if an angel had gently flapped its wings nearby. One cannot sign such a peace treaty; one has to walk naked with that six-year-old secured within one's chest. Those other kind of treaties, the ones signed by various parties or nations, they are not peace treaties: they are agreements to not have war during a given time and meant to be broken when the times are propitious. Peace can only be found within us. Peace is an individual experience. A nation can never feel peace, which is why it is said that a nation is at peace. Peace is momentary and musical and silent and when experienced, leaves us not with the desire for more, but with a sense of fulfillment, if only temporary.

It is dark and the night is half gone. The eyes scan the bedroom and simultaneously feel comforted and anxious to find the usual objects, as they should. Have you noticed that darkness at night is almost never that dark? One can always see something. Objects lose their color and yet we are able to tell what they are. It means that colors do not define objects. We look at the clock by the night table and become aware that it has been only fifty minutes since we turned the light off. What now? Darkness will reign for another six or seven hours. We curl and grab the back of our thighs with our hands in a vain effort to relax the legs. It feels good. Perhaps now we will go back to sleep. We begin feeling the pressure building up at the tips of the fingers, we have to let go and the legs straighten somewhat and we feel the coldness of the bed as the knees touch areas not yet heated by the body's heat. We have not been assaulted by any thoughts –at least not yet. We look at the clock. Surely thirty minutes must have elapsed, but in fact only four minutes have gone by.

Can you hear the sound of the hair as the head slides against the pillow? A hair is so fine, so thin and yet one can hear the crepitus as one hair rolls against another. Too tired to count the creaking of hair against pillow. Turn to the other side. For sure that will bring sleep. That's it, turn, rearrange the pillow and relax. Again, with the eyes closed, finally about to fall asleep once more. Silence and then a creak, just a single creaking sound somewhere in the house. Why? Where? Did anything break? Surely it was nothing, just a board cooling off in one of the walls. Or was it something more evil, more mysterious than just a wooden board moaning. Could it have been someone walking barefoot on the wooden boards? But no one is supposed to be out there. I am sleeping alone. No one but me lives in the house. Or, even worse, could it be a monster? No, monsters do not exist. Only in comic books one can find monsters: Monsters like Frankenstein, or Dracula. Forget it, they don't exist. Go back to sleep. But what if it isn't Frankenstein but rather a giant tarantula that somehow managed to enter the house and now is advancing with its polygonal eyes and hairy legs, slowly and cautiously towards the bed. No, there are no giant tarantulas; it may just be a robber. Go to sleep. The ear against the pillow begins to feel somewhat uncomfortable, it is not pain, at least not yet; just that one is aware of it, I mean the ear. A little rotation of the head to save the ear and now the eye feels like if you are trying to pop it out. Back to the previous position. The ear is now fine but you detect the thumping of the heartbeat. Oh no! I can hear the blood rushing through the ear or the inside of my head. Need to move, but where?

Flat on the back. Now both ears are free from pressure. What time is it anyway? Have not looked at the clock by the night table for fear of waking up. Keep the eyelids closed. Yes. Not too tight or I will begin to see the lights as pressure built-up on the retina can produce, besides, no one can go to sleep forcing the eyelids tight shut. Just think of good things, soft things like sheep: One sheep, two sheep, three sheep. Wait a second. I don't like that greasy sheep odor. I had to give away my sheepskin carpet because of that damned odor, I cannot think about sheep. Water, think of water, a river or a brook. Oh, God! Sheep are known to transmit a variant of Creutzfeldt-Jacobs disease better known as mad cow's disease. I could get infected and start walking just like the cow they always show on TV when reporting on mad-cow-disease. The poor cow trying to walk and falling down every time she tries to do so. Horrible! Think of water. Yes, a brook. That's better. I am looking at a brook in the middle of a meadow. The ground curves in a series of rolling hills or monticules and the brook meanders as the shadow of ancient oak trees keep the waters cool and shaded from the sun. The water rushes against the rocks generating that magnificent sound that can be heard from miles away. Occasionally, the wind swirls dried up leaves from under the branches, carrying them a few yards away. That sound is not going to let me go to sleep. What time is it anyway? I face the clock with resentment, it does not care if I am sleeping or not, dreaming or not.

Ah good, time has flown by; it appears that I did doze off for about forty minutes. Time is a strange thing. It does not matter whether or not you are paying attention to it, one thing is for sure, it keeps going on. I wonder if time is an entity by itself. In other words, if I did not exist, would time still pass? I don't know the answer, but my gut feeling is that it would. In other words, other entities would still exist and for them time would be passing. It is the way of the land, or you might say, of the universe: as long as something exists, time will also exist. And now I am totally awake and my back is beginning to kill me. I am going to lay belly down, or like it is said in more elegant terms, prone. Ah, finally a good position, now all that remains is to sleep. I did not dream anything last night, or at least I don't recall I did. I imagine that my dreams must be so horrible that I don't remember them as a safeguard against going insane. The question of course is, am I already insane? I doubt it, but one could say that I am a biased, involved in the matter, person. How many Napoleons have there been around, and virgin Marys, and who knows what else? They all claimed to be the real thing, but look where they end up. The worst part of it is that they really, honestly, believe they are Mary or Napoleon. I, personally, doubt even the original ones, but that is just my opinion and we are already questioning my sanity as well. I think I am becoming a little sleepy. . .just got to adjust the pillow. . .my neck is killing me. Did I sleep? For how long? I don't want to look at the clock for fear that I will wake up.

These are the kind of thoughts that go through the mind of a person that finds difficult to sleep at night. It does not mean that it happens to me, for a person with nothing to hide and nothing to fear should sleep soundly night after night after night.

5

The smell of rotting flesh follows me around: it originates in me. If you were as old as I am you also would emanate such an odor. I am he who has lived all these years, I am he who has all the wisdom of the world accumulated in his mind and I am he who stinks to rotten flesh. After all, when one is born, floating in the miasma of placental effluvium, one hardly smells good. But even that odor is preferable to the one that begins pointing to the tomb. As they say, the price of glory is having won the battle and you know that, although highly glorified, battles come with a special sale on dead, wound and rot. Who has walked a battlefield the day after? Cadavers clinging to the ground, desperately grasping with whatever power they had left seconds before death clemently took them away while they spilled their blood and urine and vomit over grass that was just moments before as clean and green as a field can be on a late spring day after a rain. But, then, after the grenades ripped away the intestines, and just for a few seconds or minutes, you walked trying to hold them inside yourself, just before shock makes one bend the knees and yield to the ensuing pain, at that very instant, one realizes that feces are dripping between the fingers and falling onto the grass. And as you lay on the side, curled to minimize the pain in your gut, instead of wondering about dear ones, the ones left far behind waving their handkerchiefs as the ship left port and as they got smaller and smaller as if nature was being gentle to you and tried to minimize the image of the loved ones left behind, you wonder if it would matter that some insects crawl inside, trying to find nurture in what once was a friend to another human being, and then, not caring that a blade of grass is touching your open eye, you die.

I carry all that wisdom within my mind, cloaked in the fetid odor of advanced age. Now that I know so much, I can hardly speak. Now that I have seen the answer to what we are and what we should be, nurses come once in a while to turn me from side to side. Society has no time and no use for me. All pray that I should die soon so that the social services' funds don't hemorrhage in my behalf. And I wonder if it had not been better had I died on that spring day so long ago, when I saw flies trying to nest inside my chest. Now, I have replaced the aroma of early vintage battlefield for the one of late vintage nursing of the old, American style. After not sleeping well all night and just as I was falling asleep caressed by the early rays of the Sun, a nurse –I call them nurses even though they may be simply hired aids– enters my room and places me flat on my back and then cranks the bed up so I can have my breakfast, and leaves. I stay in this position for about an hour and a half before someone comes and places a plastic tray covered with plastic flattened domes that serve to keep the food warm. All along, the bones of my hips press what was left of my buttocks against the bed, draining the tissues from their nourishing blood and enlarging the bedsore that is eating me alive even though I have not yet touched my breakfast. Finally, long after the protective thermal effect of the dish coverings has lost its magic powers, another aid comes in and attempts to feed me the cold scrambled eggs void of salt and fat to protect me from high blood pressure and, God forbid, cholesterol deposits inside my arteries that could threaten my health. Then, after I finish with half the morning offerings, she or he leaves the room to feed others like me. Another aid comes by and moves away the tray with the remaining cold food and lowers the head of my bed and turns me on my right side. And I live moment to moment, each moment being as long as a long lifetime, waiting for the weekend when my daughter will visit.

Did I mention I have a daughter? Well, it is not that I had forgotten, rather that I am a private person and matters of family sometimes are better left alone. You know: wash the laundry inside. Oh yes, I have a daughter and two sons. They all work and pay taxes. In fact, they have become what you may call the American public: Joe and Jane Public. Yes, they care too much about the elderly to let them die in a noble, shameless way; they are more into ugly pain and slow wasting away. It all derives from the morality we taught them at school, you know: a human life is priceless, i.e., has no price; we are made in God's image, that kind of stuff. So, when the time comes and we get old, when we cannot care for ourselves any longer, then, instead of welcoming us back into their adult and vibrant homes, bolstered by a sizable government subsidy to help with the added expenses of a difficult extra mouth to feed and care for, instead of that, because of our great values, we place people like me in these homes for the elderly where society pays in full, thus washing its hands, these workers that don't care to take care of us. Hellholes! No matter what you are told, what you are brainwashed with, no matter how often they show you the well-cut grass and flowers at the entrance, all that matters is that inside they are hellholes. I don't want to hear that there are people that care, that there are good nurses and good nurses' aides. Of course they exist, but where it counts, that is, where most of us live –or are dying– there is nothing but waiting for death to come for us and while we wait, we have the privilege of smelling how we, little by little are rotting away.

And on visiting days, when some designated member of the family comes for forty-five minutes at three in the afternoon, they take us from our beds and place us on the lounge chairs by the shady tree, next to the fountain, where we get to see that there are still birds flying and hopping from branch to branch in search of a small meal. And sometimes that is all that we get to see.

I can detect the odor of rotting flesh, in me and on the person next to me. But the world keeps turning no matter what. My daughter couldn't come to visit last weekend because the guy that was going to come on Thursday to clean the carpets did not make it on time and had to come, as a special favor, on the weekend. So, I got half an inch more of bedsore and she got clean rugs.

My sons don't come to visit. They live in cities too far away to make it convenient for them to travel at the spur of the moment to visit their old man. Ah, they are all grown up. One is an architect. He designs beautiful homes, not that I have seen them, so I'm told. Homes, I imagine, where families move in and have children of their own that grow up to become architects, as their parents grow old. My other son is a doctor, great job! Of course, I had to work to pay for his college and then for medical school, but even after, I had to give a little to get him started with his first home, one that his brother the architect built for him and his family. I am so proud of my family!

I don't like to talk about my wife. It brings too much pain back to the forefront. I have invested great effort in burying the pain. In fact, it got buried with her. Yes, we met and fell in love and smiled and walked together along the winding paths that all lovers manage to find. We got married and lived happily ever after and had three wonderful children to whom we taught all our moral values and chose for them the best teachers money could buy to prepare them for a productive life. But one day, the call came informing me that there had been an accident and I had to come to the hospital right away. That's when the nightmare began. When two persons marry and they truly love each other as a couple should, then they become one: One person with two separate bodies. And when one of the two gets amputated off, then what's left is not really a nice thing to gaze at, just a macerated stump. That's what happened to us. One morning, another human being approached her and asked her for her watch and wallet. All happened right in the very center of downtown, with people walking right by where they were. But apparently the thief was not satisfied with taking her watch and wallet; he had to take more, so he stabbed her. He stabbed her seven times. And seven times is all that takes to down a person or a city. Like Jericho, the walled city, it too could not take more than seven days and seven go-rounds. The doctor said that if she had not been stabbed in the neck, she still would have died from the two stab wounds that ruptured her heart. So that all that love she had for me, all the love she ever told me pointing at her heart, all that love came gushing out with her last drop of life. No one remembers my wife. Not even during those tumultuous days right after the murder and then the trial. They all expressed how sorry they were for my loss, but the papers were really concerned for the man that was forced to rob people because society had not done enough to protect him against the evils of our nation. I was left amputated, not bleeding, but dying just the same.

We are a civilized society. We care so much for the poor, the needy, the abandoned dog, and of course, we care for the aged and the infirm as well. Tonight, I am looking for the nine-hundred-and-twelfth time at the off-white ceiling with its crack and the little spot of peeling paint by the corner next to the window with the drawn blinds, waiting eagerly for breakfast.

And you know, I cannot complain too much. After all, our compassionate society not only cares for those like me, but also cares for dogs. Yes, I am the first to say we should care for dogs. Just think. What species of animal has given away part of its DNA just to befriend us humans? That's what dogs did. Well, they were not dogs. At the time they were wolves: powerful, cautious, shy but determined. Wolves live in families, social clans if you wish, structured according to genetically specified dominance patterns. When the time comes to find food, they get organized and after determining their prey, they perform this fantastic hunting dance that ends with the object of their attention mortally wounded and being eaten by the clan, preserving their social stratification at the dinner table, leaving the least dominant wolves with the least amount of nutriments. And yet, among all this apparent savagery, there is also tenderness. Little pups are taken care of like royal princes and mother wolves tend to them and defend them against any danger. And adults lick and caress each other and on frigid winter nights, they cuddle and give warmth to each other.

To the wolves, man was nothing but an object of danger and a possible meal. But some wolves, very few and very cautiously, began to lose some of their natural tendency to avoid humans: opting to follow man and eat some of the spoils, the leftover spoils. Some of them got really close to our ancestors. Of course, humans would kill wolves. After all, they were natural enemies, and very often competed for the same prey. But among the humans, some were not so scared of the wolf; some might have even admired that magnificent animal. However it happened, one day, perhaps one very cold winter night, a wolf and a person gave each other warmth and even shared a portion of their own kill. It does not matter how it came about, what matters is that it happened. From that day on and through centuries if not thousands of years, the wolf began to shed some of its instinctual genes and humans began to morph its very appearance, so that presently, a Chihuahua and a Rottweiler and a Toy-Poodle all are but the end product of man flirting with natural selection. We say that we have a dog, a particular dog, but in fact, it would be closer to reality if one was to say that a relationship has been established between a particular human, her family and a dog. In fact, it is more like an adoption; that's it, an adoption has taken place, a social contract.

6

"Let me out! Please, someone! Let me out!" No one wants to hear what I have to say. They all pass by me as if I did not exist and yet, I know they are aware of me because at least once a day they come and feed me. I would vomit if I could, but the way I am, I hardly can do that.

I am not that old; I shouldn't be here. "Please, please someone, talk to me!"

I was like you or for that matter, like me. I had a job, went to work every morning and came back to my apartment every afternoon around six-thirty. Like most people, I have moved around. Away from my parents first, in that attempt to let my own wings take on the flight we call independence or assertion of one's self. First, I worked as a messenger in a law firm downtown and later on, as the person in charge of the interoffice communication system. Then, tired of this, I got a job at Macy's, in charge of the toys section. I had to test and learn how all the toys worked so that I could show the other workers. I was also in charge of assessing if a toy had potential dangers that could result in injuries and liability suits for the store.

One morning, I tried to get up from bed and couldn't.

"Can anyone get the flies of my face! Please!" I can't stand it anymore. I lay here, on this dammed bed, like if I was a piece of furniture, the only problem being that I have needs, I want to talk, to kiss, to urinate, to vomit, to defecate, I need someone, anyone! The flies will lay eggs on my eyes!

There was nothing I could do– I stayed in bed, unable to get up the entire day and night. The following morning, the building engineer came in, accompanied by my Macy's supervisor (I guess they had been worried about me) and found me in bed. I could hear them and see them but could not move, could not talk. They were asking me how I felt, but I could not reply. The ambulance came and the paramedics placed me on a stretcher and brought me to the emergency room of a hospital. They kept me there for several weeks, not in the emergency room, but in the intensive care unit. I could hear the doctors speaking of me having potential problems breathing and that they needed to intubate me. No! No! No! I shouted in my mind, but they went ahead with it anyway. It was horrible. They thought that since I could not move or talk, I was also unable to feel. But I felt everything, every wrinkle on the bedsheets, every needle stick for blood, the catheter in my penis, the dryness in my nose, the foul odor inside my mouth, and the raw pain of the plastic tube into my lungs.

I was under intensive observation for several weeks. They decided to replace the endotracheal tube for a tracheostomy, so they cut my throat so that now I breathe through a plastic tube coming out of my neck. I feel intense pain in my bladder and penis and have listened to the discussions about the urinary infection I have because of the catheter there. When they come to move me, I suffer horrible pains along the back of my buttocks and hips –they are saying I have bedsores.

What happened to my life? I wanted to get married, to have a family, to take my kids to the park, to baseball games, to the movies. Instead I am rotting like a ripe fruit that someone forgot to turn. I can smell the sweet odor of rotting. I want to die. I want to die and no one listens.

I remember one day when I was around nine years old. My parents took me to the Catskill Mountains in upstate New York. We stayed in a kosher hotel that had a lovely pool and every evening there was a show. I loved the potato soup they served at the hotel's dining room. I don't even know why I remember the trip now. I guess that the liquid they inject into my stomach is whitish like the potato soup of my youth. Now I want for my life to end.

It was a sunny and clear day, brisk air, with the trees along the winding road shaking their branches and saying hello with thousands of fluorescent green leaves. We didn't have a car. We were riding on a bus. When we arrived, the air that met us outside was like totally different from the city's: it had a fragrance and was full of the sound of the breeze caressing the dark green woods that surrounded the hotel grounds. It smelled of pine and wet deciduous leaves. The building did not look like a conventional hotel, more like a very large clapboard house. On the back, there was a large swimming pool and a lifeguard. The pool and the grounds around it were cluttered with people. There were many parents, just like mine, and many kids, although I must have been one of the younger ones. There was this particular girl that excited me the way I had never been exited. We never got to talk. I was shy, I guess, and by the time I promised myself I would talk to her, she had already left.

The restaurant was on the first floor and all the large windows and doors were opened to the pool area. The dining room was filled with large round tables. We were seated around one of the few tables for four. My parents asked if I wanted barley or potato soup and I had said potato. Potato soup I got and I was conquered for life. What a soup! What a great soup! Thick, slushy, slightly off-white, it would congeal and form a membrane on its surface that concentrated even more the flavor. Heaven! And the waiters were coming and going at vertiginous speeds, like magicians, holding so many plates at a time that people wanted to applaud them when the meal was done.

I know there was a fourth person seated at the table with us, but I can't remember who he or she was. I don't know if it was a child or an adult, or if in fact there was a person there, or if we were only three at the table. But I could swear we were four. It is as if someone cut part of a photo and there might or not been another person there. What a potato soup! And now I am getting injected some thick, white concoction right into my veins and into my abdomen!

At night, the dining room turned into a theater of sorts. Most nights a band played and people danced and sometimes there were comedians on stage. They made everyone laugh. That laughter still rings inside the wrinkles of my brain. So many years later and still I can hear the cascading sound of a wave of laughter as the comedian delivered the punch lines of his jokes. It was mostly Jewish humor, but I believe that it really was universal humor: we all feel a little bit foreign no matter how familiar or how close we think we are with anyone else around. And let's face it, this is one of the essentials of Jewish humor.

One morning all the bags came out and mother packed and off we were on the bus, pointing south and getting away from the living trees and the whispering breezes and the people laughing and the potato soup and the girl I never got to talk to.

7

When I was a child and the time came to play with dolls, I played with them as if I was a nurse. I don't know from where I got the idea, all I know is that I had the idea. I remember mending my cousin Lydia's doll when she broke its arm. I remember making little bandages for my dolls and rolling them around their heads. In high school, when other girls went out with their boyfriends, I volunteered in the hospital near my school. I remember how I felt the first time, after two months of distributing candy and magazines in the wards, when I was permitted to walk with the nurses and visit some of the patients and the feeling of warmth that filled me when I began to read a magazine to Mrs. Rosalie, my first patient. When I saw the peace reflected in her eyes, I realized at that moment that my childhood fantasy was going to become my life's work. From then on, my studies were geared to becoming a nurse. When I finally got my degree and my symbolic white hat, I felt in heaven.

All my life I wanted to be a nurse. It wasn't because I was too lazy to study medicine and become a doctor. I simply liked the idea of caring for people, of lending my strength to help the weak get out of bed, of helping them walk after their surgery, to bathe them when they couldn't do it themselves. Being a nurse to feel their bodies with my hands –feel how little by little life overtook them– and give them hope to live again. This is the true nature of nursing. It is not some kind of computer directed ministering of pills and injections, even though some may see it this way; it is about nurturing the damaged and the fragile with a delicate touch and eyes that inspire in the patients confidence that they will recover from whatever horrible illness or condition may be affecting them. It is about listening not only to what they say, but what they are feeling. It is about bringing solace to those that become patients and depend totally and utterly on a kind touch, a kind gesture, a smile when it is time to administer medicines. In a way, being a nurse is to share the pain of others in a way that makes one understand the fragility of life without souring one's own life.

For years I have been serving patients. I have laughed with them and cried with them. I have suffered their pain and been elated by such simple things as the first few steps after hip surgery, or the first bowel movement after abdominal surgery. To see the face of them gleaming with happiness just because they were able to have a bowel movement, or to take a few steps on the parallel bars, is like watching a beautiful morning coming to be. And I cannot complain of the many happy events that have studded my life. But time has a way of tarnishing things. Some years ago, patients became more demanding –perhaps their expectations had shifted– and more bitter. They began to see us nurses as slaves, as employees hired to satisfy their every whim. The lawyers began to include us in their lawsuits against the doctors. The doctors were not called any longer doctors, rather, health-care-providers, and so were we. Medicine was pushed into becoming a trade no different than plumbing. Personal touch was looked upon as a possible aberrant behavior, good enough to hang a lawsuit from it, or more commonly, as an unnecessary waste of precious time.

What is happening to all of us? Has the rotten matter lawyers feed upon spilled over into the rest of society? These days, people appear to walk assured, freely, just until they have to sign a waiver whenever they want to ride the carousel, or swim in the public pool, or be admitted to a hospital. Just tell me who is not going to sign a waiver when coming into a hospital. You are stretched on top of a stretcher, breathing as light as you can so that the pain does not get worse, curled like a snail to minimize the intense cramping in your belly when a hospital worker comes with a paper for you to sign, even before anyone sees what's wrong with you. You don't sign, you don't get to pass go and be ushered into the sanctum of the emergency room. The doctor orders some laboratory tests and if you do not sign a waiver, you are not going to get any tests done. And if you need surgery and you refuse to sign what is known as an "informed consent form", that is in fact a waiver, forget about having surgery. All of this, just because the lawyers have invaded the minds of the common people. Like a cancer that has metastasized to society, legal intervention is at the very forefront of any and all endeavors. By the time a patient is resting comfortably on a hospital bed and a nurse walks in to greed him or her that person is already fuming with suspicions and totally paranoid about all the possible things that can go wrong while inside the hospital. You want to be kind, they want to watch you every step of the way, just to make sure that you are not intent in maiming or killing them. Frankly I miss the days when I was mending dolls for my cousin; I knew deep down that they were not capable of feeling anything, the dolls, but at least they permitted me to be kind while I mended them.

I have thought of killing myself many times. Suicide is not that bad, I think people get kind of emotional about it and overreact to it, but sometimes it is the only way out. My tombstone will read: "Mary Who Nursed Herself to Peace".

Wait a second! I am not a nurse. You have to excuse me but I have not been myself these last days –or were they months? What was I saying? I must have imagined it and yet, I am left with the curious impression that I was a nurse, even if I was not one. The mind of a patient doused with pain and bedsores can play tricks; if you doubt me, just wait some time, sooner or later you will get ill or old or both, and then, assuming you are able to recall my words, you will know.

Just to show you, last night I had a dream. I had a son in this dream. Someone told me that he was involved with a prostitute. Yes, he was having a love affair with a lady of the night. Needless to say, this was a lurid affair. This was a high society whore with many high society connections. My family's name was being soiled. But things have a way of coming to a point, not a boiling point, but a decision point, and this came to me one day when my daughter, who was dating a high-society millionaire, came one day home with tears in her eyes. They were planning a big wedding sometime in late spring, but the very public life of her fiancé was complicating matters. He was the managing partner of one of the largest law firms in the state. He had a public image to maintain and it was about to be tarnished, albeit indirectly, by his fiancée's brother's sexual proclivities –imagine, tarnishing a lawyer. The situation left only one possible action for me to take, and I took it: I decided to speak with this beloved whore of my son's. Of course, at the time I saw her, I had no idea that even if I had not taken any steps to finish with their relationship, things were destined to end in just a few weeks. You see, she had a terminal case of tuberculosis that was inexorably eating up her lungs. But at the time she was still a most beautiful woman and I did not care to look deeply into her eyes, or even care for her. So, when I visited with her at her own apartment, I just explained the situation, no ifs ands or buts. I did not see her recoiling, I did not see her tears, although I was surprised to notice that she was quite aware of the consequences of her love for my son, and even more surprised to find she would comply with my demand. That was all, or I thought that was the end of it.

My daughter's wedding took place as announced and the world continued its course. But nothing is easy in this world of ours. My son became a drunkard and a gambler, and in fact it was during one of these occasions, when I was following him that I saw her again. This time she was attached to some rich banker or hedge fund manager. I saw her from the distance, across a large room where there was dancing and card playing and drinking and rejoicing. As I said, I was following my son and I am glad I did. I could not recognize the handsome, innocent, good fellow I had produced, instead, I watched him getting drunk and after a short while, becoming verbally and physically abusive of his ex-girlfriend. I left in a hurry but decided to visit her one more time. It did not happen for several weeks, I got busy with some business affairs. Anyway, when I finally got to visit with her again, I was shocked to see how shriveled and consumed she had become. She even was glad to see me –imagine, me! She told me she had never stopped loving my son, and I realized that he had turned into a drunkard because he never stopped loving her. Oh, I had done my deed indeed! I needed to act without wasting time. I called my son and risking it all, told him what I had done. I asked for his forgiveness, but more importantly I asked him to come to her apartment immediately. Unfortunately, when he arrived, she was dying. She recognized him and smiled and they embraced and I could see the happiness in her face and then I saw how she turned somber and I saw the light from her eyes escape as stillness engulfed her haggard body. There was nothing that her doctor, her few friends, my son, or I could have done to save her. You can't imagine how bad I felt. Even now when I remember this episode of my life, I feel shame and infinite regret. But I often am not sure it happened, or if it was just a dream, but how could it be since I don't have dreams, maybe it was a movie or an opera I saw years ago. Funny how a dream you had when you were a child tends to be remembered so vividly when you are all grown up, even old, no matter that you have not had that dream for decades. The problem is that I am beginning to blur memories and dreams.

8

Lately I have been thinking about death. Well, it is not completely true. For a long time, I have been thinking about life. And you know, if I could summarize it all, it is not about life I was thinking, it was about how much life there was left in me or for me. But in a curious way, it was not even about life I was thinking, I was thinking more about realized dreams and dreams I still had not made into a reality. Now I am confusing you but stay with me and you will see that I am not delirious. When we are young, we sense there is an entire life ahead of us and we may or not prioritize our goals and dreams. Whether we choose to do this task or that task is not that critical in general, for we know that after we have completed one chore –realized one dream– we can move onto the next one. We ride this wave for a long time; so long in fact, that we lose sight that life is passing us by, that we are like a machine that requires, instead of gas or oil, time. Yes, time. This is how we measure our lives, by time. And it is not so much that life is passing by us, rather it is that life is passing into us. At the end of a certain time segment, we look back and we judge whether we accomplished what we set out to do or not. But during those first three-quarters of our lives we are not too concerned that some of our dreams have not been realized yet, there is still time to do so. It is like an eagle soaring over a vast landscape, flapping its wings on occasion, knowing well that air will make it float above the ground, slicing silently the ether of life, with more to come as it is needed. This is how I felt during my earlier years: that I could do any task I set to do, that accomplishing a task and attaining a goal was part of me –and it was. But sooner or later, we find ourselves in the midst of something that clearly demands certain effort from us, but also needs to be performed within certain time parameters, and often without the cooperation of our fellow humans, and we realize that although the flesh is willing, there is no air supporting our wings. And then, we notice, perhaps for the first time in our lives, that we may not be able to complete that task, to fulfill that dream. It is then, and only then, when we began to visualize, to glimpse at the finiteness of our life and by corollary, at the proximity of our death. And even at this point we are not strictly speaking of death, just of lack of time. Here is the amazing thing I find myself immersed into: that in spite of knowing I may not finish the task, I persist in pursuing it. It is my foolishness, perhaps, but I cannot help doing otherwise. I must continue plowing, even if they are just stones. Continuing in the pursuit of my dreams does not keep me alive; rather, I am living because I am pursuing my dreams. But the horrible conclusion I derive from this situation is that I am like a dog howling in the midst of nowhere, in the middle of the night, perhaps even a moonless night, not even knowing if other dogs are listening to my palaver. But I do care, I do care that other dogs hear my bark, and not knowing gives me pain. So here you have it, a confessional. Without any ailment in my body I am still in pain. When life abandons my body, I will cease to feel this pain of mine. At that point, you can say I am dead, at that very instant I will have ceased to be alive.

Sometimes the mind can play tricks with you. Like, for example, last night —or was it this morning? I think that it was the heating pipes within the walls of my room. They began to vibrate. It must have been that, otherwise I have no explanation why I remembered the events that happened so long ago.

Have you ever leaned you ear on the ground and listened as ten horses come at you in full gallop?

Well, if you had that experience, then you know what it feels to fall down –did someone trip me when one of the transport trains approached our extermination camp? The whole earth trembled (and perhaps the heavens as well) as the train, sensing the end of the line, began to apply the brakes to slow its nefarious march to a halt. Being on the ground, with my right ear pinned against the dry, fine dust that so many shoes had created on their last march in this world, I could hear and feel the weight of that train transmitted by the rigid parallel rails. I could see or perhaps imagine the crusted earth giving up in a series of soft waves, like if god was shaking a blanket. And then, that final stop and the swishing sound of the vapor escaping and the metallic screeching of the doors being opened. I felt the pain in my back as the soldier's boot began its task of raising me so that I could help control the new arrivals. I was a worker at the camp. I had the job of being a kind of an escort; this is why I was still living. I was to guide the incoming prisoners to walk in the direction of the pointing baton –a kind of deadly karaoke following the jumping dot—and herding the new arrivals to the right or to the left. I served at the discretion of the camp commandant. It was I or any other I, for we all were ready to help if it got us an extra portion of bread, or less abuse. All these past years have served to blunt the specifics of memories I might have formed during those horrible days, but not the horrendous feeling I keep in the very middle of my chest of knowing that because of me, hundreds went up in smoke on the very day of their arrival, while others remained alive so they could waste away during their brief stay surviving on a diet of meager portions of food and strenuous physical demands that sooner rather than later, metamorphosed their bodies into mere sacs of dry skin and bones.

One day, early morning, I felt the same slow rumble and felt the earth trembling. This time I was inside the barrack, I had fallen to the ground and I could feel very distinctly that powerful surge, like a giant serpent clawing its way toward us. But this time there was no transport train. This time I had not been forced into formation, this time I was weighing 80 pounds and was not aware that I was alive. The bulking iron fortresses rolled into the camp and then stopped. When I woke up, I was laying on an army field hospital. It was the first time in three years that the blanket that covered me did not emanate the odor of pus, of feces, of vomit, or death.

A rumble of the ground! That was the best way I can describe the sound of those racing horses the time my grandfather took me to the races. What a show it was! The power, the speed, the beauty of those animals impacted me deeply. I felt warm and whole touching their foaming snouts after the races were over. My grandfather must have known someone in the stables that let us get so close to the animals. The smell of the horses' sweat and the hay and the horse manure was like taking in a single breath history of mankind.

"Nurse! Nurse! There is a bee in my room! I need to urinate! Hello! Someone? Room 231!" Sooner or later the nurse will come. God bless them. Maybe I can sleep for a short while.

9

It is too dark to see all the details. It is not night yet, at least I don't think it is. Of course, with artificial lighting and not leaving the room very often, it is not easy to divine if it is day or night. On top of everything, I am not sure I have my eyeglasses on or if the prescription is so old that I cannot see clearly with them. No matter the reason, all I can tell is that on the far upper corner of the wall right in front of me, the one with the television, there is some bug crawling. I hope it is a roach and not a spider. I hate spiders, even though I have no reason to feel this way about them. It's big enough to be a roach, the distinctive *Periplaneta Americana* species. Blamed for all the maladies that can infect urban human hoards. But the truth is probably close to it being more like a telltale sign that hygiene is not a high priority where the facility is concerned. And who can blame them, for Pete's sake, if they fumigate with heavy toxic compounds, they would probably kill half the population in the ward, and you can imagine the lawsuits flying right and left. And let's face it, these are rooms filled with old people, incapable of remaining clean, even minutes after they are washed, if for some reason they are hit with a bout of diarrhea, or if there is a sudden bladder contraction that releases a quarter cup worth of urine right over the freshly changed bed sheets; if... After a few minutes it will start smelling to uric acid and in no time it will begin to macerate the skin, and add to it the fact that they, or I, have not been moved from the bed in some hours and you have the beginning of a bedsore. There, there you have it. So, I am now almost sure it is a roach that is crawling on the ceiling. I lost track of what I was saying. It had to do with the roach and with fumigating and...I just remember. So many people want things to go back to a kinder gentler time, a time without automobiles spewing all that horrible pollution, a period when people were courteous and wholesome. But here is the thing, I think. Not one person that wishes to outlaw the polluting cars, that so much wants to see the return of the horses, wants to also exterminate three-quarters of the human race. That's what one would need to go back to gentler times. Imagine what it would be if we were to remain seven billion humans inhabiting our earth. In other words, imagine that we get rid of the entire gas combustion fleet in the world. The first thing to visualize is that if there is no alternative way to mobilize foods and garbage, thousands of inhabitants would starve to death, the remaining ones would be involved in turf wars, real wars. But even if one were to replace the motorized vehicles by horse-drawn carriages, you can see that crossing the street on foot would be rather adventurous, like walking with horse manure up to one's waist or perhaps chin. Horse manure is rich in many bacteria, among them, *Clostridium sp.* These type of bacteria cause horrible diseases that block nerve function and paralyze muscles, most of them deadly unless treated, and you already can tell that in that new world, antibiotics would not be readily accessible. People would be dying like flies, and yes, flies would be thriving in our newly conceived heaven on earth world. Factories and hospitals would depend on electricity to keep operational, but without adequate supplies of energy, soon they would start failing and going into rolling brownouts and decreased production, driving our decay even further down the perilous road to our idealized world. All the tall buildings with all those sealed windows and highly dependent on cooling air conditioning, would need to be abandoned. Assuming you are one of the survivors, imagine going to the dentist. The dentist would not have energy to move the high-speed drills; carving out the bad cavities from your teeth would have to be done manually, with a metal hook. I can't bear thinking of the scraping sound transmitted by bone sensation into your ears and the numbing pain that each pass with the hook would generate as it scratches the nerve endings. Hey, but that is part of this ideal clean world. Vegetables and meats needed in great quantities to keep big city dwellers alive would rot before reaching destination. In the cities, people would begin to feel real hunger, and with the hunger and the sense of deprivation would come real gangs. Marauders with weapons would patrol the cities competing with each other for weapons, food, potable water and any other thing or person of value. The world of computers that we so much have gotten used to would go by the sideway, Facebook would be replaced by the face of death. Yes, those roaches are like the legendary mine canaries. And what would happened with us, the ones that cannot take care of simple tasks, that depend on others to survive from day to day? And who would feed all those horses?

See? The question is, or should be, are we afraid of death. I know people that will do anything in order to not die. It sounds reasonable until you realize that they are as old as one can be and still be alive. So first, what is death and then, should we be afraid of dying. But who am I to talk to you about death, for that, there are experts. Wait a second! Experts? What is a death expert? I am not going to take this just passively. I am not going to let some proud, ivory tower insulated, badly dressed professor with rotten teeth declare that he or she, as the case may be, is an expert and I am just a mere mortal that should believe to all and any statements about death that come out of his greasy mouth or pen. The fact is, one does not have to be a murderer to be an expert on death. In fact, one does not need to be a scholar. What one needs for sure, is to be alive. No heartbeat, no thinking about death, no expert. Just that simple. At present, according to all the vital signs, I am alive, I am thinking about death, consequently I am an expert. It really is not a complex topic. The reports from the true experts on the subject, i.e., those that have died, are extremely rare. I remember the first dead person in my life. Perhaps it was one of two dead persons in my very early youth: My grandfather. He, of course, was alive at the time of my remembered interactions. The old man probably was not that old, but when you are two or three years old, a fifty-year-old person definitely looks old to you. It is more like sensing than knowing, that the other person is old. I can tell now a days by the way young people look at me, or more precisely as young ladies –teenagers, women– don't look at me. It was the first time that I realized that I was becoming an old person, the day when I was walking in a shopping mall and a group of attractive young women was walking in opposite direction to mine. When we approached each other, I could see how some of them were truly beautiful, to the point of imagining having sex fantasies with some of them; but when I looked into their eyes, they were looking through me, as if I was furniture, landscape, a non-entity. The insight that I was not any longer perceived as a male of the species hit me right on the face like if each one of them had slapped me for having those dirty thoughts. The only thing I had left giving me sustenance and keeping me somewhat alive was the feeling that my muscles and my body still felt youthful. But I digress. The relations between a three-year-old and a fifty-year-old can only occur at a symbolic, emotional level. Spoken language is not well developed at such an early age. Nonetheless, there is plenty to remember and curiously, the memories carry no sound –at least no sound of words. In my case, I feel comfort and warmth and a delicate and gentle soul. And then, I remember my mother ushering me out of the house so that I would not confront the old man's death. Of course, I already had seen him, lying on his bed, straight, supine and totally motionless. I had become a death expert at that very moment. It was many years after that furtive look at death that I would confront it again. By then, I was in medical school and this time I had my own cadaver to dissect. A cadaver is not death; it is the carcass of what at one point used to be a person. That person is dead. This time, I had plenty of time to contemplate the dead person on top of the cold, smooth cement table. He was naked, cold and deformed. When people think of the dead, they do not really imagine it quite as it really is. A dead person becomes immobile. Whatever position is assumed, it keeps.

So, if a person was facing down with the head resting on its side, there is a flattening of all the surfaces in contact with the floor, or table and a migration of fluids brought down by gravitational forces. These factors produce a deformation of the cadaver; at that very instant it is no longer handsome or pretty but deformed. There is no arguing about it. These are the facts. And there is another thing working: utter immobility. More than anything else, it is this immobility that is capable of penetrating deep into oneself and makes one aware of death. I have noticed this same act of realization in animals other than man. I noticed it when my Rexi died. She was a sweet female Rottweiler that had waited to die until she could see my wife returning from a trip to Alabama. By the early hours of my wife's return she was dead. Popey, our other Rottweiler, came into the room and walked carefully towards Rexi, got about six inches from her, lowered his head and then walked back and away and began seven months of mourning. It was looking at her, utterly immobile, that triggered in all three of us the realization that Rexi was not any longer alive. It was immobility that defined death, because death can be equated with immobility. A year later, Popey became immobile and it was our turn to mourn him. Often, I have seen people asleep on their hospital beds. They seem immobile, but they actually are moving slightly. It is at the very instant that one of them stops moving that I realize that death is in the room. You can see it also in the face. At any given moment the face belongs to a person that is living and then, a second later, without any major external bleed or deformation, just suddenly, the face becomes frozen in time and the eyes become the windows to the unknown abyss we call death. It is the very opposite of a water fountain with its cascading flow, or a brook cutting through a meadow. They too can die, but when the water flows, they are alive like any of us. I never have been comfortable in the presence of death. I, like my dog Popey, approach gently to confirm it and then walk silently away from it, and if it is appropriate, I mourn.

It is curious how persistent certain events are to all of us. There were many questions that I needed to ask my parents and I never thought of doing so. In some instances, the question never occurred to me, in others, I kept postponing asking, perhaps because I did not want an expansive and lengthy response, and then one day they became immobile for eternity and I was left with no answers. I know that it has happened to all of us and yet we keep doing it, we keep procrastinating in asking questions and often the answers become forever cloaked in obscurity as those that could respond are frozen in the eternity of time. And so, death can also be defined by questions never responded to and now left with no solution for eternity.

I often stood by a person dying and wondered if I could see or sense the soul as it escaped the body during that last gasp of air or the following letting it go. I knew exactly when the person died and yet never was able to see the soul. Instead, I felt, if only for a moment, a sensation deep inside of me that carried no form to be able to explain. Perhaps this is how my life energy responded to that instantaneous conversion of a living organism into eternal quietude.

So, I return to the initial question, should we be afraid of death? The answer can only be given by experts and by definition they are all dead. But if it were up to me, I would phrase it somewhat differently: should we be scared of perpetual motion? Can you imagine continuous movement of body parts? Not being able to rest, to put our head down and after decades of turmoil being able to say, it is time to not be anymore. I would be terrified of such perspective and in a way, I must say I am not afraid of dying. For those that think that it is OK to die, but it must come at a timely time, a propitious occasion, the question can be rephrased: when is it propitious to die? And one could then embark on a diatribe about the appropriate timing for dying, and that would require me to think of an issue that I do not want to pursue at this moment.

10

Today has been a very special day. All has gone well. When I woke up, the sun was shining and the birds were singing outside my room. The nurse came and gave me the medications and washed me with a soft cloth. Dietary came by and delivered the food tray on time; they even placed it close to my bed and rang the bell so that a nurse's aide came in time to feed me warm food. And those birds kept singing and chirping. Come King! Come King! I said. We started walking down this sandy path. It was shady by segments, almost as if nature knew that I was beginning to heat up and needed some protection from the bright sunlight. King and I shared this walk many times, actually for many years, until he died. He had the good sense of dying. But on this day, death was far away. The trail curved gently, shaped by giant trees, mostly oaks, but also pines. It had rained early that morning and there was no dust and the sand was packed. King walked next to me, wobbling with his massive body, gently touching me on occasion with his cold nose so that I would caress his muscular head; the short stump of his tail wiggling from side to side and his face smiling. Yes, dogs can smile. Up on the high branches, birds of all kinds perched, serenading us, or courting their mates. After a mile or so, we found a large rock, its edges rounded by the passage of thousands of years, and we sat down on top, right under the shade of an oak branch. From my sack, I got out a container with water and an apple and we shared both; I, drinking from the bottle and King drinking from the cup of my hand. He loved apples, and that particular one went almost all to him. I laid down, resting my head on the empty sack. Clouds, in small puffs were crossing the sky, changing their shape and daring me to divine what they were telling me. I could swear that King was doing the same, but perhaps I am anthropomorphizing just a little. We felt so well, so close to nature, almost at peace with the world. Up above, really high, a hawk circled silently. Down below, the wood mice were scattering, trying to go back into their little burrows, their brains triggering alarm signals predetermined by the genetic wiring, their instinct to survive. A gentle breeze was blowing from the west, sometimes picking enough strength as to move some of Kings neck airs in little ripples and waves.

There are times in one's life that can be alarmingly pleasant. We tend to not remember them well, or not at all. This is just the way we are wired. We tend to remember unpleasant things and events much more often and vividly. But in this life, this short and temporary life of ours, we should try to remember the good and forget the bad. Can I do that? I really don't know. All I can affirm is that when I am not too down on myself, when the rot of my flesh does not reach my nostrils, when it is not too hot in the room or too cold, I am invaded by some happy memory, or at least a happy thought invades my brain.

A path through greening hills is pretty enough. But find out what were you doing there –or why– and then it becomes a major problem. I once walked such a path. Perhaps I was six years old when, after riding in a car over a dusty and bumpy solitary road for hour after hour –a time that seemed to be eternal to my dust covered eyebrows– finally arrived at the destination: a small village of white painted mud houses surrounding a little grassy plaza crowned by a big church. This is what I recall now from that first breath I took in after standing on the ground, I recall the aroma of wood burning coming from cooking stoves, and not any kind of wood, but eucalyptus wood. I did not know then that those majestic trees swaying to the gentle cool breeze were called by that name, but I learned it soon enough, because they also brought with them a soft murmur, like if phantoms from who knows where were trying to tell me a story carried by the mountains' winds. That day we had dinner served by a person just a little taller than I was then, that moved silently over the red-ochre tiled floor with flat and short feet that left no trace. I could swear it was cabbage soup, but the fact is that all I remember of it is that it had a particularly special taste entirely new to me.

The following day I went walking, following a narrow path up a gentle hill covered with soft and fluorescent grass. You may suspect I was not alone, that at that age my parents would not let me go by myself anywhere, and even less given that we were in an entirely new and strange place. My nanny stayed close to me, my nanny of whom years later, I would learn had come to us from those same mountains and hills. We walked one in front of the other, or one behind the other for a little while until we arrived at the top of the hill. We could see the village below, extending over a narrow valley, a river to its left and eternal pastoral hills and woods to the right. Where we were standing also stood a little white building, a one room church, made of thick adobe walls finished with a coat of white calcium paint except for a thin blue line that went all around the building about two feet above the ground. A double door was the only entrance. It was painted blue (or was it brown?) and was ajar enough to tell us that it was opened and we were welcomed in. And in we stepped onto the hardened mud flooring of the little church. There were a series of wooden benches with no back supports arranged in two lines. The walls inside were also painted white and on the two sides close to the altar, there were two statues of saints dressed in real cloth resting in two nooks carved into the walls. Each stood about a yard tall: one was of the Virgin Mary and the other of Saint Joseph. I remember the little statue of the virgin, it had tears painted on her cheeks and the top of her head had a crown of stars. The altar was empty; I don't even remember having seen a cross. Some of the white paint was peeling off and there were a couple of holes on the ceiling through which I could see the blue sky above and hear the cooing of some doves.

Outside the church, there was a piece of cardboard stained green underneath. My nanny told me to sit on top of the cardboard and she pushed me over the grass until the slope of the hill propelled me gently down for about sixty feet or so. Up I went again ready to slide back on the hill with the cool wind refreshing my face. Far away from us, coming down another mountain path, there was a family walking in the direction of the village below. They were far enough that I could not see their faces, only that they walked slowly, swallowing the path, as it were, with the larger of the figures in front and the rest in descending order of height, behind. All wearing light yellow straw hats, all in white shirt and blue ponchos and black skirts, all walking in silence towards the plaza down below. Watching them affected me more than any other event I can remember from my childhood. I was, I realized even then, witnessing mankind in its inexorable descend.

Yes, I had a nanny, and no, I was not a spoiled brat. My nanny taught me gentleness and kindness and how many can say they had a teacher that did that for them? She had moved to the big city from a village even smaller than the one we were visiting that week. There had been no future in her hometown for her. She stayed with us for many years and then I left and later she left, and we both think of each other and take a deep silent breath and by now she is probably dead. A silver spoon in his mouth is what you are thinking, what I am thinking. But deep down I know it is not silver but honey that is coming down my throat. My nanny was "mine", it is true, but I belonged to her as well, her protégé. There was never acrimony between us. There was a sense of belonging comfort, a sense that she was an island of permanency. My mother was also an island of permanency, but I also give her the added quality of having given me support, or rather, that I sought support from her even though both supported me. Both of them loved me. I could not tell you who loved me more. I know I loved them both and I can tell you that I loved my mother more deeply, even though my love for the nanny might have been purer, not attached to so many emotions. I can tell that although at the time I did not realize it, now I am quite aware of how much she meant to me. She might not have been wind under my wings, but perhaps she was shade.

Pleasant and beautiful days can bring with them the oddest things. Like today, the word "persuade" entered my mind. Persuade. I recently ran across this word, but it is today that I am noticing it. It is not that I don't know the word or that I do not use it, rather, it was the fact that seeing it in print, I became aware as to how beautiful the word "persuade" really is. I would say that it even has a sexual connotation, as in I tried to persuade her that having sex with me would not be a great inconvenience and that she could continue shopping the rest of the afternoon. The word is in itself beautiful. After repeating it several times I am left with a meaningless name of a beautiful woman: "Persuade please come back to me', said the tall man standing at the edge of the abyss as the wind fluttered the wide lapels of his raincoat." I guess that in a way, I somehow am seeing this word as a feminine entity. Even if it can be used along with force to alter someone's behavior or to extract the truth from a prisoner, as in, the soldiers applied the electrical terminals to the man's genitals and let the electricity flow in a vain attempt to persuade their prisoner to reveal where his comrades where hiding. But in general, I don't associate persuade with violence, rather, I feel it as a gentle word. It is as if the wind, with gentle persuasion bends the shafts of the tall grasses as the storm approaches. Persuade is very much an intellectual word as well, for only by studying one can find enough arguments to persuade someone to alter an attitude. Human history could have been altered if the main characters would have been persuaded to change their behavior. I remember the time when I argued with my parents about studying architecture, but they persuaded me to pursue medical studies. It was not a violent argument, if anything, it was a rational argument, and in the end, it worked out for the better, or so I think. Is it not funny how one rationalizes that things turn out for the better the way we end up, rather than if we had done differently? We often are left with a question mark after we do something or embark in some great enterprise that will send our lives on a route where not even the wind can deviate us from it. Some people withhold marrying because in their minds there is always the possibility of finding a more attractive partner. I thought so at one time in my life and after my own rational arguments persuaded me that such thoughts were conducive to nihilistic behavior, I went on to marry a person that proved how wrong I had been and how lucky I was to have permitted rational thought to alter what would have been practically a suicidal decision to keep looking for what I obviously already had found. Such is the power of persuasion. But things have not been always pleasant when I think of "persuade". There have been many instances when I failed to persuade people to act in the manner that I wanted them to act, when I was unable to bring down the barriers that stood against my success. All that I can say is that there are not enough curses in this world to wish upon them for their sins of being stubbornly passive, for failing to be persuaded to act in a manner that, I am sure, would have brought success and happiness to all parties involved. But this is the very miracle of persuasion that, like a piece of paper standing on one edge, it can go either way. Because of this, some believe in destiny, determinism, or even absolute chaos.

11

I am King Saul. Yes, the biblical King Saul, or Shaul as my landsmen used to pronounce my name. Yes, I know, I know, you think I am crazy. Crazy because how is it possible that I should be using a computer to write about my thoughts; crazy because no king would degrade to this level just to vent some of his anxieties and feelings. Well, you are very circumspect and very politically correct. You have not said it, but you really think that I am crazy because I have been dead for so many centuries that it would be physically impossible for me to be talking to you. Because talking is what one does when writing to a reader. It is a very personal matter, perhaps forgotten by many writers and never learned by too many readers, that is, that there is a special relationship established between a writer and whoever picks up the product of his or her writings. But let me tell you that in fact there is such relationship, almost as if the writer teleported into the room where the reader is. It does not happen very often because readers these days often skip pages and very often speed read those pages and paragraphs they consider boring. But when a reader captures the phrase, when the reader can in fact read the words as the writer meant them to be read, then, and only then, there is magic in the room and there is in fact teleportation and yes, the reader and the writer might as well be laying in the same bed or sitting in the same chair. So as you can see, I am not that crazy when I am telling you that I am King Shaul, the first king of Israel, the maker of the kingdom that eventually became the State of Israel, the very essence of what a king should be and do for his country. But you would not know it from what the Bible says. I have been relegated to trivia, my life is trivia, my family is trivia; where are my descendants! Certainly the Bible does not account for them. Well, I have news for you, and here is my prophesy, there will not be peace until I am recognized for the true value of what I achieved and did, for only then, humanity will become objective and will cease to live in a world of distortions and misinformation crated by and fostered by the followers and adorers of King David. Oh, he was a king all right, but what he did and what was later done in his name has marred history, marred morality, marred the very essence of religion for thousands of years.

It all started where it shouldn't and by means that speak against free will. You see, Hannah, Elkannah's wife, happened to be barren and bitter and desperate and envious of the other woman that shared Elkannah's bed, I am referring to Peninnah. In any event, it turns out that one day, Hannah went to the temple at Shiloh and prayed to God that he would give her a son. Her bargaining chip was that if He did so, she would dedicate her son to Him. Well, as it turns out, He did and she did. Her son became the famous priest and prophet, Shamuel. But in between lines, one can already see that there is certain abandonment, certain lack of complete dedication, because it appears that Hannah did not return to the temple at Shiloh but when she had weaned Shamuel. Clearly, she had to reintroduce herself to Eli, the high priest. In addition, she made good on her promise, she handed Eli her son to be dedicated to serve the Lord. True, Hannah did speak beautifully about the Lord and her words remain an example of what Jews may comprehend as what is God. But the fact is that she, not Shamuel, made the decision to have him serve the Lord. In other words, my story, my destiny is intertwined with the life of a person who had no free will; I am talking of Shamuel, the very man that eventually anointed me, by God's will, King of Israel, the very man that eventually betrayed me. Don't misunderstand me, I am not saying that Shamuel did not serve well the Lord, not at all, he in fact was a great man and a great priest, but what I am saying is that he did not start his service to the Lord of his own volition, he was planted inside the temple by his own mother. Even worst, he happened to be at the right place and at the right time as well. As it happened, Eli the priest had been tolerating his children's wrong doings for too long and God finally got fed up and basically cursed him and his offspring and chose Shamuel to fill the vacant post of high priest. One thing is clear from the events up to this point and that is that God seems to get more upset and displeased by acts of omission than acts of commission. I, Shaul, gather this from the very evidence. God did not obsess against Eli's boys for their travesties, he was displeased by Eli's tolerance of the ongoing sins his children were committing against the Lord, thus, God did not directly punish Eli's children for their behavior, he punished and cursed Eli and his family for ever and ever. But I digress. In any event, Shamuel became Judge of all Israel and he occupied this position until his old age, at which point he appointed his two sons as judges, but as is the case so frequently, they did not turn out to be of the caliber of their father and became corrupt to the point that the people of ancient Israel asked Shamuel for a king. As expected, from the writers of the Bible, this displeased God. Apparently, he was not so displeased with Shamuel's sons and their corruption, but he was displeased with the people of Israel for asking for a king. The concept here is to understand that God considered himself to be the King of Israel and consequently he felt betrayed. So, when Shamuel asked for God's advice, God acquiesced to giving the Israelites a king, but this king already was, even before he became a king, on the wrong side of God's throne. Shaul was innocent, he was a young fellow, strong and intelligent that was searching for his father's lost donkeys when he came upon Shamuel. God had already spoken to the high priest about his choice for a leader, and when Shaul approached Shamuel, God signaled to his prophet that this was the man to rule over Israel. Now, you got to believe me that up to this point I had no inkling of what my destiny would be, moments before I was Shaul son of Kish son of Abiel from the tribe of Benjamin and the next moment I was chosen to be King. And according to the very same Bible, it is clear, if you check it, that I was reluctant, I even hid so that they would not find me, but it was to no avail. Thus, I became King and it started with a battle. Oh, I remember well, it was my first army; three hundred and thirty thousand men and we destroyed the Ammonites at Jabesh-Gilead. My first battle! It was after this battle that I was formally crowned King, I was thirty years old at the time, I had no evil in me and yet, somehow, Shamuel was already building up an aura of negativity around me.

I was doomed whether I did or did not. In fact, and even if you do not believe me, God cut off my dynasty because I made a burnt offer to him in preparation for battling the Philistines. It was a dirty trick from Shamuel. He had asked me to wait until he came at such and such a time, but he did not come at the assigned time, so I proceeded with the offering to God. Well, this act was apparently bad enough for God to withdraw the lineage of power from me and choose instead David's. David! I am sure you have heard some of the bad things he did, and I say some because he did many more bad things that never were reported in the Bible, but I was there, at least for some of the time. It is not to me to talk ill about David, in those days I was busy fighting Israel's enemies, and there were many, Philistines, Moabites, Amonites, Edomites, Zobahites and the Amalekites. Oh, I was building up Israel's power in the region; in fact, I was following God's commands. But once, just once, when I fought the Amalekites, I permitted my soldiers to bring the best of captured cattle for sacrifice to the Lord and I spared Agag, their King. Yes, the high priest had instructed me to kill everything alive: animal or man, woman and child. When confronted by Shamuel, I felt repentant, I asked for God's forgiveness, but He did not. God did not forgive my sin of omission. Needless to say that from that day on, Shamuel never came to visit me. The Lord ostracized me. The Bible is so set in hating me that it even made a mistake in reporting about Shamuel, David and me. The Book of Shamuel 16:1 reports that the Lord orders Shamuel to go and anoint David in Bethlehem. He tells

Shamuel to stop mourning for Shaul (the previous writings report on his death at an old age). To this, Shamuel responds that he is afraid that if Shaul hears of his doings, he will try to kill him. Well, you be the judge! Am I dead or not? The Bible is so biased against me that it even calls for evil spirits taking hold of me and the necessity of having David play the harp to soothe me. Evil spirits? My foot! I was worried and continuously at war with many enemies of Israel and of course I would get depressed from time to time when things were not going well, but evil spirits? I know there is no way to win this contest: who can win against God! But more importantly, who can win against evil innuendo perpetuated for centuries in the holy writings of the Bible? Ah, but it was not enough, not enough with all the dirt they had written so far, no, now they had to make me a murderer, so next in the biblical agenda is me ordering the killing of the priest Ahimelech and all his cohorts in the city of Nob. The fact that they had conspired, in effect, against the king appears to be inconsequential, but in any event, now I was also a murderer. Mind you that at this point, I already had been dethroned by Shamuel (and God), so is not like this bad act on my part was the cause of me losing the crown. And just in case you are thinking that God had known in advance about this particular atrocity and many more as of yet not committed, and that it was because of this that he withdrew the crown from my head, that would speak very much against free will and much in favor of determinism and consequently it would make ridiculous to start with why God had chosen me as king. There you have it. Look, I don't want to continue reviewing all the other writings describing me like a crazed savage that appear to justify God's selection of David and his bloodline for Israel's management, I know I have no chance to win this argument, but I can tell you that I did not brake so many commandments as David did and was allowed to expiate for, and that ultimately, all that I wanted to do is to raise in you the specter of doubt, that I, perhaps, was dealt an unfair blow by the writers of the Bible. And if you had any doubts about David's cunning and disregard for human life, let me remind you that he was aware of the presence of one of my man when he asked for the collaboration of that priest, Ahimelech, in Nob; he knew that there were going to be repercussions once I had been informed about such act of treachery and he did not care. That is the very essence of David's actions throughout his kingdom, and he always was pardoned and on top of that, blessed with being the seed for all the rulers that were to come.

Hey, you don't want to believe me? That's your problem. All I can say is that I am King Shaul, the son of Kish, the son of Abiel, the son of Zecor, the son of Becorath, the son of Aphiah of the tribe of Benjamin. All I can tell you is that in most of David's victorious campaigns, he killed every man, woman and child, although he brought for himself the treasures of their lands, the very action that had gotten me in trouble with the Lord. But it appears that the Lord found no evil doing in David's actions. So, I was damned for it and he was blessed. Damn, it makes me mad! And I am not talking small potatoes here, suffice it to consider that when David came to my camp and took from me my spear and a jug of water to proof that he could have killed me, I and all my men were under a deep sleep brought up by the Lord. In other words, the Bible does not mind establishing the bias. But wait, it gets even better.

The Philistines were amassing forces against me near Mount Gilboa. I asked the Lord for guidance but he did not respond. I needed to know if my forces could attack the enemy. This had always been the Lord's job before my battles, but this time there was no response. So I conjured Shamuel's spirit, consulting a woman that knew about these things who lived in Endor. Well, sure enough, Shamuel told me that the battle would be lost and that my children and I would die on the battlegrounds. All speak of me committing suicide, but by the time that my three children had been killed by the Philistine hoards, I had been critically wounded by their archers. At that point I knew that they would capture me and torture me to death and then desecrate my body, so I asked my armor-bearer to kill me with my sword, but he refused. I had no choice but to hasten my death, so I fell on my own sword. You can call it suicide, but it would be like taking the life of a person that is imminently in the process of dying. They said I committed suicide when I was 72 years old, but technically it is not the case. As it turns out the son of an Amalekite gave me the fatal blow, so technically I did not die by my own hand. Isn't it crazy, that I needed so many wounds to die? First the many spears of the Philistine hoards, then my own sword and finally the lance of one Amalekite. And I am not counting the Bible itself and its many attempts to cover my name in shadows. Now you know why I cannot really die, why I have to keep fighting my battle, why there cannot be peace until the wrong is righted out.

So you still think I am crazy? Well, welcome to my world, for it is you who is deranged, for not accepting my story; not believing my word places one more time the world at peril. Don't you understand that the reason things repeat themselves is because there is a need to correct history and history will continue to happen until it is finally lived well?

12

Yesterday it was a beautiful day. I believe it was yesterday, but it could have been a month ago, I just don't know. I have been somewhat ill lately. When I woke up, I was in another room. I don't even know if I am in the same place or a different building. I don't see the same walls I saw before. The crack on the ceiling is not there anymore. Perhaps they fixed it while I took an absence of my awareness, I just don't know. I am thirsty! I would like a chocolate ice cream soda, but I don't think this is the place to get one. "Nurse! Nurse!" Oh, it is no use! I need to move my bowels. I think I am constipated; I don't recall when I had my last bowel movement. But I digress, I was not talking about kings and social injustices, I was talking about…Well, I forget, but it is not important. What I was trying to say is not important. Nothing that I can possibly say is important. I am nothing. However, one cannot really say that everything is unimportant. Saying this is tantamount to minimizing the universe, the world, even worst, mankind. Thusly, I will have to retract my previous statement; perhaps some of what I say may be important. It is just that I forgot what I said. But never mind, what I said is probably unimportant in the sense that there are very few humans that care or would care about anything I say, irrespective of the validity or veracity of the message. Such is the way things work in this world of ours. Take for example a newspaper, go to the social pages, and then look for who is being honored. You will find that more often than not, the honoree is a millionaire that has given a ton of money for a certain cause or to a certain organization. He (or she as the case may be) is not a particular expert on the subject matter of the organization or cause, the recognition is simply because he has given the money. But if you look closely, there is more to it than just recognition. Such a person is often named to serve on the board of the organization. Suddenly the person is not just a giver of money, but also a director, a person that can influence the events of the future, even if this person is not an expert on the subject matter, just a sympathizer. And in a matter of a simple signature, we have a cause being directed by people who, although are believers in it, know nothing about it. It is so prevalent, I mean this practice, that if one looks into the makeup of a hundred organizations or museums or opera houses or medical institutions, or universities, one will find that at least half of those governing these institutions know little about the matter that needs to be carried out. And so, we have an opera house that must adjust to the likes of a powerful board member, and a museum that may need to exhibit certain items to please the tastes of so and so, or a medical center endeavoring on certain aspect of medical research not because the researchers wanted it so, but because a major donor that lost a loved one to a certain disease donates millions of dollars on the condition that the money be earmarked for research on the disease that took the loved one away. And all the meanwhile, the people that are dedicated to those same causes get to perform their tasks with devotion and for the most part in total darkness, not being recognized for their knowledge and their dedication. This is what I was talking about. But in a certain way, this kind of makes sense. Figure it out, that such an apparent unjust, random distribution of donors and beneficiaries, at the end, are able to make some sense. For if there ever was a true statement it is that there is a trickledown effect, and somehow, even though in a certain inefficient manner, these peripheral controls somehow prevent the inmates to control the asylum, and so, artists are not totally free to control the Arts, and scientists don't have total freedom in choosing their projects, and so on. This is the axis that permits the earth to rotate in its pursuit of eternity. And I, just walking down the dusty road, feeling the pebbles against the sole of my shoes, and looking at a landscape as vast as a horizon can be, looking for a tree tall enough to cast a shade under which I could take refuge if only for a few minutes.

Curious that I end up looking for a shady tree, as if life was just but repeating itself, as I stand under another shady tree with my grandfather decades ago, and we look at the distant mountains and fields and he takes out of his left coat pocket the onion wrapped in newspaper and bites it as if it were an apple and I am cuddled by the memories of the sound of his chewing the crunchy onion and it does not go away. So, I can tell, without fear of being wrong, that conscious life is just but a series of memories that start under one shady tree and end under another. And isn't it funny that even death can be included as well. Just think. Think that when you look at a postcard or an advertisement for a cemetery plot, the parcel of land that is most desirable is the one under the shade of a lovely tree. This is not esoteric philosophy; this is hardcore philosophy, the kind that no philosopher dares to talk about because it is real and it is simple —no mathematical formulas needed. Not simple minded, just simple. Which reminds me: How often people ask or want to know about Jewishness. Well, here is the one answer that comes to my mind most often when I want to distill the essence. It comes to the memory of an old man, born and dead long ago, that came to this country from another country and never learned to speak the language of his adoptive nation, that walks like an uprooted tree, searching in vain for something that has been missing, that speaks like the Bible was written, that always is dressed in a suit and that even after he dies, when you look into the pockets of his jacket, you will find dried onion skins. But it is too late, too late to ask who he was, what he liked, what made him happy or sad, where did his family come from and what his dreams were: onion skins cannot talk, they cannot tell us what Jewishness is.

Imagine, if you will, a fountain in the middle of a peaceful garden: On one side stand two large Piñon trees and on the other there are two Bristlecone pines; in between them stands the small fountain. Water spouts up for about two inches and then falls on an upper stone dish about twenty inches in diameter and from here into a larger pool and then re-circulates. The water cascading in the shape of small chains made out entirely of droplets creates a waterfall sound that reverberates throughout the vicinity. On a tree, about ten yards from the fountain, on a small top branch, sits a small bird. To venture as to what kind of bird it is would surely bring someone protesting that such birds do not inhabit this kind of habitat, proving that the author is wrong. But I am not wrong, instead, I can tell you that it is a tiny bird, a little larger than a hummingbird, that its little feathers are tinted by various colors of which a creamy gray and a faint yellow predominate. Its beak is short and its body and wings are compact. The little bird is eyeing the fountain, I know it, it has happened before. I am seated very quietly on a chair about ten feet from the edge of the fountain. I wait. A test of wills if you will, between the little bird and I, intent in not moving so that I can enjoy this magnificent bird flying close to me and, her, deciding if I am a predator or just a bystander that represents no danger to her –I don't know why I am calling it her, but it sounds reasonable to me that such a beautiful and delicate animal would be a she. She moves her rounded head from side to side and begins to flip her tail and flicker her little wings. I am sure she has made her mind: she is coming to the fountain. You can appreciate that this is an idyllic situation, and it is. But just for a moment let me digress. What I have described so far is nothing but astounding. I have described thought processes in a bird. You have a little bird standing on a branch, clearly wanting to come and take a few sips of water and then a bath. In her way, so to speak, there is the danger of a predator. My presence a few feet away is not comfortable to her. She is making a decision and as the outcome comes closer and closer, both her body posture and the level of activity change. Then, she flies to the edge of the fountain, her little delicate feet submerged in the water and resting and grabbing hold of the stone beneath. Again, she pauses and evaluates the environment from this new position. I am now even closer to her than before, even though my position relative to the fountain has not changed and she becomes aware of this fact. In other words, her previous estimation of a relative danger-free zone remains valid, assessed by some form of trigonometry. Her attitude changes, she is now more relaxed and then she dips her head in the water and comes up again and looks around: nothing has happened to upset her. She now ventures a little more into the water and begins to flap the wings and give little jumps of happiness. Ah, incredulous minds! You think I am anthropomorphizing. Well, swallow the bitter truth. She is fully enjoying her bath and she is truly happy, perhaps not at an intellectual level like when a person goes to the opera, but certainly at an emotional level like when a person goes to the opera, no different that the happiness that a one-year-old child may feel and express as a series of little sharp cries when given something pleasurable to play with. The scene continues for about sixty seconds and then, fully wet and content, she flies away until I lose her among the density of branches of a Piñon tree not too far from where I sit. It has been a brief encounter, but a deep one. You cannot be in a hurry to fully realize this miracle of nature, when two species as different as man and bird, can share the beauty of the same fountain. And then, one can ask: if two so varied entities can share so much, why we, mankind, cannot live in conviviality with ourselves. You can see how one can escalate events, how one can learn from simple facts, how suddenly, the philosophical issue of happiness can be posed in so different a light than when one simply studies the "philosophers". Happiness cannot be studied in writings; it has to be felt with one's senses.

It is difficult to assess what is happiness, or fulfillment, or any of these apparently simple concepts that so much surround our daily living. Each of us experiences events in a different manner, even if at the end of the day we tend to call them by the same name. What is fulfillment, what is homesickness, what is realization? Sure, we can consult a dictionary and read about these words and from that, even conclude that we have experienced these particular concepts. But what is contentment to me may not be experienced as such by someone else, contentment may be happiness for another person and realization may be happiness or closure for someone else.

I do know that there are certain occurrences in one's life that irrespective of what one may call them are in fact monumental in their nature, even if they are simple in their description. Take for example the memory I have of my father taking me to school. God knows that it was my mother who often interrupted her activities to take me or pick me up from school. Perhaps she did not interrupt her activities, it was part of her routine. And how many children or adults can really remember with so much love, that their mothers acted as mothers and not drivers when they were driving them back and forth all over the place in their youth? But I am not remembering my mother at this moment, rather, I have the memory of my father and not driving me to school but taking me to school on the first day of school, and not in one particular year, but in all the years when it was the first day of school. And here is the crazy thing, all these memories are not clear, I cannot remember details, I only remember the feeling of being taken by my father on the first day of school. The last time he did this was when I was going to begin my surgical training. He already had taken me to school for my graduate program that eventually resulted in a doctorate in pharmacology, and before that, he had taken me on the first day of school during my medical training, and before that, during high school. So there had been so many first day of school openings escorted by my father that I cannot remember the details of all of them and yet, I can remember, deep into myself, engrained so vividly and so permanently, that in each one of them we held hands as we crossed the threshold of the school, the university campus, the hospital grounds. We never made a pact that it would be so, it just happened and then, there was no way to stop it from happening. It was only the fact that I ran out of schools to attend to and eventually he not being able to accompany me, on the account of him having died. But you know, I am not so sure that death did stop us from our little ritual. I distinctly felt him by my side every time I began a new project. And another funny thing: clearly during my childhood days, he accompanied me to school, perhaps to reduce separation anxiety, I was very young in those days, but in later years, especially during graduate school, he did not have to accompany me, but both of us needed the gesture, as if I was sharing with my father the very accomplishments that were coming my way. It was not a case of me returning favors, a kind of pay back for his emotional support, not at all, it was more like if we were sharing life. Parents often are seen as something of the past, they are necessary to start us in life, but once we take off, they become obsolete. But I did not look upon them in this way. During my entire childhood they were there backing me up, pushing, pruning, plowing so that my education and future would be assured, and in later years I could not conceive of them not being part of whatever I had achieved. And even though it was my father the one walking with me, my mother had established that she would be with us in spirit, this was to be an activity involving the "two men". As long as she lived, there she was, backing us as we walked toward the entrance door. A delicate line to walk on, but this was not childhood fixation, this was no need for recognition, certainly not from them –they had seen in me all that I could be– and it was no insecurity on my part, it was simply sharing, sharing as it must have happened thousands of years ago, when our world was somewhat simpler, and people would share supper time, seated by the fire, the mountains' edges revealed by the dying sun behind them and the gentle breeze beginning to cool the rocks and sand overheated during a cloudless day. What name does one give to such events! Clearly, there is no eponym; it would be as erroneous as thinking that one knows a complex painting simply because one knows its name. Guernica is the name of a painting, but there is much to be discovered beyond that. The name may catalog the item, but how can one put a name on the experience that I shared with my father during those days when school opened and I was about to confront the challenges that one more year of learning would bring? How can two people experience Guernica from the same pair of eyes?

To tell you the truth, I have no idea why I was assaulted by those memories. I opened my eyes one day and noticed it was a beautiful day: that is all.

13

I believe there is a new ulcer brewing on me. More specifically, the ulcer involves the lower ribcage on my right-back side, right where the ribs protrude the most. The liver is cradled by these ribs, huddled and protected like inmates by the bars in a jail cell. I don't know how long I have to go. One can live with these bedsores for months, even years! I woke up and have no idea of the time. My glasses are on the night table, but I am so far away from them, that they may as well be in Timbuktu. Blurriness is not so uncomfortable if one does not have anything specific to look at. Years ago, when I was someone else, my vision was much better. In fact, there were times when I would leave home without my glasses, not noticing their absence until I looked at my wristwatch just to find it blurry. Its face was out of focus, and so is my life. Except that now that I see blurry, I really have a clear picture of my life. In many ways, it is like a piece of Swiss cheese, the meaty stuff represents our hits, the things we did and accomplished; the holes represent our misses, the many goals we were never able to bring to fruition. Have you had a piece of cheese in your mouth and have been unable to resist feeling with your tongue the smooth surface of a hole, haven't you? I often ruminate about the things I did not accomplish or miss in my life.

I always wanted to live next to a big body of water, preferably the sea. A lake, of course, would also be wonderful, but it has this inherent sense of being constrained. In a lake one can only go from here to there and back. It is too finite, too constrictive, even if it is one of the most beautiful landscapes nature has given us to delight our senses. I much prefer a house by the sea, with its infinite shores and horizon. Even though in practical terms, one only makes use of just a small portion of this seascape, it is there, immense, awe inspiring, god-like. Well, I got close, really close to accomplishing this. There is a certain magic in the sound of the waves caressing the beach. It is as if the sea and the earth were lovers involved in an infinitely long copulation: the waves coming and going, sliding over the tender slope of the sandy beach. Sometimes, I just imagined that the sound of those waves is closer to the murmur of hundreds of persons reading from a book the same lines in a kind of rhythmic disarray that the wind brakes into a broken message, the meaning of which I can never get to comprehend. But there are times, when the seashore is just that, a magnificent gift of nature. Curiously when I think of the beach, or the seaside, I am not under a hot Sun, I am rather, suspended in an amorphous environment where I am not sweaty, not cold, not hot, not standing or seating, just being there. As I said, almost got to live by the sea, but in one of those twists of destiny, reality confronted me and made me realize that opportunity resided elsewhere, and so, my dream never came to be, becoming one hole in the Swiss cheese of my life. So now, in days like today, I can hear the distant surf, its sound unresolved as if it too cannot find the beach. But like my vision, memory is becoming more and more blurred.

The bed sheet is sticking to my back. I am oozing my life through this damned new ulcer. I hope that someone will tend to it today, or if not today, perhaps this week. I hope. There are certain experiences that can be called sacred, not so much because one visited a church or a temple, but because one witnessed or became part of an event that was sacred. I was visiting a patient in the intensive care unit one day. Frankly I don't know if it was day or night, and I don't remember what year it was. As I arrived, the cardiac monitor by the nurses station was going wild. You know, these monitors have a life and language of their own. They are like dolphins, chatting with one another with their clicks and beeps. In any event, it was clear to me that that person was in its last moments on this earth. In the room with me there was a nurse. She was finishing suctioning the secretions from around the breathing tube that was the only connection with life and that moments before was being obstructed by tenacious mucus. I had never spoken with that patient. I had no idea of the sound of his voice. He had been admitted comatose to the unit after a car collided with his bicycle – massive head injury. There had been no hope that he would recover. No one expected him to survive. Suddenly, the cardiac monitor stopped beeping and its broken chirps were replaced by a single lonesome tone: his heart had stopped. The nurse excused herself and left the room, really there was nothing else that could have been done for the patient. I was also going to leave. I had no emotional attachment to that person. For some reason –*le cœur à ces raison que la raison ne comprend pas*– I stopped by the door and turned. The patient was still, only his face and arms exposed, the rest under an immaculate sheet. The respirator had stopped and the cardiac monitor was now silent. I knew that in a matter of minutes the brain, without oxygen, would cease to function completely and irreversibly. I stayed for a few minutes longer and then suddenly, there was a brief and final letting of air. All was over. I was struck by the realization that if there was a soul, it had just left his body, and that I was in the presence, if only for a fraction of a second, of a soul. We had shared that room, his soul and I, for a moment. I felt an intense emotion, as if I had witnessed some magnificent sunset, or some other great natural occurrence, that lasted no more than five seconds and then, as ephemeral as the soul had been, it was gone and I was left alone. A moment ago, there had been a person in that bed, a person with friends and relatives, with accomplishments and failures, and in an instant, there was no person, just a body, a cadaver that within minutes would start to rot. And now, so many years later, the memory is still ringing in my brain, so vivid even though it all had been about death. Yes, this is the miracle of life, that we are alive because we are aware, we are thinking. This is sacred. And I was taken to another time when my grandfather had died. No one told me he was dead, but I knew it. I guess no different than an animal knowing that its companion is dead; knowledge that doesn't need to be verbalized, an emotional wisdom. I was taken away from the room —everything in that room was colored in a variation of brown to ochre— and brought to the street, like if not being with him would protect me against some evil. But I had seen enough, I had seen the large stand-alone wardrobe closed, covered with its fine burlwood veneer, and the light brown bath robe hanging from the hook behind the door, and the bed with its large wooden headboard and the old man lying very still over the bed. How could they keep away from me the fact that I would never see him again? How could they fill in the gap left by my grandfather's death, when the time came to take a walk to that old tree by the hippodrome, and who would munch on that onion and make it as appetizing as if someone was eating a crunchy apple? You see, this is what life is, a tapestry knitted with memories. Each person uses a different set of memories and ends up with a different brocade, but at the end, that is all that is left: a rag or a king's cape.

There is a cricket in my room. I don't see it, but it is here, somewhere. It has been with me for more than 30 years. The only time I don't hear it is when I go to sleep, but as soon as I am awake, there is the cricket with its song. At first, I tried to hunt it down, but this is easier said than done. I looked for that insect for months and months on end, until I finally realized that I would never find the little beast. It was too smart for me. Nature had equipped it with preservation instincts more powerful than my hunting skills. After a few years I gave up hunting for the cricket and changed my strategy to poisoning it. I placed one of those insect bombs, locked the place and ran out, but the damn beast had read my thoughts and somehow had managed to escape as I exited the premises.

Finally, after almost giving up, I consulted a specialist and he referred me to an ENT doctor who made the diagnosis of "Tinnitus" within seconds of my beginning to tell him the story. In other words, I carry the cricket inside my head. It is my cricket and no one else's. My consolation is that when I die, it will die with me; I don't think it can escape the enclosure of my skull. "Nurse! NURSE! There is an insect in my room! Can someone please catch that cricket!" No use. No one pays any attention to me. I am just another Medicaid bed to them.

14

I can see the blurry line of the blue horizon between my feet. It moves from right to left, from up to down, never really horizontal but always on an incline a continuous zigzagging. I am lulled by the gentle sound of the wind. How far is it from where I am? I cannot tell for every time I try to calculate the distance, I keep moving forward again. I gave up with metrics; I just enjoy the lullaby of the warm wind plucking my hearing cells in a rhythm that almost puts me in a trance. This is life! Reclining on a chaise lounge at the end of the ship on level 9. Next to me there is a side table with a book and a perspiring glass of icy vodka tonic. On the other side of the table there is my wife and she is as more relaxed than I have seen her in many years. Our moments of dissonance come and go like broken waves, the flotsam of love. We don't really have fights; we just have unpleasant arguments imposed by a set of circumstances about which we have no control –more like feathers on the wind than feathers in a wing. And so, we are resigned to exist in this flow of peace and dissent that shapes our lives, like an able sculptor does with mud. Life on a ship is good. After the shock of signing the last payment before the tickets are issued, there is an interval of silence and then, as the time to cruise gets closer and closer, the excitement begins to fill the glass. The next thing you are aware of is when the crew is welcoming you, ready to serve you. But here is the weirdest part of it: it does not matter how many times one has cruised, your heart gives that little extra kick against the ribcage and you look around feeling you are once more coming back home, even though you came from home. The stateroom is never big, but it is clean as a surgical suite and welcoming. Walking along those long corridors, finding again that the dining room is where it's supposed to be and the small bistro with its coffee and pastries still closes at six in the early evening is reassuring in a way that only an old comfortable pair of pajamas can be. We laugh at the same jokes, sometimes told by the same or different comedians and we rejoice not caring that we heard those jokes before. And to tell you the truth, often when one thinks it is a new joke, it's simply because one forgot it –brain cells crumbling– but no one cares. We are on board to enjoy, to live in a world that is almost imaginary, where nirvana often touches from high above the clouds.

Did I ever cruise? "Nurse! Nurse don't leave me!" I think another piece of skin just got stuck to the sheets. Oh God, I am wasting myself into the linen. This should not be the way to live or to die. But I think I have experienced bruising sometime in my life. Not so much because I remember it, but because I have this image of a large gray form lurking and erupting from the morning darkness. I remember that it was not a cold morning, or at least not too cold. In fact, we were surprised of how mild it really was on that early day of May. Like the soul of the dead, rising from the low fog amidst the cemetery crypts, there she stood, at first just a mass and then the giant shadow of a woman with her right arm raised high. She was holding a flame, rather a torch and was covered by a mantle and crowned with a multipoint crown. As big as she was, someone had made her stand on a pedestal as high as she was tall. And there she was, Liberty Lady, chanting in that voice that made so many cry, so many years ago, the song that so many have forgotten:

"Give me your tired, your poor,

Your huddled masses yearning to breathe free,

The wretched refuse of your teeming shore.

Send these, the homeless, tempest-tossed to me,

I lift my lamp beside the golden door!"

They say Emma Lazarus wrote the words in 1883, but by then, my grandfather had not yet thought of moving to America and my father had not been born yet. By the time my parents came to America, they could not hear Ms. Liberty sing those magic words. The doors were closed to the tempest-tossed Jewish masses. It was the guy standing next to me and towering by a head that broke the silence with teary eyes saying that his grandparents had come through these gates listening to her song and kept repeating it like a mantra. That is why I believe I have been on a cruise before, otherwise how could I have remembered this particular scene if not because I lived it? Am I living a nightmare or is my life a nightmare? Surely, I will not die wasting away my body against the bedsheets, like if I was an eraser rubbed against sandpaper! There has to be more to life than this.

I am extremely tired and no wonder, I had the most exhausting experience. I still cannot believe it, how could I have been so stupid, so daring. The point is that no matter how it came to be, it did come to be: I began walking in a northeasterly direction. That much is clear to me. The roads were too noisy, too busy and too dangerous, so I kept to the fields and the woods. Eventually, I got to the end of what one may call the Continental USA. There was nothing to be done but refill my thermos with water and my pockets with food and keep walking into the sea. It was horrible; there were sea monsters all around me. Everywhere I looked there was nothing but sand dunes and death. The wind blew the sand into my eyes. The sun was burning my skin. The coral reefs were ripping my cloths that by now looked like an old forgotten flag assaulted by savage winds. My hopes surged when I got to Iceland. I felt it in my bones that she would be there. The snow was melting on the frozen ground exposing patches of greening grass that extended as far as the next rocky outcrop surged. The ground was mostly solid lava and the mother volcano that had spewed it rose just yards away. The sound of geysers spouting burning water like monstrous whales surrounded me constantly, pushing me to go further and further to the next basaltic hill, just to find that she wasn't there (perhaps never had been there). I kept walking when my shoes had lost their sole and my back was covered in scaly sores. I got to the edge of the island and I kept walking. The northern seas were as brutal as I had heard they would be. The winds hauling like phantasmagoric wolves and the heavens raining frozen rain that wanted to drill right into my bones, but I kept walking for nothing would stop me from finding her. There was a moment when I thought I would die. Several weeks had passed since I had left Iceland and had lost any sense of where I was going, or for that matter coming to. My canteen was dry like a desert bone and there was no more food in my pockets. Then, when I turned around, there it was. I knew it was the coast of Norway –don't ask me why– even though I saw no welcoming sign of any kind. I simply knew. Norway was really tough to walk on. The rocky soil cut the soles of my feet like a hot knife cuts butter. I was bleeding but I could not stop. I walked and crawled from one fiord to the next one, from Geiringer to Bergen. I thought I was going to lose her, that I would never see her again. Then, I saw a green hill coming into downtown and many people getting into a tramway that clearly was going up the steep hill. Not wanting to wait a second longer, I began to run up the side of the mountain in the same direction that the tram was going. When I got up to the top, my lungs about to burst, I saw her. I could not believe it, but there she was, seated on a bench catching the shade under a bushy tree. She was licking an ice cream cone. I ran to her, and just before I could say anything, she looked at me and said: "There you are, I was beginning to get worried". All went dark.

15

This time there is no foul odor. All is the same and all seems to be somewhat different –different as it can be. It is not morning, and I am not turning into a giant beetle, rather, I am inside, under a roof, and all seems normal. That is to say nothing can be farther away from normalcy. After all, I am confined to a nursing home, or if you prefer it, a long-term care facility. From where I sit, I can see the reception area. On occasion, the sliding glass door opens and a person enters. They all approach the reception desk. Behind it there is a large lady, her unexpressive eyes half covered by lazy lids. Her lips seem to be like to sausages added over a large balloon as an afterthought. Some acknowledge her, sign in, and continue their pseudopodian march in. Others aren't as lucky and they have to show their identifications and wait for someone to come and escort them to wherever they intended to go, presumably their loved ones, or what is left of them.   Here and there, a few exit the facility, leaving behind the hard squish of the wind after the glass doors slide close, as if a faulty chapter in the book of someone's life has just been given a last rewrite.   Nearby, the delicate sound of some small bird cooing to its loved one comes and fades in waves, like if coming from a distant lake too far away to see or smell. For a moment I look at the large glass enclosure containing a small replica of a piece of nature.   Several tree branches with desiccated leaves; from one of them there hangs a little trapeze. A few straw sticks scantly covering a sandy floor. There seem to be three different kinds of birds within the enclosure. Two of them can fly. There is a pair of doves perched on a high rim –I guess they are the ones cooing.   Two little birds with black shields on their breast, probably some chickadees, are constantly hopping from branch to branch. On the ground, there is a pair of flightless birds. I know that from the rounded bodies, the lack of tails and disproportionate small wings. One of them is walking across the floor back and forth, as if looking for something. I begin looking with her trying to see if from my height I can find out what she so desperately cannot find from her ground perch. I see five little eggs in a corner. Then it dawns on me, where is the other one? Where is her companion?   It was I who initially assumed there was a pair. Nature can't be so cruel. Can it? But what am I saying! Am I not here myself? For a moment, this beautiful vivarium had given me some pleasure. Now it was showing me once more –as if I needed it– the cruelty of living. I was going to shut myself off to all of this, when from somewhere, I hear music. It comes from farther away. A concert is taking place somewhere. How could it be? Lovely classical music, Gershwin actually, floating right into my ears. Only piano notes played with exuberant and tender expertise. It was as if a brook of crystalline water had just sprung from a rocky soil. There were no stormy clouds, no thunder, simply life floating on the airwaves.

Gliding like a pebble over smooth ice, that's the feeling I got then. That is how she looked when the volunteer pushed her wheelchair past my room. The door was sufficiently open so that I could watch the corridor. Nurses often passed by pushing their carts replete with drugs –the very poisons that keep all of us alive. It was like standing on a bridge when a sailboat breaks the virgin water, barely making a noise. But there were no sails gloating on the wind, no elegance to this silent procession. It appeared as a gentle glide, but what rolled by on that wheelchair was the living carcass of an elderly woman, balding, with white strands of wispy white hair radiating in disarray. She was partially reclining and partially on her side. A position that had been given, as a present, by the arthritis that was converting her into a rigid caricature of a wrecked ancient jalopy, with her skeletal legs straightened, too stiff to bend under the infinite pressure of chronic muscle spasms that had escaped the brain's message to relax. In a way, she reminded me of an Olympic sprinter, that having been frozen in mid step had been laid on its side. She was wearing a typical hospital gown, her skin was white and streaked like marble from Carrara and from her mouth, hanging in a thick strand of saliva, the word "Harry" played over and over again like an old, scratched phonograph record. "Harry…Harry…Harry…" the sound waxed and waned and then was gone.

The birdcage was the same and yet was so different from when I had seen it months before. On the corner, as before, there were the five little light brown spotted eggs. On the artificial tree branch the little chickadees were hopping around, and over the ledge were the two pigeons. The thing was that the sandy ground was void of any living thing; there were no birds. Rather, the single miniature chick-like bird, the one that had lost its mate not so long ago, was now missing as well. I asked a nurse's aide that was walking nearby if she knew about the missing bird. To my utter amazement, she was not aware that there were any missing birds. She mentioned that there was a birdcage near me, which appeared to be something new to her. Was this not how the world is? I was saddened by the five little eggs that were now nothing more than five little coffins. I was saddened by the two parents that had died –one of them for sure had died of desperate loneliness. And here was a person that had not even noticed that once a little piece of paradise had existed just but a few feet away from her daily routine, her daily trail among all of us that were for sure dying with every passing week.

Don't ever make the mistake of waiting too long. Taking one's own life is no shame. All religions pompously argue that life is precious and that no one has the right to take it away except for God. But what if, what if they all are wrong. What if God never uttered such a dictum? What a cruel joke on us all! Perhaps there is nothing as precious as life, but it must have a certain quality. Life for living's sake is not necessarily a life. During my life, I had many opportunities to watch someone dying. It is a drama where there is only one actor on the stage, a human being. You know all along that that person, whomever it may be, is a human being. And then, suddenly, he or she stops being a human being, stops being a person and becomes a cadaver. There is no better way of saying it, although there may be more elegant ways of expressing it. But let me tell you, there is a very distinct feeling when that person ceases to breathe. After some moments, realization becomes quite clear that one is not in front of a person. Of course, there is too much religion and superstition and what not attached to the dead, and for a while, one may even think that such a cadaver is a person, but believe me, it is not. A cadaver is not a person, and within a few minutes it begins to decompose, to rot away. The first observable sign is the abdomen getting bigger; it is all because of the accumulation of gas as a byproduct of the bacteria. In a few days the odor emanating from that body will be shocking, and in a few weeks the rotten meat and fat will change the appearance of that person to the point that the dear ones will not recognize it, the only thing remaining as a person is the memory that others keep. Who will remember me? On whose memory will I live?

As I was saying before, there is a point in our lives when living becomes the product of habit, losing all its pleasures. It is just at that point, when we still have our faculties, when we still are lucid, when we still are capable, it is at that moment when we can terminate our own lives. The problem, as always, is in the details. Even those that want to see their loved one live, are well aware when a life is not worth living.

"Aaaaiiiih…uuooououuugh!" The sound came out of a distorted mouth, drooling mellifluous saliva onto a chest shrunk and bony by old age and chronic disease.

"Why are you crying?" Said the large black nurse's aide that was pushing the wheelchair out of the elevator, with a surprising tenderness, as if the incessant repetition had bounced off of her, somehow not making her impervious to human suffering.

"My mamma, aaaiiiiih!" I could barely make out the words that came from a body ravished by contractures and terminal cachexia. She must have been at least 85 years old. No one came to visit her, not on weekends and not on weekdays.

"Your mammah's okay. Don't cry no mo. Tell you, your mammah's just fine." The nurse's aide reassured her.

"Aaaaaiiiiih… uuooooooououuuuigh!"

Do you see what I mean? Do you understand what I am trying to convey? That woman was a dry, ancient, dilapidated sponge and all that she could say over and over and over again, day and night was "my mamma". And it was not a comforting utterance, rather, it sounded to me as if she was remembering something painful that had occurred a long time ago. Not even that memory was pleasurable. Pleasure had left that body years ago. Now all that remained was living in what seemed to me eternal agony. I don't call this living. Do you understand? Do you understand me?

My bed is wet again. I am not sure if I had a bowel movement or if my bladder just decided to empty, or if I am bleeding again from one of the ulcers on my back. I know that my time is arriving. At least I hope my time is arriving. Oh, how I wished that on that autumn day two years ago I had paid attention to what my body was telling me. One is conceited when the body is healthy. There are no thoughts of death. We are all mighty. But you see, it is all a fallacy; there is no health, just the absence of the perception of disease. When we are ill, it is not because we are not healthy, it is because we become aware of something bothering us, something not being right with our bodies. And I did not pay attention to my body telling me that something was in disarray. It's nothing, I said. Then a few weeks later, when that feeling had not gone away, I made no attempt to zero in on what it was that was bothering me. And that started me on the slippery road, downhill and without brakes. By the time I knew with certainty that there was not going to be a return to normal, by then, I had been taken to a hospital and from there to here.

I don't know why I am thinking of a quiet morning during a late spring day. I am high in a mountain valley. It came unexpectedly after a turn on the narrow, rocky path. The evergreen vegetation was so verdant that it looked as if there were lights illuminating them from within. Everything was perfect. The path was beginning to bend down so the slope was not so demanding, my dog had stopped to smell some invisible message left behind by an anonymous friend, my wife was coming along smiling with that cherubic smile that opened the heavens for me. And there it was, that small valley surrounded by tall mountain peaks, as if nature was speaking directly into my ear saying, "you see, there can be gentleness and brutality within the same breath". That's how I took it, because those mountains were made of black basalt and rose a couple of thousand feet almost in a vertical slope. But nestled right at their feet was this incredibly gentle valley, fluorescent green, pierced by rocky outcrops instead of mushrooms, and right in the middle of it all, there was this lake. Perfect still waters, crystalline blue, as if the sky had settled on the meadow to take a rest after a long day: Nothing but absolute beauty and silence. We walked to the water's edge holding hands. This was life splashing us with utter beauty. Infinite happiness. A moment like that does not get erased so easily, not even after all these years, not even after all are gone. Or perhaps, it will also leave me one day, but then I will know that I am finally dead.

Have you been in a canoe, gliding over still waters, almost as if you were flying, only the occasional gurgling sound of water caressed by the cutting edge of your paddle interrupting the silence that sometimes nature can offer? Oh, I am not a nature kind of guy. Frankly, I can count on the fingers of one hand the times I have been in a canoe. But those memories, those images of a perfect moment, where whatever unpleasantness has been erased by the passage of time, those images are worth a lot. Surrounded by all this putrefaction, it is just about the thread, the string that keeps me sane.

16

Death. I never was really afraid of dying. Never thought with any serious concern about the existence of an after-death. I have always known that life is being alive, and that there is no such a thing as being not alive. As a child I did imagine Death as an ugly, cold, evil monster, but that was the lore that surrounded me. By the time I was a teenager I had stripped away from Death all its ugliness, leaving her, or it, as the final state that awaits all living beings. I had once the privilege of seeing Mary Espinosa on a concrete slab in the pathology lab. She must have weighed 80 pounds. Her left leg was bent at the hip and knee, protruding out from the slab, and her abdomen was opened with a trapdoor incision. Her intestines had been retracted away, exposing her uterus. It was partially submerged in a thick, milky fluid that proved to be pus. The large cancer that had originated from her left ovary had corroded the inner wall of her vagina from where the infection had arisen. It was impossible to be in that room, with Mary, and not be submerged in that sweet, putrid, warm, clawing odor. Each breath I took made me understand how much she had suffered and how definitive death really is.

How much has there been written about Death. It weakens my arguments to stand, side by side, next to the mountains of documents and books written on the subject of dying, but if one stops to think about it, who is an expert on the subject? Who has died and revived over and over again and remembered the experience to become such an expert? During my life I have been next to the living at the very moment they passed away. I was witness to life and within an instant, to death. But does this make me an expert? All I can say is that I am not afraid of being no more. I am afraid of the road to dying.

It must be the end of a shift. I hear stirring in the corridor, on the other side of the door to my room. "Nurse! Nurse!" No, no one will enter. They never do unless they are required to do so. I can rot in my bed, swell in my own feces, drown in my urine and not a single soul will come to my aid. It is not in the nature of these healthcare givers to do so. It is the little secret that our society does not want to hear, even though it is being shouted from so many rooms. But you see, it is a cry that cannot be heard, for if one were to listen to the agonic syncopation of those trapped in their living carcasses, one would have to come, one would have to pay attention, and then care or go mad. And so, the presence of pitiless caregivers is tolerated and supported by our social institutions while those not yet requiring of such humiliating help, can repel their guilt by ignoring the agony of those in need, hidden behind colorful façades. How else can we even begin to comprehend the savage cruelty institutionalized inside nursing homes? Normal brains cannot capture the stagnant odor of the unwashed elderly, the deep hurt of lying over pressure ulcers, the utter loneliness experienced, as thousands of seconds become minutes and hours and mountains of days.

Death is nothing. Getting to it: there is the rub; as they say, the devil is in the details. And for those of us that can notice them, those details are the only companion we have. It is the crack on the ceiling slab, the chip in the paint on the wall we are forced to watch hour after hour when the nurse turns us in bed, the small insect trapped on a spider web too high and too small to be noticed by the room cleaners, it is the noise made by the condensation of droplets inside the top of the toilet, the slanted screen over the window, the ever present distant voice asking for help or calling a name that once meant something to somebody, the sound of one's blood rushing near whatever hearing one has left, smelling decay in one's own body. These are the missing details that I am so fearful of and losing my own history as the brain erodes its cells and with them the footprints and traces of past memories – My few friends, my pony, my dogs, the little birds, the tranquil waters.

Funny how memories are. There must be a trick as to how one evokes a memory. Lately, the only memory –unwanted memory– that invades my wellbeing, if you can call this wellbeing, is the memory of white. It is not a purifying white, not relaxing, not existential; it is not the light at the end of the tunnel that the frustrated dead claim to have seen. Rather, I am inside of a white environment, almost like a tube, that if I was a daring man would say almost like being submerged in a brook, where surrounding rocks cause enough turbulence to make bubbles and the sound of rushing, except that all of it is white, the fluid, the sound, the feeling of the liquid around me, all is white. There is no particular odor, but if there were one, it would be white. There is no special tactile sensation or for that matter, no pain. Wait, I spoke too soon, there is pain.

Folks tell me that all began Tuesday, but curiously, I only remember that on Saturday I made a point in remembering that on Tuesday I had to see the doctor. My wife was with me. That much I know. In those days, we were inseparable, like a captain and his ship. So, on Tuesday we must have gone to see the doctor, some top of the line cardiologist he was. We arrived on time and he didn't, but that is not new. Eventually, he did come and explained to us about the test and the procedure he was going to perform on me. He said, he had cleared the calendar for that afternoon. He was going to enter my heart by way of a long catheter inserted into the femoral artery on my groin. Then, he was going to inject a liquid that could be seen on x-rays and that would permit him to see the blood vessels that feed the heart muscle. What would you know, the heart that is completely wet in blood, needs blood vessels to feed itself! He expected to find one vessel narrowed enough to give me some of the almost nonexisting symptoms I was feeling, as it turns out for months, without realizing that it was my oxygen-starved heart clamoring for more blood.

I remember my wife showing me a drawing of the heart with a bunch of thick black lines all over it. She was saying that there had been too many narrowed vessels, too many to place stents into them. I needed surgery. Real surgery. Then, I remember white. All the white images are only interrupted by a large dark woman, whom I interpret to be some sort of hospital worker approaching me and asking for a signature at the bottom of the page indicating that I agreed to pay from my own pocket any extra days if I decided to stay hospitalized beyond the insurance decreed discharge date. Then all is white again. "Take a deep breath and cough so that we can take the tube out" they kept repeating at one point. But, how could I? I had a tube stuck in my windpipe! Finally, they took the tube out and I began to be me, more or less, again.

My wife said that it was Friday afternoon, but I only remember a little bit about a drawing of a heart and then being suspended inside the color white. Then I became aware that I had three tubes coming out of my chest. A large woman dressed in green came to me and with a single sweeping pull removed the bandages that were covering the front part of my chest and the upper abdomen. I felt intense burning pain and was told that after a few days the skin would cover it all up; that I had sensitive skin. When I became fully awake, I realized that I had also pain in my left leg from the groin to the ankle and that my chest was sore and numb and painful, and so were my ribs. "You need to cough", they said. I found I had been cleaved open, lengthwise, in two halves from my neck to my belly. I was told not to use my arms to push myself out of bed because I could snap open my chest. I was told to take deep breaths and to push them out and cough, as if doing that weren't going to split my chest. And don't worry, to avoid becoming like a carved chicken carcass I was supposed to hold tight against my surgical wound a little foam cushion every time I needed to cough, or sneeze, or take a deep breath. They took away the morphine pump two days later and gave me a pain pill once every twelve hours, if I asked for it. Have you ever had a soldier in full gear step on your chest and keep his boot on it, hour after hour, day after day, week after week without ever pulling the boot away? Well, I and perhaps others felt that boot all the time.

For three days I was normal if I kept my eyes open, but the instant I closed them I saw right behind my eyelids dark orange-red worms, tightly packed, moving without ever stopping. When I opened my eyes, after a few beats when the room passed by me on its way up like if I were inside a tumbling drum, I could see all normal again and as soon as I closed my eyelids the worms appeared again, or a distorted face or a scene from a battle where all the soldiers were dead and bloated and gyrating like if I was swinging a photographic camera 360 degrees around myself, and yet, my thinking was clear. I could hold conversations, think abstractly, speak and reply to questions with my eyes opened or closed, but the images were there. I figured that this phenomenon was secondary to all the drugs I had received during the surgery. Finally, after three days of free movie tickets, the images stopped, I was free at last! Free to be able to concentrate on the bedding. It takes some kind of evil genius to design a bed and mattress that no matter how you position your body, after two minutes you feel uncomfortable and in pain. The skin of my back was always wet and itchy; my lower lumbar spine in constant pain. The position of my head was always wrong: the pillows were too low or too high, the inclination of the bed in too much or too little of an angle and my body in a constant fight to slide down. The gadget to control the bed position was never at the reach of my fingers, the gadget to control the television set was beyond my control. "Nurse. Nurse, I need to turn!" Silence from the other side of the door to my room. There had been voices right by it, but no one had heard me, they all were gone. I waited until the voices returned: "Nurse. Nurse...Nurse". I hated when my wife left me alone in the room and I knew it was necessary and important that she did so. She needed to go home, to shower, to be confronted with the rest of our lives and their demands. She needed to have a few moments without being a witness to my misery, to the very possibility of being alone. She never left me for too long. After two or three hours, she would show her face at the door and as if by miracle, the room would get brighter and the time easier to support. There are angels, but they don't have wings and don't belong in the netherworld. At least one of them, I could swear, has my wife's face.

Ah, those were the days of roses and hope. "Nurse, help, I am rotting here! Help". I know I am dying, or I am dead and went to hell. It is difficult to conceive of a society crueler and more self-righteous than ours. Oh, we respect a human life so much that we allow it to become me. Great! Once one falls into these nursing holes, the sun never rises; compassion never penetrates these bunkers. It is not allowed to. If by some mistake some compassionate person gets through the impeccably clear glass sliding doors, the infinite prevalence of indifference and oblivious cruelty soon drowns any tender gesture. These are the empires of the lazy refuse of nursing, kept afloat by the effluent magma of government fostered social services: the flotsam of hell.

So, I know about death and about living too. As I said, one moment you are alive and the next moment you are not: that is, becoming dead. But if there is nothing after, as I suspect, what is the living hell I find myself suspended in? Because if I already died, then surely this is living proof of Gehenna, of inferno, or of hell. Oh god, I feel wetness on my legs and I fear it is not my urine, and no one has fixed the sound of dropping water from the toilet and if I am not wrong it is just morning, there is an entire day ahead. The kitchen lady will come and place a tray in front of me with non-descript mushy something, low in salt so that I don't swell up. Sometimes I cannot tell if I ate an egg or a chicken or a piece of soggy bread. All taste the same and all look about the same and, in the mouth, they have a spongy consistency. The chef is the great equalizer: he can make strawberries taste the same than beef patties. But enough complaining, you may think I am inventing all this.

I don't know why lately I have been thinking of an old friend. His name was Aldo Serpico. He has been dead too many years. Sure, he died too young, but look at me. I am rotting into myself, leaving pieces of my body on the bed sheets like snot on a well-used handkerchief. He was living his life and died instantaneously at the very peak of it without any premonition or pain. Sure, his life was cut short, but mine has been stretched too long. Anyway, I have been having these flashing, vivid images of him. He was 5 years older than I until the day he died. We had known each other since high school. I was just one year behind. I guess he had not applied himself to progressing in his education, not until I met him, when he scored at the very top of his class. He looked like Mario del

Monaco, the operatic tenor. In fact, his voice was not so dissimilar to his. But Aldo could not sing. He had, what our choral director used to call, "*Oreille faible*", weak ear. Put it more bluntly, Aldo was tone deaf, or now a days, musically challenged; although more precisely, he would not have been musically challenged within the confines of atonal music. He just could not carry a tune by Puccini, or Verdi, or any melodious line. He would start singing an aria with that magnificent voice he had and within a few bars he would be off the road, lost, derailed. Then after a few more bars, somehow, he would come back to the original tone and then do it all over again. He was aware of it, of course, and we would laugh and laugh until tears came running down and then laugh some more. Of course, Aldo had no operatic voice training and did not dedicate himself to that particular venue, rather he took the path of a medical healer. He applied his efforts to medical studies and then enrolled in the psychiatric training program after he finished his studies at the university. His patients adored him.

Aldo was going to write my biography and also a book of my preferred and original metaphors and aphorisms. He was going to do it because he loved me as his best friend. He was going to get married and have children. He was going to help his parents that lived in poverty and that had helped him to become what he was. He was strong like and ox, a small ox. On Wednesday nights we liked to go to Pasmin's Bar. The establishment was located in one of the worst sections of town, right in the middle of a profitable sex for sale business operation that pleased anyone who came, without discriminating race, religion or political party. Pasmin's Bar was a square shaped room with one half dedicated to the bar itself and the storage of alcoholic beverages, and the remaining area occupied by a few, well dispersed tables, and oh yes, a coin operated music box. You insert a quarter, make a choice of musical selection and then listen in utter calm to magnificent arias from famous operas, sung by the very gods of the early Twentieth Century. We would sit, the two of us, ask for two beers, and then, cleanse the mud from our soiled souls with the likes of Fleta, Tagliavini, Caruso, Tebaldi, Di Stefano. The outside world ceased to exist. Only those few souls inside Pasmin's Bar would quiet down and listen to the music pouring out like crystalline water from a mountain brook. That was it. That was what fed us until the following week, when returning to the bar, we would acknowledge the same characters that had been there the week before, occupying the same places at the bar or the tables, listening with teary eyes, with faces that if you did not know better, could have sworn were under the influence of some forbidden drug. That is the image that has been assaulting my brain lately. I try to use it to cover my bitterness, to wash away pain and sorrow, but to no avail; the stink of my own body rotting trumps opera, trumps anything, except hell itself. Aldo and I were not religious. One cannot be too religious living in a world that offered us sickness and suffering and death for breakfast, lunch and dinner. Religion requires of some beauty to survive, no different from a boat requiring some minimum amount of water to float. Never mind that religious people surrounded us wherever we walked or looked; for the other side of hope is religion. But we did not have a coin named "hope", there was too much rot surrounding us. We were not in despair, not by a long shot. And it wasn't a matter of rationality either. Being cognizant of human suffering is not a vestment one wears with comfort. One doesn't go shopping for a medium short suffering jacket at the local store! Awareness of suffering, human or not, is wired into one's brain. You either got it or not. You doubt me. You think that anyone can learn about suffering by simply reading or watching the news, but you would be wrong thinking so.

17

One may be informed about suffering, but to be aware, there is much more to it than just reading. There is a...

"Nurse! Please nurse, can someone clean me?" There is no one coming, they are all busy writing their reports in the new computerized system; there is so much more that is required. Awareness requires a resonance, not different from a guitar, or a cello, when someone plucks at a cord the instrument vibrates with it, resonates and sculpts the sound. So, reading about suffering is like plucking the cord, what determines the quality of it depends on what organs are attached to the reader, or viewer. Aldo and I resonated to the world, but even so, we were not made of the same material. We complemented each other, we overlapped, we vibrated to similar happenings, but just like two musical instruments can play the same note and sound differently, so were we. My sound wanted to sore, scale the mountain, climb the wall of our prison and see and touch the other side of the world; Aldo's sound liked to stay around the town where he was born, to linger by the river that flowed through our city, content with the calming winds and placid valleys.

How peculiar the mind is! I was remembering my friend's happy surroundings and a river comes into my mind, the memory of a river, one totally different from the one that cut our town in two. This river of mine had more water, yet it ran more placid. I don't even know its name, or origin, or where it ended, but the segment I remembered was surrounded by tall bamboo trees that bent inwards toward the waters as if wanting to caress the very source of their life. The sun penetrated the plumose branches in an infinite dance obedient to the wind. There was a short stretch of land cleared of trees and covered by naturally short grasses that reached almost all the way to the water, stopping a few feet from it and exposing a hard, sandy soil that ran in a gentle slope toward the calmed waters. I remember walking with my naked feet over the soft grass and then on the hard sand, and wetting my feet in lukewarm, light brown water and feeling that the floor had become soft and was hugging my feet up to the ankles. The water surface was smooth and ran in almost total silence, barely uttering a murmur as it slid against the opposite curving side, where some of the bamboo branches touched the water, creating a musical ripple. And distantly, the songs of birds.

Perhaps things would have been different if Aldo's horizons would have been as extensive as mine, but reality has a way to quench one's thirst in manners totally unexpected. He was to stay where he had been born and died where he had lived all his life. My road turned out to be more convoluted, more circuitous, and much longer, way too long and now, well, now it is not a road anymore, more like if I had walked into a treacherous sewer. A sewer with a purpose, a good intention, if in practice nothing but a sewer and nothing else.

The song of birds, always filtered by the ever-present glass of the window imperiously blocked from opening by a lock painted over thousands of times preventing possible jumps from willing inmates, reminds me of music. Yes, music. I still can remember that I loved music and as you may suspect, mostly classical and within it, the human voice. Since an early age I placed great composers on a pedestal reserved for few mortals; more like the Greek semi-gods. How could I close my mind to Verdi, or to Puccini, or Mozart? And what of the great compositions of Mussorgsky, or Schumann, or of the music of those great ones that did not compose so much for the voice, but rather were inspired by their voice, what about of the great Beethoven, or Brahms, and what about the simple and magnificent songs that came to life in the form of boleros and tangos. A lifetime could not be enough to enjoy all of it and yet I tried and found orgasmic pleasure in all of it. The sweetness of a great orchestra following the directive, dance-like, hypnotic gestures of a sensing conductor, the sound of a classical guitar or a cello, the trivial and touching operettas and zarzuelas. The inspiring, movements of ballet dancers singing with their bodies in a legato of hypnotic impossibilities, all of these fantastic sound and visual expressions of man's creativity, I swallowed without ever satiating from its inexhaustible fountain. I am now almost completely deaf and my vision is not too far behind. My mind, or whatever is left of it, still can remember on occasion a full passage from an opera. I wish I could dream of being at the opera and listening to those so sweet final notes of Verdi's Traviata or the horrifyingly repentant notes of his Otello. Why is it that they bring the director of the production at the end of a performance, to take a bow, why not the bust of the composer so that the public recognizes the infinite talent that the composer really had. No, recognition has gone the same way that our world has gone: life in the present, live in the moment, for the moment, not caring to go deep into anything for fear that one may find that sometimes the world was actually better, that someone else in another time and place had more talent than our currently talented people. There is no use to wish that I could dream of an entire symphony. God has not been so charitable with me lately. Perhaps Cornelia, the late shift nurse, would be inspired by God to pump some twenty cubic centimeters of air into my veins so my life, if that's what you call this life of mine, can be finally terminated. And there is no use to call the nurses today. They have been very busy making everything spick-and-span for the site visit of Medicare/Medicaid tomorrow. Yes, our nursing home has to comply with all the rules and bylaws and among them there is this qualifying visit. I imagine that we all will look just wonderful when the government dignitaries come poking their noses into our rooms. No pus odor, no urine - soaked bed sheets, no turning me so they can see the exposed bones in my back.

Years ago, in a place called the Third Reich, ordinary citizens were being killed by the thousands every day. Don't ask me how, for I am bound to tell you. Suffice it to say there has never been such a selective mass killing performed in such a cruel and magnificent way. However, even the mighty Nazis had to be careful with the World as a whole. They too had a site visit of sorts. In the early summer of 1944, the Red Cross paid a well announced visit to Theresienstadt, the citadel that the Germans had prepped up for the purpose of erasing once and for all the crazy idea that the Nazis were mistreating Jews in Europe. So, with plenty of time to prepare, Theresienstadt or Terezin, became an idyllic village populated by happy Jews that spent their time composing and playing music and theater and of course painting and enjoying life, and their children bathed in the sun playing soccer. The Red Cross had no intention of finding anything wrong with the treatment of Jews in Europe, hence the well-announced and propagandized visit, and of course, they were not displeased. All was found in perfect order –and no one asked why the need to keep Jews in a ghetto. Needless to say that, within hours of the Red Cross departure, seven thousand Jews, a small percentage of the total imprisoned at Terezin, were deported to the extermination camps of Auschwitz-Birkenau. This is not to say that I am comparing the distinguished visitors to our nursing home with the Red Cross, or that I am saying that my nursing home is behaving like the Nazis at Theresienstadt, although the thought has crossed my mind on more than one occasion.

Why do the images of verdant hills keep popping into my mind? I once saw a perfect verdant hill. I was driving on a narrow road towards Paris, not Texas but France. It was just a two-lane road, smooth enough so that the tire noise was minimal and hypnotic, giving the impression that one was gliding rather than driving. It wrapped around the landscape as if it had no hurry to leave what was clearly a beauty to behold. The hills that came kissing the edges of the road were not higher than hundred or two hundred feet, I would venture. They were covered in the greenest of green grass, not taller than a cup of tea. Here and there a tree stood with enough foliage to provide a solid shade for the sheep that were scattered throughout. All was silent. That landscape has stuck to my brain for the longest of time and I have no idea why it has popped into my mind just now. It was so idyllic, ethereal and jet so definite, like a fluorescent transparency.

The inspectors from the Health and Human Services will come and they will find all is well within the walls of my current, terminal prison. Perhaps, they will encounter a couple of minor infringements in the kitchen department where conveniently they will find —horror of horrors! — one upside down dead cockroach in a corner behind a stainless-steel cabinet, and a small patch of sticky surface where once stood a glass with milk. Such findings will be noted, written and tabulated in their exhaustive four-hundred-page report. The extensive document would certainly justify the millions of dollars our government and our society spend funding such studies. But more importantly, it will surely assuage that gnawing feeling that we, such a civilized nation, don't want to admit into our consciousness, that we have failed in the compassion and rationality departments as it concerns ending suffering for those that suffer so much. The report will be looked at by willing eyes eager to accept the findings and will wait for the results of the next yearly inspection with equal expectations. Would they find me written about in the reports? Could they accept photos of me lying in my own rotting body? Could they dare smell me? You dear readers are the judge.

The sound of the condensed water over the cold pipe in the bathroom falling in a drop, like a tear, is driving me crazy. No one seems to hear it when I have complained. They come, listen for a few seconds, hear nothing and saying: "Here you go dear, there is no dripping sound", they leave the room. But there is too much noise from the corridor and the air blowing and their own talking for them to hear the sounds. These sounds can only be heard when you lay down in a bed motionless for hours. Then you hear them, the sounds, and you feel your scalp ache and you feel the minimal crunching noises that your hair makes as you try to turn your head to one side.

Sometimes I ache for a friend. Not even a real one. But these days friendships can be reduced to contacts in a telephone list. Such friends may give you a "thumbs up", may even write they "feel you man", but do they even possess a face, an odor, a timbre in their voice? Have they spoken with you for hours on end? Have you watched, together, in silence a beautiful landscape or a painting? I guess that having a family would help. But if I look around, when I am rolled on a stretcher over the long corridors of my facility, I see lonely people filling every room. I don't see smiling faces, I don't see anything but my own image projected in every alcove. I see those eyes looking at me, or through me, without shine, without hope, not focusing on any object. There is no reason to look at something when all is dark. One could say that if life was at one point like a boat under sail on a beautiful breezy morning, waiting for death is like a sailboat with no wind stranded in the ocean on a moonless clouded night: The sound of those waves against the prow are nothing but muted memories of images blurred by pain.

It has always amazed me that we, that are all born and that most surely will all die, have not learned anything throughout all these thousands of years as to how we should die. I am sure we think that to leave some old person without food and water to gather itself to heaven in no more than a week's time is a cruel act that reveals a thoughtless and cruel society. Primitive societies might have done that, but we are civilized, we are enlightened, we are god-fearing believers, and if not god-believers at least moral people and we certainly cannot permit such barbaric acts to be committed! No! That "No" reverberates inside my head like rocks inside a delicate vase. The Greeks, and I don't mean the modern ones but the ancient wise ones, knew that if life was not smiling upon you, it was best to finish it off. Philosophers have argued throughout the ages that perhaps the Greeks were right and that perhaps they were wrong, but I am telling you they were right. A life not worth living is worth dying for. Yes, my old friend would have copied this sentence for his book, the one he never got to write on the account of having died young. But he would have known a pearl of wisdom when reading this one. And there rises the frustration, the futility of it all. For I always knew that that is how I would like to go. But fate has a way to interfere with the best-laid plans. At home I have all the means to end my life. I could have ended it by not defeating gravity on a frenetic fall from up high, from asphyxiation after ingesting enough sleeping pills to down a horse, from the sudden shock that lead would produce upon penetrating my skull and so many more ways. But for that I need to be at home. Sure enough, from the hospital they transferred me to this nursing home so that I would have time to recover before going home. But it was not meant to be that I would recover. It was not meant to be that I would be permitted to finish both my agony and society's guilt, instead I got worse.

163

The system that was so happy to discharge me after twenty days of rehab because, and only because insurance companies pay for those twenty days, now, with a new diagnosis was able to obtain new reimbursement. With the new diagnosis they could keep me indefinitely. My life in hell was to begin.

That is the joke Mother Nature played on me. I had planned how I should die since I was a young man. I always knew that when the time came, I would terminate my own life and that of my wife if she so wished. At first, I had no specific way to accomplish my goal, but life brings knowledge and experience and one learns from these. It was not a matter of committing suicide because one is sad or crazy, rather, it involved an intellectual sphere beyond normality, one has to be super-rational in order to accomplish this goal. On a beautiful day under a clear blue sky, when the early morning is being announced by pigeons cooing in their pursuit of happiness, when the neighbors walking their dogs greet each other with bright smiles, when the news delivery truck makes its daily rounds, when all one has to do is look forward to a predictable rewarding day at work, one does not think to activate a plan to end one's life. But that is precisely exactly when it should be planned. The topic is too serious to be left as a last minute detail in our life. Yes, it should be the last thing we should execute in our lives, but the notes for this orchestration should have been written long before –and I was not an exception. First of all, one should have several options. If one can drive, one can hit a concrete pillar at high speed, say somewhere between 60 and 80 miles an hour (disregard the speeding ticket). If you don't want to die a violent death with the car, you can re-direct the exhaust gases into the car; just make sure that enough time is allowed for the carboxyhemoglobin to do its task. If one has a gun, one can aim the barrel towards the head making sure that the bullet is not tangential but perpendicular to the point of entry; the ideal aim should be towards the junction of the medulla with the brain and the two ways of aiming at this point are either through the mount or through the back of the head. If one has pills, then hoard them so that eventually you have collected sufficient quantities to surpass the LD50, that is the dose that will kill 50 percent of the subjects taking such an amount. Whatever pill you may use, make sure that enough time can elapse before you are found, to prevent that you be rescued from death's clutches. If they are sleeping pills, you can combine them with alcohol to maximize the depression of the central nervous system in order to suppress respiratory drive. Other types of pills can severely damage the kidneys or the liver –the body's detoxification machinery– permitting the accumulation of so many toxins that you enter into a state of coma and then death. This latter method can be preceded by several days of malaise so I would not recommend it unless there are no other options. Other medications can affect the heart to the point of blocking its normal contractile function and consequently resulting in a rather quick demise. If you are not too bothered by heights, jumping from a tall building would do the trick; just make sure that it is at least from the six floor, preferable higher since the statistics show that it is possible to survive, albeit in pretty bad shape, a fall from a height equivalent to five stories. To minimize the fear of falling, one can drink a good amount of liquor before. If you don't live or work in a high-rise building, one can certainly scout for the appropriate one. Hanging is certainly another way to terminate life, but better make sure it is a solid construct from where you will hang to avoid failure, and secondly that there is enough height to avoid dying from asphyxiation, the goal is to damage your medulla-brainstem region. And there are many other forms of killing oneself, including the combination of any of the above, and for that matter, the taking of a good number of psycho depressant drug combined with a plastic bag over the head closed with a rubber band over one's neck and maintained open with a finger that will stop the action when one goes into a deep, drug-induced sleep. All of the above I had planned. All that I needed is the right moment and the access. And I was denied both!

So all this philosophical ideation is for naught if one does not find the right moment. My right moment was going to be some variation on the theme of becoming aware of not feeling well at all, and of knowing that there is not going to be a return to normal or even close to it. It encompassed also the concept of finding myself in such state of poverty that institutionalization could be contemplated by the state, i.e., society. It also included my wife's wishes. It was a complex formula, but a rather achievable one. But formulas have a way of containing these variables, some of them difficult to predict. In my case, the access to my home was an absolute and important constant, all other situations being variables. My ability to be independent for those few final hours was critical. Nature denied me that. In my next life, if there is such a thing, I will have to contemplate including in the formula a factor for this. There probably is no other right more important than the right to terminate one's own life. Without this absolute right, all other "rights" are conditional at best. All other rights may depend on someone else, but this one, the right to claim death, should come from within. Perhaps someday.

18

Occasionally, when one least expects it, something out of the ordinary happens that, if only for a moment, brings some balm to the soul. Nights are sometimes brief. During those occasions, I am actually able to sleep. In one moment, it is dark, I have been fed whatever concoction they loaded me with, the lights are turned off and by miracle, the next time I am aware, it is light again. No sounds of drips, no moving shadows, no awareness of body parts, of skin, of bone. But there are other times, when Morpheus does not oblige, and it is during those nights that time becomes elongated like a strand of melting cheese. Then, there is no position, no thought, no breathing pattern, no mattress or pillow that can bring comfort. And yet, it was during one of these nights, when I experienced the most vivid images I had seen in many years. I was aware of being awake and had no other option but to remain in bed. In the hope that lying quiet and still, with eyes closed, would bring sleep, I remained motionless. My eyelids draped over my eyes. I was lying on my right side when all of a sudden, the lights came on and I was able to see with utmost clarity a table with a crisp tablecloth over it and a basket of fresh fruits. For a moment I thought I was hallucinating, or dreaming, but just to check myself, I moved my eyes behind my closed lids. Clearly, if all that I was seeing was some visual memory of something that I once saw in a magazine, I should not be able to explore further into the room, there would only be the image of the table. But that was not the case. I saw all the other furniture that was in the room. To check that I had my eyes covered by my eyelids, I closed them even tighter and indeed, they had been closed. In effect, I was seeing images with my eyes closed. The amazing thing was that these images were not real, even I was aware that they were too crisp, that their colors were almost fluorescent, that the edges were so well demarcated that I had never seen objects so well, so perfectly in focus, not even as a young person. I had to be sleeping and dreaming, even if I thought I had been awake all the time! But such an event was preposterous! I was awake. I was not dreaming. And yet, how was it possible that if I was not asleep, I was experiencing such magnificent visual imagery? I was afraid to put the situation to a test and fearful that there might not be an easy answer to such a potentially difficult question. All that was necessary to do was to open my eyes and see if the images I was so mesmerized by would match what my eyes saw when I opened my lids. I already had proven that my eyelids were closed; now I had to prove that I could open them. And I did. There it was. The dark room, the night table, the dilapidated window coverings. I closed my eyes again. Do not think that the thought did not cross my mind. Was it possible that I had been dreaming that I was awake? Was it possible that all these nights I experienced as eternities had not been anything but dreams of being awake? Was I living a nightmare or was I dreaming it? The magnificent picture I was contemplating was similar to a Cézanne's painting of fruits on a table, but not distorted by his expressionistic brush, my landscape was distorted by its more than perfect style of reality.

How would I know? One cannot live life again at will. One is not supposed to be able to write one's biography at will, making editorial changes when one is not pleased with this or that outcome. But can one be so wrong about life? If I looked at a blue cube, did I see a black triangle? If I was in love with my wife for so many years that we melted into one another, did she exist or do I exist? Am I the person I think I am and not my next-door neighbor? You may think me crazy, but I can say without fear of being wrong, that I am cogent, that I am who I am, even if it is a leap of faith. The question is vital to me because I must know if I have been awake all those nights that stretched to infinity, or was I just dreaming I was awake? And following the rules of engagement in the field of sleep, does one relax and have a "good night" if one dreamt that one had been awake? You see, this is not an unimportant question. The answer is much more existential than you may think. For if I was just dreaming being awake, did I also dream of being bedridden in this miserable place?

Don't even assume that all this is a creation from an overactive mind. For if I can in fact be deluded to being so wrong, what about you? Are you who you think you are? What if at one point in your life, towards the end, when the days forward are counted in one hand and those back are in the thousands, you were to wake up and realize you have been dreaming all along that you were a capable banker working on Wall-Street, with a wife and two grown-up children and a Bentley, when in fact you are an old woman, an ex-druggy that earned her keep doing tricks in an alley behind a supermarket in Detroit? Would that be a source of surprise to you? Would you then understand how important it is for me to know if I have been dreaming all along? Did I imagine that I had a fawn, a two-week-old horse? Oh, I do remember it well. At the time he had soft, inch long hair, the color of Roy Rogers' horse, but lighter, a light tan. His snout was as soft as the softest of velvets, but more so. He used to nibble at my hand and push me with his head. I was a child then, older than he was, but a child non-the-less, and he was my friend. I was not an orphan, but he was. His mother had died during delivery and had left him alone on this Earth. At the farm, they were going to kill him because it was too inconvenient to keep him alive. But then, I had visited the farm. Like most weekends at that period in my life, the man I knew as John had picked me up at six in the morning. He had a light-gray Dodge pickup truck with an open back. We drove on the road south of the city for about an hour until the streets ceased to be streets and became a long paved two-way highway sided by few and far between houses, and little by little we lost the pavement, and the houses, and were driving on a dirt road. After crossing a village that had no reason to be there, the road became even more bumpy and dusty and finally, we made a right turn into the driveway. I would go down and open the gate and wait for John to cross into "*Méjico*", that was the name of the farm. I would close the gate, climb on the truck and after about a quarter of a mile on a deeply rutted muddied road we arrived at the main house. There was about a quarter acre grassless area fronting the house and across it there were two structures, one the workers' dormitory and the other a relatively small corral. Between the corral and the workers' house there was a grassy space about 25 yards wide that led to a placid small river that crossed the farm length wise, providing plenty of water for cattle to drink and cool down and a growth of giant bamboo jungle some ten acres in size that served no specific purpose except to give the workers an eternal supply of posts to fence the various corrals and pasture lands. All the cattle fields were seeded with imperial grass that grew lusciously except in those occasional spots where the terrain was so shallow that the soil became just too muddy for any grass to grow. It was here, in this paradisiacal space on our planet, that I met my little friend. I can tell you that as vividly as I can recall that little horse, his name escapes me. All I know was that on one particular Saturday morning I got down from the pickup truck and saw this little horse horsing around near the house. His neighing was all I needed to fall in love with him. As I approached him, he made no effort to run away from me, in fact, he extended his delicate neck and smelled me with his oscillating nostrils and neighed again. It was then I learned they were going to put him down because his mother had died and there was no other mare around with foal that he could be given to. I begged John to let me keep it, and he agreed and gave the order to the foreman in charge. And so, I became an adoptive father at a tender age.

The following weeks were heaven for me. Every weekend John picked me up in his pickup truck and off we drove to the end of the dusty world and into paradise. As the weeks passed, his little hoofs were still pink, but were beginning to harden, my little companion was maturing. His neck had acquired a certain thickness that told me he had passed the stage of being a baby and was now a little child, in human terms equivalency. His pelt was still long, but less wild, the color of his mane was darkening to a light brown and so was his tail that still was too short to be called a horse's tail. When I arrived on the weekends, he would come trotting towards me and push my shoulder gently with his head and wait to be caressed. We would take a walk by the dirt trail that had been carved by the hoofs of much older horses carrying the field hands on the way to the fields. Nothing grew on these trails. After about a quarter mile we would turn around and head to the corral where I would give my little friend a brushing. This was the way happiness filled me during those few months. But happiness, if escalated to a high peak, can result in much pain if one fell and this was to happen three months into that same year. I arrived on that particular weekend and noticed that my friend did not come to greed me. The foreman approached John and murmured something into his ear. Then, John turned towards me and said that he had died. One of the workers had left a bucket with an insecticide mixture in it and my dear childhood friend had drunk from it. They already had disposed of the carcass two days before. And so it is, that although life can bring one unexpected presents, destiny can take big slices from one's heart. But I am sure I already had told you the story, after all, old age is the time to tell the stories of our lives over and over as we make new friends, when our old friends die. And every time we tell these stories, we tell them slightly modified, not so much because we are lying, but because we have new scars that bend the memories hidden in our hearts.

Can one be living in a world that only exists in one's own mind? How cruel can destiny be? I know I am alive, if you can call this being alive. But, are the memories contained in my consciousness my memories? Are they someone else's memories? Am I someone else's memories too? I have nothing to do. All I have is time. This is assuming that time exists, for even that is being put into doubt by physicists. Yes, by physicists, those most exalted of scientists that having the gift of mathematics, but lacking the gift of being useful, spend their time deconstructing the universe to a point in which matter and time and space cease to be what they are and become a formula that, according to the most generous of gifts, lacks a set of factors constituting at least 90 percent of it. In other words, putting it crassly, they inhabit a world missing 90 percent of itself. But going back into what I do have, time, then I only can but spend it thinking since I am not able to do the things I used to do before I fell into this cloaca.

Out of nowhere comes into my mind the often-repeated sentence that if we don't remember history, we are condemned to repeat it. Even though I am almost blind, I still can see the sanctimonious faces of those saying it, and the complacent faces of those hypocrites listening and acquiescing with it. Just stop and think. Given the amount and intensity of the wars we have been involved in during the past, let's say, five hundred years, it would appear that we have not remembered our history. But if anything, we are getting better and better at recording and preserving history. First, we used hand-written accounts recorded on sheep's skins, then we invented a mechanized way to print on paper, and now we don't even need the paper since we can go to computers and read all about anything. And yet, with all that information, we still –I am sorry, I think I just regurgitated my lunch. It came up without any preamble. Lately it has been happening to me. Not only I am losing my feces and urine without being able to control them, but now it seems, my esophageal sphincter has lost its magical retentive powers, and the food or what passes for it can come up to my mouth or down to the intestine with equal probability. I am a rotting living piece of flesh that can, on occasion, still think or speak. "Nurse! Nurse, please somebody clean me! Please!" They will come when they decide to come– We still have civil wars and international wars, and we still continue to tolerate all kinds of violence. And the same sanctimonious faces still keep decrying these wars and they still keep fomenting them. I see the faces. I see the faces even though I am almost blind.

19

After all is said and measured, clearly life in a nursing home is a struggle to die. On the one side there are the inmates eagerly awaiting death and on the other side there are the nurses saving them from succumbing to dying not because of pity but because it is a war. In Jewish tradition it is said, in a most convoluted way, that the creation of the world is justified even if only one righteous person, a *tzaddik,* lives in it. It is said that God does not allow the world to exist free of a righteous person; before one dies at least one other *tzaddik* must be born. In fact, tradition holds that at any given time, in this world of ours, there are 36 *tzaddikim.* As to where, or who they are that is a mystery. But mystery does not make something become false. As to what characterizes a *tzaddik,* well that is an entirely different story. I don't think that we could ever find agreement as to a righteous person's definition. All I know is that there are probably some *tzaddikim,* somewhere.

Now, you may ask, what has brought this topic to the frontline. Well, I don't really know. I think that it is comforting to know that somewhere at this very second, lives a *tzaddik* in this world of ours, and that being so, it justifies our existence. I personally am looking for a way to kill one man, me, and in doing so completely disqualify myself from the *tzaddik* category. But then, I never claim to be such a man. All I am claiming to, is the right to put a limit to one's own life so that one can depart this earth with dignity, still knowing that one is oneself, still having fresh memories of love and friendship. Dying in a nursing home involves a slow replacement of good for bad memories. It is as if one is not allowed to die until all that is left inside the carcass is bitterness, darkness, and grief.

Isolation is a beautiful word. It sounds nice, it even sounds as it is written, perhaps because of its French root. But here, something weird happens to its meaning in that the word can be self-imposed, or can be imposed by others, or it can be passive. In a way, it reminds me of the Italian word, *isola*, island. I once visited a most beautiful island, Isola Bella, in Laggo Maggiore in northern Italy. It is so far north in Italy, that the beach on the other side of the lake is actually Switzerland. I remember that morning as if it were today –what an irony! When I woke up, the sun was warming up the room and the light, almost luminescent with its own life, reflected inward the movement of the tree branches that radiated an intense green that flickered under the morning breeze that came over the water from the distant Alps. When I opened the window a chorus of birdsongs, as pure as one may imagine heaven itself, blanketed me. After breakfast, I walked across the hotel's garden and the busy road and approached the lake's water edge. Of course, not a beach by American standards, merely a pebble beach with small waves lapping at the rounded, gray stones, like a loving dog welcoming its returning owner. Farther down, perhaps some hundred and fifty yards, there was a small concrete pier next to which a small motorboat, reminiscent of a gondola, but not quite like one, bobbed at the rhythm of the waves. A man in his early fifties was climbing onto the open cabin, helped by the captain of the boat. I walked in their direction and soon was also inside, seated on a wooden bench. After some minutes, finding no more passengers, the captain started the engine and we began our slow-motion trip to the island that stood, or protruded, about three hundred yards away. It was a small island by any standard, but it was a beautiful one, colorful and textured by a series of townhomes and buildings, stacked one against the other by centuries of trial and error. Colorful laundry hung from wires and windowsills and undulated and vibrated with the wind like a thousand hands welcoming us. At the far end of the island, separated from all other structures by a luxuriant park, there stood a small palazzo, the old ancestral home of the royal family of the Borromeo's. Like all tourists, I also went in and felt victim to its charms. That is all. That is what came to my mind this morning, the beautiful island in the middle of Laggo Maggiore; that island with those gardens and that small palace that had been the home of a happy family centuries ago. Clearly rich people. Clearly, they had chosen to live the isolated life of islanders over the more connected life of those living in their palaces and villas across the waters, on the verdant shores and hills, or in the cultural center that Milano had been even at that time. They had chosen to be in some relative isolation. It was a self-imposed isolation.

When the Jews arrived in Venice in the early 1500's, they were welcomed, but they were told in no uncertain terms, that they were to live within the gated area assigned to them. They were to reside within the confines of what is now known as the *Ghetto Nuovo* (the New Ghetto). Jews had left Spain, their homeland for almost fifteen hundred years. Many of their families had not been as lucky as they had been. They had fallen prey to the Spanish Inquisition, a soul-cleansing movement that lasted almost five centuries. Jews had been asked to convert to Christianity or to be saved by burning, or quartering, or exsanguination, or asphyxiation. Those that could, left Spain; those that could not, were 'saved'. Many who converted were questioned about their sincerity. To be sure of the commitment of their conversion, they were tortured. This way, as promised, their souls were saved if not their bodies.

Now, you may ask, or perhaps you may think that I have finally gone berserk, what all of this has to do with me. But if you ask, you already missed the point. This morning –or is it night –I was asked to leave. Nature has been asking me to leave this world many, many times. But I have not been able to follow the instructions, for I have been placed in this charitable institution, that I may call my ghetto. Mankind is keeping me alive, at all costs, so that Mankind can sleep comfortably at night knowing it has done the Samaritan dance with me. I am not being murdered by quartering, or stretching, or

Saúl Balagura

burning; no, I am being disposed of by putrefaction: The new societal arsenal against human dignity. I am in no *Isola Bella*, although the names of our institutions may be as attractive and compelling as *Isola Bella* sounds, I am in 'Isolation', while my body is subtracted away from me by the incessant rub of the bed sheets, and my mind is allowed to be eaten away by the moths of time and miniature strokes that erode my brain as surely as I am dying.

Can you imagine all of humanity kept alive just because there is one saintly person living among us? Who is this person, man or woman that is keeping me from dying? Is it a child? Is it an old and decrepit man? How can someone so saintly be so evil? Is he not aware that by its mere existence war is happening? Is he not aware that by being alive he is keeping millions of sickly and suffering children from finding the peace of death? Has he not seen into the eyes of hatred? Has he or she not seen into the lightless eyes of those being hated? Has he not entered my room during those few moments when I slumber, and smell the scent of my suffering? And if the answer to all these questions is yes, then, how can this person be a *tzaddik*, a saintly person, and even worse, how can there be more than just one?

20

Magnolia House and Resting Home is a sprawling complex of two-storied buildings arranged in a horseshoe fashion in the center of a seventy-acre, well-manicured park. Although this part of the country is flat like an ironing board, the landscape architect had planted copses of trees dispersed throughout the terrain, so that one could never get bored contemplating the land that surround these buildings that housed the Institute for the Mentally Ill, also known as the Behavioral Division.

The cluster of buildings was approached by a winding road bordered by dark and tall Italian Cypress trees that yielded to the winds like tall grasses in the African savanna. After driving about 300 yards, the imposing façade of the Administration and Visitors Center intruded into the idyllic landscape. It was here that one would make the arrangements to intern a person. It was here the papers to release a patient were signed, and it was where one would sign in before being escorted to visit any given patient. In this building were located the offices and conference rooms where the clinic's Board of Directors met on the third Thursday of every month to discuss the future of the clinic and of its inmates.

Dr. Jane McKensie had been chosen by the Board to run the clinic. She had come from Pilgrim State Hospital, where she had finished her training just before the hospital was closed and the inmates had been vomited out onto the streets of New York City, and into the homes of the families that years before had decided that they could not cope any longer with the aberrant behavior of their loved ones. It had been the repository of convicts, of schizophrenics, of extreme obsessive-compulsives, of severely depressed, of suicidal, of mentally retarded, of brain-damaged epileptics, and of many others whose behavior, abnormal as it was, prevented them from living a free life in our society.

Dr. McKensie had had a long career in private practice and retired on her fifty-fifth birthday. She wanted to travel to exotic places and to cities she had not had the opportunity to experience. Her self-imposed week-long vacations made it impossible to visit during her psychiatric practice. She had cared for her patients. She had listened to their stories and those of their families, and had taken thousands upon thousands of notes, and had ordered any and all available treatments for them, from counseling, to pharmacological, to electro-convulsive, to surgical. She had been eclectic in her clinical approach and had measured her cases in terms of success or failure, and for that she had paid dearly. She now was haggard, with a wrinkled forehead that extended down to the underside of her chin, exposing a turkey neck that added ten years onto her biological age. She walked erect and her voice was sonorous and pleasant. Having been protected from the sunlight throughout her life, she bore no sun stigmata on the dorsum of her hands and arms. Her vision had been corrected with Lasik surgery, complementing lens removal and replacement with the latest version of artificial lens implants.

Two years into her retirement, a headhunter had approached her after an initial contact on LinkedIn that had resulted in a full-time job as Clinical Director of the Magnolia House and Resting Home. Visiting the rest of the world had to be postponed once more.

The next building was the recreation building. It

housed the movie theater, the library, the dance hall. The movie also doubled as a small lecture hall. The dance hall served as a performance hall, and most Sundays brought to it some musical group or instrumentalist that offered their services for free –America is a most charitable nation, and this nursing home was living proof of it.

The following building was devoted to kitchen services and also housed the dining room where breakfast, lunch and dinner were served every day to any and all inmates that were permitted to exit their unit building. It could accommodate 150 souls without any signs of congestion. Food was served at the tables, mostly by volunteers. At one time the clinic had tried to make it "cafeteria-style", but a nutritional panel had shown that the inmates were not choosing their food on a nutritional basis, but rather tended to under or overeat whatever dish they liked, some eating only carrots and others eating only chicken. By serving the food at the tables, they also solved the problem of those patients handicapped by wheelchair or crutches that had difficulty with the buffet servings. The patients that could not come to the dining room where served their trays of food by uniformed employees. Volunteers would help those that could not feed themselves.

The following building contained the Treatment Center, where small procedures were carried out, as well as the occupational therapy and physical therapy facilities. It also housed the Nurses' Club and offices.

The next two buildings where dedicated to housing patients, with the more delicate ones, or the ones that needed the most attention located next to the Treatment Center, and the ones dedicated to housing the most abled inmates almost at the end of the horseshoe arrangement. The last structure contained the laundry services and a small area dedicated to communications and mail. At the center of this arrangement there was a three-tier fountain fed perpetually by two unicorns spouting water from their mouths. From here radiated walkways to each building. A semicircular walk bordered the front and back of every structure. An enclosed walkway connected the end of each building with the next one.

The morning when Sharon Benjamin received the message that Dr. Jane McKensie wanted to see her at the Clinic, Sharon had been writing to her cousin in New York. It had been quite some time that they had spoken, or written, but Sharon always felt certain proximity to Miriam. She intended to tell her that she was, perhaps, ready to travel. After all, she had not been in Manhattan for so many years that she was afraid not to recognize her old neighborhood. But truth be told, she never was sure if she could leave, if she could go so far away from Moses. What if the doctor called her? What if suddenly he wanted to see her? —All those years waiting. She had gotten used to waiting. Waiting for a phone call. Waiting for an improvement. Waiting for a day when he would look at her and she would realize that he, the man she had married, was looking at her. But the time had passed, and she had to go on living and working, and visiting New York had become blurry, more like looking at a distant seagull flirting with the wind over the far horizon. And now, it was raining and thundering and the telephone had rung, and when she had picked it up, she had heard the voice of the operator saying, "Mrs. Benjamin, this is Dr. McKensie's secretary, she would like you to come to her office, if possible, this afternoon at two." It had been five years since Moses had to be interned in the Clinic.

LIFE'S PALIMPSEST

21

Sharon was born one bright spring morning, after 17 hours of painful contractions, in the Obstetrics ward at New York University Hospital. She had a normal childhood, if having two brothers and parents that were dedicated to their children can be called normal. After finishing college, she had pursued a nursing career, obtaining a master's degree in Nursing. Sharon was an attractive woman with blue-green eyes and blond light brown hair of medium built and height. She began working as a daytime nurse in the General Surgery ward at the very Hospital that had heard her first cries and tended to her loving mother.

Moses, Sharon's future husband, was also born at NYU Hospital. He also was a product of a normal household, and lived during his entire life, up to going to college, in a Bronx neighborhood not far from the Zoo. It had been a Jewish neighborhood for many years, but by the time he left it, a relentless process of integration was taking hold of many historical national quarters. Brooklyn, first Jewish, now was half Italian; Bronx was now half African American. Moses enrolled in the City College of New York when a degree from there meant something, getting a Master's in Organic Chemistry and graduating from medical school at Columbia, followed by a Doctoral degree in Pharmacology. He joined the Department at NYU as an Assistant Professor, but after two years, was lured to the private world of "Big Pharma", triple the pay and quadruple the research money. His new employer had seen the brilliant mind that was destined to find new drugs for horrible diseases.

It had been during his first year at NYU, that he met his future wife, Sharon, while she took the basic Pharmacology course under his leadership. If it had not been love at first sight, it had certainly been attraction at first glance. Soon thereafter, they went for coffee and a bagel at a coffee shop across from the Hospital where they had tried to speak amid the noise of police and ambulance sirens trying to negotiate their way into the emergency room entrance. Within one year they had walked under the chuppah. Neither of them was a religious Jew, but marrying under a chuppah had been a tradition as old as the Bible itself, and no Jewish wedding of any merit would lack a cloth –no matter how simple in design– suspended by four posts under which the bride and groom were promised to each other. A year later Moses was offered a position as a team leader in a private pharmacology firm, and they had moved out of New York, into the wilderness of New Jersey.

The Benjamin's married life appeared to be blessed. Sharon got a job at a local hospital that offered her the same salary that NYU was paying her, with similar benefits but with less stress. She dealt with patients that seemed to be more gentle, perhaps not being exposed to the daily grinding life of New York City dwellers, where the code of conduct was shove or be shoved, especially if you were trying to get a taxi during rush hour or when it started raining, when the thin layer of civic behavior would wash off New Yorkers' surface with the first drops of the grayish water. At the Jersey hospital, her call schedule consisted of 12-hour shifts and one Sunday coverage every month. She could hardly complain.

The pharmaceutical laboratory that had hired Moses gave him a standard office, with three metal cabinets and a Formica topped metal desk, with one reclining desk chair and one guest chair, and two walls with metal bookcases that soon began to fill with his scientific books and journals. A window looked onto a neighboring park with a small lake and two willow trees.

In his laboratory, directing a team of seven other scientists and technicians, Moses studied certain biochemical processes natural to cell reproduction, including the interference with the formation and maintenance of DNA. His experiments would eventually contribute scientific knowledge that led others to create medications that would interfere with DNA's chain elongation and repair, a pathway that in practical terms became useful in the treatment of certain types of leukemia. However, Doctor Benjamin's methods were somewhat antiquated and were replaced by a new emerging science of biotechnology where computer algorithms took over many of the trial-and-error experiments that Moses would run in the laboratory with his experimental mice. In a way, he had been born at the end of one era and before the new era of genetic engineering had come into its own. He had been a victim of circumstances, and thus, after a while, his experiments became antiquated, the invitation to scientific conferences dried up, and so did the funding he received from the National Institutes of Health and his employer. It took him a couple of years to begin experiencing depression, but once it took root in him, it only got worse. He was disappearing into a deeper and deeper hole where no one and nothing could follow him, not even his wife's love.

Sharon's most difficult decision ever was to intern her husband into the Behavioral Division of the Magnolia House and Resting Home one beautiful autumn day five years before, give or take a few weeks. He had clammed up and ceased to speak. The paucity of movement was unnerving; standing he looked like a statue, in bed he looked dead. Dr. McKensie had been honest with Sharon. "It is possible that you may never have your husband back again", she had said. "He probably suffers of a major depressive disorder with psychosis". And now, half a decade later, on this awful autumn day, she was again driving through pastoral fields in the middle of a rainstorm and fearing what destiny might bring upon her.

Five years visiting her husband had been painful. Sometimes she thought she had visited a body in a morgue. Moses, forever silent, not acknowledging her presence; Moses looking out the window; Moses seated; Moses lying down; Moses rocking back and forth; Moses crying. Sharon's visits had decreased in frequency as time went on, for she could not stand the sight of a man that looked like her husband, but who lacked the brilliant intellect and the sweetness, and capacity to relate to others that so much had defined the person she had married. Her heart had been broken those first months of internment. She began to make excuses to avoid going to the Clinic. She felt guilty. How would people judge her? But who could judge her? Only those that had experienced what she was experiencing were entitled, and those people were not judging.

Eventually she settled on visiting Moses once a month, and sometimes she would stay for a few minutes at the most. And at home, she never stopped loving him, she kept his things untouched, and she kept cooking those foods he had loved. The dinner table was always arranged for two people, and she looked at the emptiness that perhaps at some point in the future would be filled again by her husband. And now she was driving to the Clinic, apparently a breakthrough had occurred.

It had stopped raining. Sharon parked in the visitors' garage and walked briskly to the main entrance. A receptionist announced her and within a few minutes doctor McKensie's secretary came for her. After a tentative knock, she heard the doctor's voice inviting her to come in. The office, as always, was decorated impeccably. A large modern Danish design rug exposing a cherry wood floor. Fresh flowers in a medium sized vase on a table in front of the window. Books arranged orderly on wood carved bookcases, and two nineteenth century Hudson River School original oil paintings of landscapes that probably only had existed in the mind of the artist, since most of them were just but composites or idealized forms of the unfathomable magnificence that nature offered before it was to be conquered by modern man. A French renaissance desk with a modern glass top, and two comfortable Louis XVI style chairs for guests placed looking at the entrance door. Behind the desk, a tailored Miller desk chair, and behind it a collection of diplomas and certificates hung in orderly and mathematical precision.

Sharon shook hands with doctor McKensie and they proceeded to occupy their expected places, connected to each other, but separated by the desk —a routine cast in iron.

"I must confess, started doctor McKensie, that I have been somewhat disingenuous with you, if one can call some of my clinical decisions unconventional."

"I don't understand", said Sharon.

"Two months ago, all of a sudden, and without any specific preamble, your husband began to emerge from wherever it was he had been in. I made the decision to not notify you for fear that any change in his environment would set him back. We will never know if I was right or wrong. The case is that during this period, your husband has progressed to a point that he is almost ready to be discharged."

"When can I see him!" Interjected Sharon, barely able to contain her hope.

"Well, first I would like to give you enough information, so that your meeting can go as smooth as possible. If you please."

Doctor McKensie continued. "One morning, two months ago, a nurse's aide found your husband sobbing. It had been the first time that anyone had seen such an emotional expression in his face." She continued: "Josephine, the nurse's aide, reported immediately to the desk nurse. Half an hour later, I walked into your husband's room. I found him seating on the edge of the bed and, I noticed him following me with his eyes as I approached. This had been the first time he had done so." Doctor McKensie changed position on her chair and looked attentively into Sharon's eyes. "He asked who I was. We began to talk. At first his speech appeared all mixed up, but I soon realized he was telling me all the things, the thoughts, that were on his mind".

"Is he OK? Asked Sharon.

"Since that time, I have spent three hours every day

talking to him". By now, I have a clearer picture of what he has endured all these years." She interrupted her explanation and looked contemplatively at Sharon. "Do you know if he had a friend, a doctor, who died suddenly in his office? I believe he was a psychiatrist."

Sharon remained pensive for a few seconds. "We have told each other everything from our pasts. I am pretty sure he did not have such a friend. He would have told me about him or of his sudden death. For sure he would have told me about it. His best friend was Jacob Landowitz and he is still around. I think he lives in Hoboken; he has a shoe store in Hoboken."

Doctor McKensie continued. "What about a little pony. He has mentioned it several times with great affection."

"What about a little pony?" Sharon asked, somewhat surprised.

"Well, in at least five occasions he has told me about a baby colt, a fawn he called it, he was nursing because it had lost the mare during delivery. Apparently, the little pony died from accidental poisoning. Do you know anything about it?

Sharon looked surprised. "He has never been in a farm. The closest he has been to anything like a farm has been at Central Park or the Bronx Zoo!"

Doctor McKensie's face appeared at ease, as if she had arrived at a conclusion, as if a series of discontinued lines would have come together in a smooth pattern. Some call this, an insight. "Your husband has been experiencing a deep, deep feeling of depression, of having had a great loss. At the same time he has felt a yearning, a yearning for an environment where he feels safe. I presume that he never lived by the edge of town and went on walks with his grandfather when he was a child?"

Sharon replied with a nod of her head. She too was beginning to understand the symbolism in her husband's stories. He had been wounded by his scientific failures and had escaped in search of a safer world, a world that on the surface appeared idyllic, but in it he had found sadness as well. He had attempted to run away, but as the saying goes, his mentation had run from the oven onto the frying pan. As a result, his feelings of worthlessness had become even stronger. The tree of worthlessness had grown deep roots into him; roots so strong that, as it happens in nature, had dug into the interstices of his soul, fragmenting it into pieces.

"For a while his spirit had wandered into religious philosophy, but it had not been enough. It seemed that God's silence had become the echo of his own muteness. He identified with the biblical King Shaul, and this only helped to undermine any support he might have gotten from religion. He had suffered in silence for five years. He had tried to inhabit a world where he could live but had found misery had invaded his very core to a point where no amount of imagination could free him from his demons. He had relived the Holocaust just to find that the world was marching inexorably towards the next one. The society he recalled within the confines of his clinic room was as rotten as the one he was imagining, so for all these years there was nowhere to escape to."

Dr. McKensie uncrossed her legs and for a short while remained silent. Sharon, that had been sitting tall in her seat, full of anticipation and happiness, now was squashed. She had shrunk so low that she felt almost part of the carpet, or at least she thought so. The sound of the air coming off the vents filled the room with a deafening roar. She began to realize that, as bad as she felt, her Moses must have gone through a veritable living hell —for how long could a person suffer such feelings? Dr. Mckensie finally interrupted her silence and began speaking again. "As your husband became more and more depressed, he began to experience sleepless nights. His insomnia became so intertwined with his depression that soon began to interfere with the welfare of his brain to the point when a process of disintegration took root. The nights must have appeared infinite to him. His space began to fill with the sounds one normally cannot hear during the day when one is standing, when the ambient noise is increased by the quotidian rhythm of our activities. He began to listen to the rub of his hair on the pillow, the contractions of his heart. This 'hyper awareness' of his environment became organic within himself and he began to develop symptomatology compatible with psychosis. At this point, the integrity of his thought process combined with his depression and his concentration of feelings about himself began to appear to him as images of rotting meat, except that in his case, it was his own body that was rotting."

"Oh, my God", Sharon heard her own voice amid her tears.

Doctor McKensie continued. "You can perhaps imagine the pain he must have suffered deep inside himself, when he experienced the beauty of having loved a fawn side by side with the decay and putrefaction of his own body". Again silence.

"He fought hard. He built an entire stage set-up where he could and did fly free and unencumbered as a condor, just gliding on the air amidst the beauty of giant trees and greenery. But even this construct was spoiled by the horrible nightmare of suddenly confronting a set of high voltage electric wires interposed on his way. This is the kind of situation he endured for five years." McKensey said thoughtfully, almost as if talking to herself.

"Is this what he did all these years? Sharon wondered aloud.

"Yes, this and other emotional thoughts or constructs. Repeating themselves in his brain like a continuous loop of tape. Even, more interesting, is the fact that the basic format for most of them was similar: a beautiful memory fighting with an ugly one. Take for example what he did with water. On the one hand, he thinks of it in the most purifying terms. Terms like peace, beauty, life. But through it, the memory of a horrible incident, the vehicular homicide of a physicist, is brought into play. One moment Moses was floating on calmed waters and at the flip of a switch, he is confronted with the waste of humanity in the form of the accidental death of a learned man. This appears as a characteristic pattern in his reasoning."

"But as I mentioned earlier, he suffered from schizophrenia as well, and this showed up more in terms of his realization that he was rotting away. Of course, we never knew about this, not until recently, when he began to communicate with us. But during all those years, he suffered an infinite amount of pain. We cannot even begin to imagine how horrible it must have been for him. It was an intense feeling with no end to it. He was losing pieces of himself and yet, he would not die."

Sharon began to weep. Her tears ran freely, unashamed. The doctor offered her a box with paper tissues. After three knocks, the secretary entered with two cups of coffee and freshly baked doughnuts. It was perfect timing. Sharon could not take in more information. It had been too much too quickly, and yet, there be more to come, much more. They both knew it, and without completing the session, Sharon realized why Dr. McKensie had not wanted for her to approach her husband. These were delicate issues she needed to be familiar with.

Doctor Mckensie crossed her legs and turned the conversation back to Moses. "Do you have any children?"

"No, many years ago I had a miscarriage that got complicated with a bad infection. It left me unable to conceive. Why do you ask?"

"Because your husband began to complain bitterly that his children never came to visit him. He felt abandoned by them, by his family, by society." She uncrossed her legs, took a sip of coffee and continued. "It is possible that even this claim was a result of his feeling of being left behind. Not only by his colleagues but in a way, by you. He must have known, deep down, that you needed to continue to live, to live your life, even if he was here, rather than out there with you. This probably contributed to his feeling of being abandoned by his family, which in turn translated into having had children and not being visited by them."

Little by little, the complex tapestry that Moses had woven with his delusions began to unroll. It was not a pretty picture, truth be told, but it was an important and informative picture. "Do you know that through all these years your husband thought you were dead?"

Sharon could not help crying again. "But I visited him regularly!" She sobbed.

"Yes, but in his mind, you had died. How else could he suffer through all the indignities his mind had constructed?"

"How did I die?" Sharon asked.

"You were killed by a robber. You were stabbed to death. In fact, Moses used this as his departing point, his excuse for breaking down. So, at least, you must give him credit for loving you so much that living without you caused his illness." This remark, strangely enough, had a soothing effect on Sharon's dismay.

Mckensie had gone over all the details of Moses mental breakdown. She only needed to tie down a few more points in the narrative. "I suppose he never went during a summer vacation to the Catskill Mountains?"

"Oh no", Sharon replied, "his parents were too poor to take vacations and even less so to the Catskills, but we did go there about seven years ago. Just for a weekend mind you. It was as long as he could be apart from his research projects."

"Well, he had warm memories from the trip, even though they were very distorted, and even though he did not get his girl. I mean the imaginary girl during his visit."

McKensie looked at Sharon and asked, more like a confirmation, "are you a nurse?"

"Yes, for many years. Why?"

"Well, he also had this memory of playing with dolls and fixing his cousin's dolls when they were broken and of becoming a nurse later on. Of course, I realize that he was really thinking about you and your dedication to your patients. Perhaps another sign of how much he loves you".

McKensie continued. "Clearly, I now assume that your husband was not a prisoner in a concentration camp during the war. Yet, I can tell you that he lived through this illusion in a most horrid and vivid way, but, I surmise, it might have played a key role in guiding him on his way to healing. In his memories, or dreams, he was rescued from a concentration camp and nursed back to health. Perhaps, in a sort of twisted way, he must have reasoned that if someone could survive the Holocaust, he certainly could as well, survive his condition."

Sharon did not look surprised this time, rather, she was beginning to understand how torturing must have been these years for Moses. "Moses always argued that the Holocaust affected all Jews, not just the ones of Europe and Asia. For him, the Holocaust had been another affirmation of the existence of Judaism; not so much as a definition but rather as a boundary, almost like a mold that does not resemble the object it conceals within its walls. So, for him to experience the horrors of persecution would not be difficult."

"Well" said doctor McKensie, "his failure in the pharmacology laboratory let him to believe that he was being responsible for the death of thousands of sick people. He transported himself into the life of a death camp to clearly establish his guilt feelings. But it also proved that he could be rescued from such an environment, thus opening the door to be healed".

McKensie continued: "During the time when he was most depressed, he had very little to do, in fact, he stopped moving, what we would call a state of catatonia. He had plenty of time to think about death while in that state. He was living proof of death. He lasted a long time in this state of catatonic depression. He responded very little to the surrounding environment. It is a miracle he survived; perhaps it was made possible by our high standard of care. He might have not made it in some other institution." As if to make the point clearer, she added: "As you know we have a ratio of one healthcare worker for every two patients".

She continued: "And yet, your husband did not give up. He created a series of memories of a childhood he never had with a set of images of beautiful mountains and villages and lovely dogs and a sweet nanny and balmy weather that caressed him when his misery became almost unbearable. These constructs permitted him to survive, to re-emerge." She changed position on her seat and after a short while she added, "he did not have a nanny, did he?"

"Sharon, Moses loves you so much that he walked through the bottom of the Atlantic Ocean, from the

East coast of America to Norway, looking for you. It was a terrible nightmare, but he managed to find you, in Bergen of all places. This is how he has healed himself".

Sharon wanted to run and hug her husband tightly. To cover him with kisses, to feel again his warmth, but she knew that perhaps she needed to follow doctor McKensey's advise.

"Your husband has healed through beauty. By creating memories of lovely moments that may or not have happened to him. He has gone through the temptation of putting an end to his own life, rescued from death by beautiful memories of nature and of you." Doctor McKensie continued: "He is greatly improved. Now we need to keep him from falling back into the abysm he was in. He will need to be kept on a combination of antidepressants and antipsychotic medications to keep his psychotic depression from overtaking him again. He will need to return to his job."

"Doctor, you know he won't be permitted to return to his job." Sharon said it with certainty and in a calm voice. She knew Moses' previous career was over.

"I understand, but it is imperative that he has a job, that he develops a routine." Then, after a few seconds of silence, "Perhaps I can help. I have a friend who is the school's superintendent, and I will ask if there is a need for someone like your husband. He could teach Biology". It was an encouragement, but it did seem like a way to give Moses something productive to do, something he was fairly familiar with, even if he had to dumb it down a bit.

"During your coming visits to your husband, try not to ask him many questions, rather, play it by ear and let him do as much of the talking as possible, without appearing to be mute. Let him gain confidence and prepare him for a return home. I guaranty it, it will happen rapidly."

And so it was that Moses and Sharon were reunited a few weeks later. He had to adhere to a strict medication regime of a combination of olanzapine and amitriptyline in a concentration that doctor McKensie had worked out not to give Moses any significant side effects. The first two months at home he spent reading newspapers and watching the news on television. He knew he had a lot to catch up, but he also knew that integrating into society was not a luxury but a must. The first week at home was spent in a kind of tentative dance where neither dancer knew how much to trust the other partner, but it soon had to happen, sexual relations began and with them, the confidence that they were once again a couple. It had lacked the furor and passion of their youth, but it had the tranquility and undercurrent of knowing themselves so intimately.

As McKensie had promised Sharon, Moses was hired by the local school system, first as a substitute teacher, but after some months, as part of the regular staff. It had saddened Moses that he could not return to his previous biomedical career, but he was fully aware that this would not and could not be possible. So, he embarked on the study of high school biology textbooks to learn how much he could deliver to his students. The students appreciated his seemingly infinite knowledge of the subject, and his classes were well attended. The number of delinquent students, of inattentive students, of troublemakers, began to decrease and soon Moses' classes, were a model for the school. He had made a mental note to not be disturbed by the lack of discipline, by the noise and the fights among the students; rather, like a small motorboat chugging along against a mighty river's current, he had delivered his lectures. Little by little, one student shushed her neighbor and then another began to pay attention, and the number of students wanting to listen to what Moses was teaching grew, making those that wanted to disturb look more like the morons they were than the glorified outcasts they had been and they, in turn, also quieted down. It appeared that the broken window theory had worked, but in a reverse order. At first, when Moses began delivering his class lectures, all the windows were broken and all the walls were covered with graffiti. Then, one student began to listen, and one window was repaired, and then another, and another window was replaced and one wall was cleaned. In other words, if one person cared it invited others to care as well. Moses was as good a teacher as he had been a researcher. Life was good for the Benjamin family.

Saúl Balagura

PART TWO

THE END HAS
A BEGINNING

22

Michael Nguapana was born in the area of Am Daga. The earth around the hut where he was born was reddish-brown. The floor of the one room house was reddish-brown. The dust blowing from the northeast, from the sub-Saharan plains of Chad and Sudan, was reddish-brown and enveloped his amniotic-covered body like a warm welcoming blanket as soon as he was born. Michael was the seventh, and last child of a couple that lived in utter poverty.

The region of Am Daga is to the north of the town of Birau, the capital of the province of Vakara, the most northern province of the *République Centrafricaine*, or the Central African Republic. Bangui, its capital, sits on the southern region, as far as one could imagine from where Michael had been born. Thousands of years before, Am Daga had been a fertile land with plenty of water from the many rivers that emptied into the mighty Bahr Oulou, but it had been a while since these rivers had dried up and the bed of the Bahr Oulou as it bordered Am Daga often became dusty and rocky. The region had seen its transit of migrating caravans both from the East and the West, but their presence became as rare as the water; the dust had buried their pathways.

Michael spoke Sara Kaba, a rather primitive variant of Bongo-Bayirmi, a language spoken by the peoples of southern Chad and the Sudan that bordered the region, and of course, he spoke French as well. The few trees around his family hut had that rough and wrinkled cortex, with gnarled branches so characteristic of the vegetation that evolved to resist the desert winds. And to the south, just over the ridge not higher than 1,500 feet, the savanna extended a deep luxuriant canopy typical of the verdant African forest and the jungles of Saint Floris. It rained mostly in August and September, and then, amidst the reddish mud, plants and bushes, that appeared to have died the year before, exploded in an abundance that provided a feast to the eyes and to the stomach as well, for animals that had barely enough muscle to survive fattened themselves on this vegetation, becoming succulent food for the family, if the hunt was successful.

Michael's father, Jean-Pierre, cultivated millet and jam in a small garden patch. They had a few goats and chickens as well. These luxuries permitted the family to survive just above starvation level, but when the rains came and the millet took off, then, his mother, Antoinette, would prepare the most delicious porridge that they would sweeten with dark brown sugar brought from the city, hauled on a two-wheel carriage by a goat.

The French Michael spoke he had learned from his parents. It was mostly a kind of patois they had picked up at the Catholic French school in Birao, before hunger and poverty drove them to walk to the north, where Michael had been raised. Cooking was done in a mud oven a few feet away from the hut, and they ate outside under the cover of a canopy built with branches from nearby trees and old pieces of cotton canvas and corrugated tin. This left the inside of the hut to serve mostly as bedroom and to protect them against wild animals, especially during the night. The family owned two machetes that were used for farming, chopping, hunting and defense. They ate with their mouth and their hands. In a way, one could say, life was good, if one was to compare the Nguapana family with others that lived in Biafra, or Sudan, or Somalia.

Morning was the period of the day that Michael loved the most. The Sun coming up from the distant flatlands, bringing on its way the diurnal sounds from insects and birds. The morning breeze tickled his face. Then, with the sun overhead, it was as if a giant hand had gestured for all to slow down and pant, and when the late afternoon winds began to pick up, even though they brought dust with them, it was like a blessing from heaven, and they would gather around a fire and listened to Jean-Pierre tell them stories of travelers that he had met years before; travelers that had come from places so far away that not even walking two days without stopping one could reach.

Michael's childhood isolation hid from him a terrible secret, an ancient history written within the crevices of the trees, and the craquelures of the rusty and dusty dried mud, on the very winds that came from the north and west. For centuries, Islamic slave traders had decimated his forefathers. It would be beyond Michael's reach to know that Arab slave traders had terrorized the European coast since the 8th century, in search of millions of white, young women, men and children to sell as slaves in remote countries. Eventually, with the discovery of

America, a new venue, a new opportunity had risen, developing the trading of black men, women and children to be sold as slaves to Europeans for use in their new colonies. Many of Michael's ancestors had fallen prey to these raids as well. True, black slave trading for the New World had basically dried up by the nineteen century, but by then, the Arabs had become quite knowledgeable of the art of conquering and had expanded their territories to include not just European coastal regions, but the very depths of the African continent as well. And now, during Michael's youth the movement, that always had been brutal, had acquired a new patina: The invasion of lands and countries by Islamic groups not only had as primary purpose the slave trade, but the forced conversion into Islam induced frequently by barbaric acts of terrorism. Sometimes conversion into Islam took second place to acts of unspeakable brutality.

Progress in navigation brought the expansion of the European world as far as America to the West and even India to the East. The Portuguese had taken advantage of coastal Africa and had established themselves in the territories of Angola and Mozambique; the French had taken an active interest in Algeria and the English on the southern tip of Africa. Most of these ventures remained of a coastal nature, but the invasion into the center of the African continent took hold during the 19th century and by the beginning of the 20th century, most of Africa, with few exceptions, was under European domination.

Sometimes it is difficult to foresee the consequences that a war may carry. We imagine destruction, holes in the ground carved by canon fire, mines or bombs, people killed and maimed. But there are other consequences, perhaps subtler but not less tangible, of wars. There is the absence of the unborn children of those people that died before becoming parents, and the derivatives of treaties ratified by the victorious and the vanquished, and of course, the lives of the survivors.

World War I, the War to End All Wars, had been brewing for quite some time. The Germans wanted African lands and riches as much as did England and France, and when they could, they tried to interfere with whatever arrangements France had with its colonies. Treaties between England and France had basically divided much of Africa so that Britain would control a north-south axis from the Cape to the Suez Canal and France would control an east-west axis from the Atlantic to Somalia. So even though the First World War had started in the Balkans, bad blood had been boiling for decades in many other regions. The defeat of Germany crystalized English and French holdings in Africa.

The ensuing twenty years were not wasted on peace, rather, nations strengthened their military capabilities and by 1938, Germany was ready once more to test man's capacity for endurance of pain. Seven years are but a blink in evolutionary history, but the devastation caused by the seven years of the Second World War had nothing to envy any previous catastrophes. At the end Germany was again defeated, and the Allies had won. France that had contributed so little with its military might and so much of its blood, governed 15 percent of the African population and had the largest control, in terms of area, of any of the colonial empires even though it was mostly Saharan and sub-Saharan land. Among its territories was the land that eventually became the *République Centrafricaine*.

Michael's grandfather had been forced by the conquering French to work building the railroad, and eventually he had reached the region of Bangui, controlled by the French General Leclerc, where he had recovered from a cholera infection and had fled to the north marrying Michael's grandmother. They had had eight children of which only Jean-Pierre survived to become an adult.

The French public had lost its Napoleonic fervor and permitted the establishment of the Movement for the Social Evolution of Black Africa. Ten years later, the Central African Republic had been established. But the new republic had not brought much luck to the Nguapana family. By then, Michael's father was 10 years old and had enough time to become a Christian and get some schooling. Colonel Bokassa overthrew the extant government and became President for Life, bringing misery to the nation, a nation rich in uranium, diamonds, oil, fertile land, lumber and hydropower. Michael was barely a year old when General Kolingba took command of the nation in yet another coup. The people eventually voted to supplant Kolingba with Patassé. Poverty and disunion continued. General Bozizé took over in 2003. Soon thereafter the Bush War had begun. Am Daga was isolated because of its relative desolation and lack of population, but these factors did not stop warring groups from passing through and pilfering and raping and even stealing children. And if that was not enough, from the east, Muslim Sudanese terrorists made their occasional pogroms as well. Several of his siblings had been killed. Michael had enough.

One morning, instead of contemplating the rising of the sun and smelling the vegetation refreshed by the morning dew, he packed a pair of pants and two shirts, two pounds of dry meat, a gourd with water, and secured one machete to his goat leather belt and walked south trying to avoid any contact with humans. He was walking to Birao. It took him several days to get to the riverbed and there, having ran out of food, he replenished his stomach with frogs he caught around the few isolated ponds that still remained from the last rains. Not until he crossed the Bahr Oulou did he begin to see more luxuriant vegetation. He expected to see a big city. He had no idea of what a big city would look like, but when he finally got to Birao he knew this could not possibly be a big city. The streets were nothing more but the same soil he had been walking on for so many days, except that it was compacted and bordered by big shady trees or some low-profile buildings, most of it were built with mud. Some of the mud walls still bore the bullet holes left by an incursion that had left 20 people dead.

Michael was lost amid a city that had not seen peace in quite a few years. It often had been considered a town to send political opponents to exile; it was a place of shame. He finally ended up at the Catholic School, where he was given room and board in exchange for sweeping corridors and collecting the refuse left by the few students that still attended its classes. He also took advantage by becoming a student. He had much to learn.

This relatively pastoral setting lasted until October of 2006 when rebels overtook the town. Living in Birao was living in a nightmare from which one did not wake up. Michael was now officially a refugee. By the grace of some divine providence, he ended on a list of people to be given asylum by France, which had intervened during many of these internecine encounters, attempting to stabilize the government.

On November 14, Michael and 20 other refugees climbed on the back of a military truck and headed southwest for a couple of miles on a ride he would never forget. In twenty minutes, with military precision, they had been driven from the Catholic School to the Birao Airport and deposited into the belly of a large French transport Eurocopter Super Puma. Flying at three thousand feet, he saw his native Africa as he had never seen it or imagined it before and, as he would never see it ever again. They landed at the Bangui M'Poko International Airport, where they were given food and allowed to do their necessities in the most modern toilet he had seen. Then, they were photographed, finger-printed and given tags with official identification, and again they were herded into a large jet plane that took them to what turned out to be Paris, France. Michael's ears still were ringing with the whop-whop-whop of the helicopter ride of his life.

23

The plane touched down at the largest, hardest, flattest surface that Michael had ever seen, it was called Charles de Gaulle Airport. They were herded to a gigantic room where men in army uniforms with side arms on their belts checked each and every one of them, one by one, with meticulous care and infinite patience. Finally, it was Michael's turn. In his ancestral home, being in the presence of an armed uniformed man raised the probability that you were about to lose your life from low to very likely. But this time, the guard smiled at him and asked for his name.

"Vôtre nom".

"Je m'apalle Michael Nguapana".

The officer read a file behind his desk,

examined in detail the identification papers he had been given and after a few minutes, he welcomed him into France. At the next station he was handed his luggage, the small sackcloth with the few items that constituted all his belongings, but with no trace of his machete. As he reached for his sack, a man in a black cassock intercepted his action and introduced himself as Father Claude. He explained that he was taking him to a shelter ran by the Catholic church in the north of Paris, in a suburb called Aubervilliers. Father Claude placed a blanket over Michael's shoulders and told him that winter was coming to Paris. He apologized he had not brought a coat, but he did not know his size until now. The blanket had been the best choice. They walked out of the building into the parking garages and were instantly met by a cold, humid and polluted blast of welcoming industrial air. Michael had never experienced this type of environment and wondered how people could live like this; he wrapped the blanket tightly against his chest.

The shelter was a charity project of the Church of Notre Dame des Vertus. Aubervilliers also had a large Protestant ministry in charge of African refugees. Father Claude was assigned to work in the program for refugees, primarily from French-speaking Africa. He knew well the ordeal that his assignees had gone through. He marveled at the resilience that the human soul demonstrated in case after case. Michael happened to be his fourth hundred and thirty-fifth case. Father Claude's soul felt heavy like the blackest thundercloud, filled with rain and electricity and ready to empty its contents with cyclonic force. But upon who would he do such thing? At least the cloud could rain itself clean, but he, different from a thundercloud, had consciousness and memories, his cloud only got messier and messier over time. He read the news and the reports. He knew that the sectarian, tribal, political and religious violence that afflicted the entire African continent would not stop any time soon. It had gone on for centuries and it probably, to his utter dismay, would go on for many more centuries to come. He just was in charge of a small group of refugees coming from the territories previously controlled by France. France's colonial involvement with the Africans had lasted about a century, but its debt would sicken the French body for a thousand years, that is, if it could survive the affliction.

Aubervilliers in the Île-de-France, like its companion the *18th Arrondissement* of the City of Lights, had seen the typical evolution of Parisian communes, from a provincial, rural village, not infrequently immortalized on the canvases of the French Impressionists to an industrialized region, to being redrawn during a golden epoch, decaying and coming back to life again. And now, they were saturated with African expatriates. It was said that about 80 percent of the population lived in government-subsidized low-income housing, and at least half of them were either of African or Arab descent. In the Greater Paris area 40 percent of the population were immigrant or children of immigrants, in the Seine-Saint-Denis area 38 percent were of African origin and most were Muslim.

The Commune of Aubervilliers had had a strange development. Located to the north, but nevertheless relatively close to Paris proper, its fertile land developed into a flourishing agricultural provider for the capital city that lasted almost a thousand years. Then, in the early 19th century, a large canal, the Saint-Denis Canal, was built and little by little industry began to sprout close to it. Industry required workers, and the need for workers created an open environment for foreigners to move in. Initially families from Belgium, Spain, Lorraine, Alsace, Brittany and Italy, but also Prussians, and eventually, during the 20th and 21st centuries, to this population mélange, immigrants from Africa began to be added. The mixture of skilled workers with unskilled refugees placed into the same caldron could not result in a good soup, the results were bitter.

Michael's immigration papers were legal, which conferred him a privileged status, given that great many others, with whom he had to interact on a daily basis, had no papers or had overran their welcome status and were considered illegal residents in France. Living in poor communal quarters close to the church, he interacted with immigrants that had been brought by the Protestant fold of Christianity and their refugee ministry, and needless to say, with many immigrants that were followers of Islam. Documented and undocumented immigrants interacted in the bazaar that Paris had become, and many of them had not assimilated well into their new environment becoming involved in petty crime, drugs and major crime as well. It is difficult to crawl into the skin of a poor African immigrant. First and foremost, one must crawl into a black skin. And then, there is the problem of poverty, of not knowing if tomorrow you will be living here or somewhere else, if there will be food to eat, if one will be attacked and robbed by another fledgling young man, by a person that carries within himself the grudges of the old country, by a religious fanatic operating with a hate he never lost, or with a newly acquired hate instigated by some role model that infected him with the virus of self-hate and its cure, self-sacrifice through obedience and violence. And there was also the constant striving for wanting better, for desiring to improve, to progress, to become a person like anyone else, basically to integrate and become a Parisian, a French.

When Michael walked for the first time into the Cathedral of Notre Dame des Vertus, he felt as if he had walked into heaven itself. This was a church! The few churches he knew in his native country were often made of mud bricks. But this church was made of solid stone, and it was large, and above all, it was crowned by a series of stained-glass windows that were illuminated by the sun's rays and that imparted in him a feeling of inner peace. Of all of them, he loved the window of Sainte Jeanne d'Arc. It brought tears to his eyes. The green of the trees and bushes, the animals, reminded him of a stylized past he might have never had, but that nonetheless, he had grown to love more and more as he confronted the realities of living as a dirt-poor immigrant among hostile neighbors. The kindness of Father Claude was not enough to neutralize the pain.

Michael had been assigned the job of cleaning and dusting the nave of Notre Dame des Perdus. He was proud of his job, and it permitted him to attend school so that he could complete his high school equivalency. One evening, as he came out of the church and began walking in the direction of the Rue de la Commune de Paris, under the cover of the trees that had been planted to beautify the region, Michael was attacked by a group of three youths from Sudan. They left him badly beaten, unconscious, with a broken nose and many broken ribs. People from a nearby restaurant found him and notified Father Claude. Still unconscious, he was taken to Hôpital la Roseraie, where he was kept for nine days until his doctors where assured the traumatic pneumothorax secondary to the ribs' fractures had resolved and would not return. Michael recovered from his physical wounds and decided to move away from Aubervilliers. But as always, decisions made in a hurry and without too much information, not always work out for the better. He chose to move to the *18eme Arrondissement*, a quarter to the south of where he was living now.

The *18eme Arrondissement* was no panacea for Michael. The region was considered a sensitive urban zone by the French government, a delicate urban center that required special attention. It contained a large number of public housing buildings, with a low percentage of high school graduates, and a large number of unemployed immigrants. Thirty-five percent of the population was immigrants, many from north, west and sub-Saharan Africa. With a recommendation from Father Claude, he began to take care of the grounds of the Church of Saint-Bernard de la Chapelle. Michael did not know that a few years before, the French authorities had to forcefully evacuate a large number of illegal immigrants that had taken refuge in the church. Now, he wanted to keep it as clean as he had maintained the church of Notre Dame des Perdus. The region was known as the Goutte d'Or, close to the Garde du Nord and its many rail tracks, and for that matter, not too far from all the rail tracks sprouting out of the Garde de l'Est. For a while, he chose to live hidden under concrete parapets that accompanied the tracks as they exited the massive train station. He was lulled to sleep by the screeching of the trains slowing down or accelerating on the iron tracks, and by the distant sirens of ambulances bringing emergencies into the ancient, gigantic and famous Hôpital Lariboisière, where he himself would be brought as another victim of the senseless violent carnage that was taken place between religious vandals. After his discharge from Lariboisière, Michael again sought Father Claude for help.

Michael had completed the requirements for his high school equivalence diploma and, with this barrier removed, Father Claude was able to get him a job as a stonemason apprentice in a monuments business close to the nearby *Cemetiere Parisien de Pantin-Bobigny*. At first, Michael was just carrying stones on a cart from the storage area into the large hangar-like structure where the stone masons were cutting and chiseling the stones into the monuments that would illuminate the lives of the dead at their final resting place. As time passed, and at the instigation of Father Claude, he was introduced to the actual art of carving. And he had proven to be an excellent pupil. He worked hard and dedicated his attention entirely at mastering the art of caressing the stone with chisel and hammer, coaxing it to become what he wanted. "Short, sharp, caressing blows, like sending kisses to a departing loved one, that will get you what you want", that was the constant mantra he heard over and over as the weeks passed. By the end of the day, Michael had his hands stained by the fine stone powder that he carved for hours on end, and looking at them he could not help remembering how he used to look at his hands stained by the reddish mud of his native Vakara after tilling the earth, coaxing it to give the few vegetables that permitted his family to subsist.

Sometimes, especially during the summer days, he would take a bus up the Boulevard Pasteur north to the *Avenue R. Salengro* and get off in front of the *Parc George Valbon*. He would climb the metal fence and then, taking deep breaths, he would take in the smell of grasses and trees and the nearby lake. This extensive piece of land covered with luscious vegetation served to calm his nerves and to bring him close to the earth, to the earth upon which he had walked as a child and that now, in this city that had adopted him, had been covered with asphalt and concrete buildings. He did not know who George Valbon was, he did not know that he had fought against the invading Germans, that he had been a communist in the city government and that thanks to him a project of developing parks and gardens into neighborhoods had helped beautify these northern suburbs. Michael's brain was not geared to intellectual pursuits, be he was thankful for being in this park.

In the meantime, Father Claude was moving heaven and earth, shaking all his contacts, trying to look for a better place for Michael. Father Claude knew that sending Michael to another city would not get him into a better situation; he would end up living in another ghetto for African immigrants and he would end up being attacked by some Muslim militant gang. He did not know why he was doing it, why was he so concerned for Michael's wellbeing, but it had entered into his head that his protégé had to leave France if he was to survive one more year. Two beatings that had almost caused his dead were just too much. The inner-city violence was getting out of hand. Attacks against African Christians and Jews were becoming more and more frequent. The government's tolerance for this violence was inexplicable to him. What had happened to "*liberté, égalité* and *fraternité*"? It seemed to him that the police were avoiding confrontations with the violent youths that roamed the streets terrorizing the peace-loving inhabitants.

He saw that a fundamental change was occurring and that it only would get worse. His France was losing its soul.

His prayers were answered when he received a curious letter from Father Eusebious, an old friend who had been assigned to the Basilica of Notre Dame in Montreal. Claude had met Eusebious on a retreat that the organization of Catholic charities had organized in Quebec, many years before, at a time when the refugees from Northern Africa were beginning to flood into France and it was clear that they were about to confront a serious immigration problem unless the refugees integrated into society; religion was one way. The two of them had kept contact through the years, one complaining how far he felt from the European church and the other how close he was to the vigilant eye of the Vatican. In this particular letter, his friend revealed to Father Claude that he had been suffering from diabetes. Fortunately, it was Type II and for the moment he had been spared the daily injections of insulin, or for that matter, taking any pills. Unfortunately, the diabetes could be controlled with diet. "At this point in my life, dear Claude, I would have never guessed that I would spend my old age starving to death so that I can live, but these are the vicissitudes that the good Lord grants us to test our faith. And if this is not enough cross to bear –his complaints continued– the cost of daily living is getting pretty much intolerable here in Canada". It appeared that Father Eusebious had been in a depressive mood while writing the letter, for he continued: "And how rare it has become to find good masters of crafts, and how expensive a simple stone carver has become, practically impossible to get one for the daily repairs that the façade of our stone Cathedral requires after all these years of abuse by freezing winters and pollution. And believe me my dear Claude, our Cathedral is beginning to look like a leper". Lamented Father Eusebious.

The vicissitudes of Father Eusebious opened a ray of hope for Father Claude. He was elated by the news and immediately felt guilty. A mantle of shame covered him and he genuflected and crossed himself with the holy sign. But the news that a cheap stonemason was needed for the daily upkeep of Notre Dame of Montreal, gave Father Claude the answer he had been seeking about a safe place to send his protégé. Without consulting with Michael, he wrote to Eusebious a short note:

"Dear Eusebious,

Perhaps your problems, at least some of them, do have a solution. I have under my tutelage a young African from the Central Republic. His name is Michael Nguapana. If we can manage to pass him through Canadian immigration, I believe your prayers for a reliable and reasonable priced stonemason could be answered. In return, Michael would find the peace he has not yet managed to find in France, where the Islamic street violence is getting somewhat out of hand. And at this point, his peace would bring me, if not happiness at least, contentment.

Love in Christ. Yours,

Claude"

24

Canada is a vast country, practically a continent, extending its territory like a mantle covering the arctic circle all the way south to the northern border with the United States. Its riches are immeasurable. The abundance of minerals buried under its luxuriant earth, the abundance of water and forests could provide for a quarter of the planet's inhabitants, and yet, given its Nordic placement on our planet, its weather makes it rather unpalatable for many, so that it's population barely reaches 37 million.

Prior to the advent of European technology, the aboriginal inhabitants numbered about one half of a million, surviving mostly from the fruits of their hunting capabilities. European technology extended Canada's ability to draw produce from the land, and yet, its population growth had been rather slow, in spite of a rather open policy of immigration. Organized immigration laws began to be orchestrated during the second half of the 19th century, mostly for the protection and safeguard of those arriving to its shores. Eventually, immigration into Canada evolved into an amalgamation of permissive and restrictive laws, a segment of which, the Immigration and Refugee Protection Act, applied to Michael Nguapana. Immigration officers had been given broader discretion when evaluating candidates. Immigration officials could look benignly at applicants that might be employable and that could contribute to the Canadian economy, as determined by the education, language skill, and work experience of the applying candidates. In addition, for several decades, multiculturalism had formed an important component in the evaluation, admission and protection of those people applying for Canadian status.

Michael Nguapana could have been the poster image for all the conditions required to enter Canada. He was a black catholic African, who spoke French fluently, who was a political refugee from his native Central African Republic, who's life had been placed in peril twice in his adoptive country, who possessed a work-skill needed, and who had an impeccable recommendation both from Paris and Montreal, and now the promise of a secure job working to keep the stone face of the cherished Notre Dame in Montreal presentable. Nonetheless, father Eusebious wanted to maximize Michael's chances and for that he contacted one of his parishioners, officer George Dubonne, at the *Service d'Immigration*, whose office was located at the *Ministère de l'Immigration*, just two blocks away from the old cathedral. He dialed his phone: *"Bonjour George, c'est père Eusebious à Notre-Dame. Je voudrais vous demander une faveur…"*

George Dubonne had been going to Notre-Dame for many years, ever since he had been promoted and given an office on the fourth floor at the Immigration Department. One day, he was intent on lighting a votive in honor of his aunt, but there appeared to be no more candles. Father Eusebious had been very kind to him on that occasion and had walked all the way to where the candles were stored in the cathedral in order to get one for George. Since then, whenever possible, they visited for a few minutes after services.

Dubonne listened to his friend explain the situation with Michael, and as he was doing so, was checking off imaginary boxes on a mental list confirming that in fact it was possible, oiling the wheels, to speed up the immigration paperwork. Mr. Nguapana appeared to qualify from every point of view for speedy processing. And so, it came to be that he reassured his friend he would do his best and he would let him know how to proceed. Father Eusebious was elated and communicated the good news to Father Claude. It was now a matter of a short wait before Michael could immigrate, once more, this time to Canada. The memories of vast expanses of open land soon would be as remote as the geographical distance separating him from his Sub-Saharan homeland.

Father Claude negotiated some local streets and took the A1 to Charles de Gaulle Airport. It had been almost two years since he had driven with Michael this same road in the opposite direction. Michael still had only one piece of luggage to keep him company, but this time he had finished high school and had learned a good trade. Unlike two years before, when he had no idea of what the future held for him, this time Michael knew that his destination was Montreal, where a friend of Father Claude was waiting for him, and that he was going to work at another Notre Dame, much larger than the one he had taken care of. Father Claude was silent for most of the trip until he parked by the passenger drop area. He turned to Michael with teary eyes, made the sign of the cross and said: "Michael, I learned to love through your eyes and for that I thank you. Only God knows why each one of us is placed on this earth. May you find the way". He turned further on his seat and embraced Michael, then opened the front passenger door and looked away. Michael had truly opened the gates of love for Father Claude. Being a Catholic priest, he had no children, but Michael with his needs and yearnings, his humble presence, his dependency, his despondency and his slow and almost elegant emerging from the very bottom of hell, becoming a stoic and gentle person, had brought out a deep paternal instinct in the French priest. And now, he had put him on a plane that would take his protégé very far from him, perhaps, for certain, he would never see him again.

CDG to YUL. Those letters printed in bold capitals on his ticket meant nothing to Michael who was seated by a window in the economy section of the large intercontinental Air France jet. After some waiting, the announcement came that the flight would take approximately 8 hours. The aircraft began rolling on the tarmac in a kind of slow and majestic tour that Michael followed with teary eyes knowing that this leg of his life journey would take him even farther away from all his ancestors and certainly, he was convinced, he would never see Father Claude's gentle eyes again. The plane engines roared and Michael felt the pressure in his abdomen and suddenly realized he was floating in midair, gaining height. His body slid towards the window on his left as the craft made a sharp turn towards the northwest, soon piercing the cloud cover to reach its cruising altitude, but by then, Michael had fallen asleep. When he opened his eyes again, the cabin steward was announcing that they were twenty minutes away from the Pierre Elliot Trudeau International airport in Montreal, Canada.

Father Eusebious stood alone among all the other greeters, like a large black pine tree among a forest of colors. He was six feet tall, bald, with a bushy rim of silver hair around his temples that curled up towards the back of his head; in addition to his black cassock, he was wearing a black shawl. He held a yellow cardboard with Michael's name hand painted in large lettering. He shifted his wait from one leg to the other to alleviate the discomfort in his feet. He had been waiting for three quarters of an hour while Michael was being cleared by the immigration officers. Eventually, the two made eye contact. Although different from Father Claude, Michael sensed immediately that he had again found a friend in a distant land.

They got to the parking garage in the middle of the airport after walking for what it seemed an eternity and during which neither had uttered a word. "Voila, this is our car". Father Eusebious was referring to an army-green, thirty-two-year-old

Peugeot 504. Father Eusebious had bought the car in pristine condition fifteen years ago, from an old lady that could not handle any longer the four-speed mechanical shift. At the time, the odometer indicated less than fifteen thousand miles. Now, the car showed its age, even though mechanically, it was still in good working order thanks to an old mechanic that had gone to high school with the good Father. "Do you know how to drive one of these?" Michael had never driven before. Certainly not in Vakara, and in Paris he had always used public transportation. "Well, I will teach you so that you can also do some other work for the church".

They drove out of the airport area onto number 20, the Autoroute de Souvenir, that eventually led to the 720, the Autoroute Ville-Marie and after going through a tunnel, they exited on Rue Jean d'Estrées and after a block or so Father Eusebious made a left turn into Rue Notre-Dame O. In five minutes, they made a right turn on Rue Saint Sulpice and Father Eusebious parked the old Peugeot in a narrow parking area next to the back of the church. They got out of the car and walked to the adjacent building. "I just want to show you the church from the outside. It has a lot of stones that need to be repaired. Come." They exited the car and began walking towards the front of the church. Michael arched back so he could look up at the walls. He loved it. He had been born to take care of this church. When they reached the front, they walked across the street so that Michael could contemplate the entrance façade and the two towers extending five stories above where he was. Perched on a central arch stood, looking at him, the statue of the Virgin Mary. Below, a giant arcade two-stories high with six magnificent arches welcomed the parishioners in. He knew at that moment that taking care of this warm and welcoming building was going to be the task and love of his life. "Tomorrow I will take you inside. In the meantime, let's go home".

Father Eusebious lived on rue Richmond, just off rue Notre Dame, on Griffintown. They parked on the street and walked to a four-stories, narrow brick building. The Father lived in a two-bedroom apartment on the third floor, overlooking the street. "From here you can take the bus to the church or come with me in the car. Or if you want, you can also ride on a bicycle." Michael placed his suitcase just inside the door to his new home, a twelve-by-twelve room with a single bed and a wooden armoire. He was shown where the bathroom was, and then the two of them, as if prearranged, walked into a small kitchen that was almost part of the living area and began to prepare dinner for that night. This is how Michael spent his first hours in a new home, a new city, a new continent, and more glamorous he could not have imagined it.

When they sat down to eat that first meal, Michael, with tears in his eyes said, "thank you". This was not the afternoon breeze of his childhood years in Vakara, it had no bird songs, no red dust, but it did have a warmth that enveloped him as a childhood blanket.

"In about a week, you will begin inspecting the stonework on the towers". Michael acknowledged by nodding his head. "First, I need to learn how to dangle from that height".

"Don't worry, you will be trained and you will be safe".

The following morning, they drove to the church and Michael, accompanied by Father Eusebius entered through the main door. He confronted a most beautiful, intensely blue corridor and the most glorious and elaborate multicolor decorations on walls and columns that he had ever seen. He felt an immense pride in being part of this saintly building. For an instant he sensed an intense proximity to his family, that by now were probably all dead, after the last terrorist invasion of the northeastern territories of the Central African Republic. "These stones", he thought, "are now my family".

The two had an agreement: Michael would get room and board under Father Eusebious roof and in return he would work for only 8 dollars an hour, which was a real bargain for the church, but not a bad deal for Michael. After all, he had no major expenses, he had no family to send money to, he was like a single leaf hanging from a naked tree.

Little by little, Michael began to get oriented with the city. Fortunately for him, everybody spoke French, just as in Paris, so he was happy that even his own patois would have a chance to continue improving, peeling off the regionalisms he had learned as a child. He bought a used bicycle that permitted him to explore the nearby neighborhoods. It dawned on him that he did not have to fear being attacked by Islamic hoodlums, like he had experienced in France. Soon, Father Eusebious began to teach him to drive the Peugeot 504. Michael was a natural and rapidly he learned to shift without the protestations of the gearbox, and in a couple of weeks more, he had learned about the rules of driving, so that he was able to get a driving permit. To his chores at the church he added doing the grocery shopping for their home, and on occasion he would explore warehouses in search of materials to repair the Church's stones and grouting. He had become a real asset.

Dangling high from the church towers, like a circus performer, he had a wonderful view of the city, the Saint Laurent River, and to the south, very distant, through a blurred horizon, he thought he could see the United States.

During the summer, when the chilling winter winds had been replaced by the rays of a warming sun and cooling breezes, suspended high above the streets surrounding his beloved church, Michael caressed the stones in search of telltale signs of a future crack or the raspy erosion of the inclement freezes. He carried a notebook and in it he would annotate the condition of each individual stone to later consult with father Eusebious. They would talk about their stones like if they were flowering plants that required the same tender care. The pair had become the talk of the congregation. It seemed that Montreal was erasing, or rather, sanding down the deep grooves that Michael's past had carved upon his soul. Time was flying by and with it, like a seed growing within him, he knew he was only missing a companion, a girlfriend, a wife. But at this point in his life, he was well aware that God would fulfill his needs sooner rather than later.

Sometimes, suspended from his harness on a balmy day, he would find his thoughts invaded by memories of times he had forgotten, of moments of intense tenderness that he had experienced amidst the utter poverty and squalor during his years living on the dusty planes of Vakara. The memory of the time when he had found a wild dog with a broken leg, the poor animal had been close to death, and his natural fear of man was overcome by exhaustion. So when Michael, by then 12 years old, had found it, the dog had not protested being lifted and taken to cover near the vegetable garden of Michael's home. There, he had straightened the dog's leg and tied a wooden stick around it. He had given it water and food and kept it for six weeks. At one point, Michael noticed that the dog began to anticipate his coming around, and even would wag its tail when he approached. He got to touch the head of the small animal and even to scratch behind its ears while the dog looked at Michael through half closed lids. Then, one morning, the dog was gone, to never be seen again. It seemed to Michael, that something similar had happened between himself and Father Claude. The good father had mended his soul in Paris and he had flown away to Montreal. He felt the emptiness that the wounded dog had planted in him that morning when the object of his tender mercies had been gone and imagined how the priest must have felt that day at the airport when they said goodbye.

Life was being good to Michael. His mind worked at its own pace, accustomed to measure the day by the sun's position rather than by a wristwatch, counting the end of one day when the sun set and each new month by the nascent moon. He harbored no hates. He was truly a simple man, and if one stops to think about it, there is an inner peace in a simple person. There is a tranquility that city dwellers seldom can achieve, a certain harmony with nature.

The ability that Michael displayed in repairing the cathedral's stones did not go unnoticed. Father Eusebious did not have to point it out to his superiors, and they in turn wanted to foster the progress of their protégée. One evening during dinner, Father Eusebious said to Michael: "Are you happy with your job?"

"Of course, I am" he replied.

"What I mean is…would you want to do this all your life? Is there something else you would like to do?"

Michael thought for a moment. He actually was quite content with his life. "Well, perhaps I would like to work the stone more. Like making sculptures".

"Well, it would complement your work, for sure, Michael. Will see what can be done about it."

With the recommendation of the church, and a few blessings, Michael enrolled in the Arts Department of Concordia University. It was located a few blocks from where they lived on Rue Richmond. He needed only to pedal on rue Guy five minutes and there he was. It was not a full-time student position, but thanks to the connections of the Church, he was able to audit some courses and was given a corner in the students' studio so he could keep some tools and get some personal guidance as he developed some sculpting ability. Michael was in heaven. His instructor would repeat over and over: "Remember, the stone or the mud are hiding your sculpture, but it lives inside your head. As an artist you must bring out of your mind whatever you want to create, it is like giving birth. That's all." And Michael knew what was inside his mind. He had seen that young women in the stained-glass window in Paris at Notre Dame des Vertus. He wanted to bring forth the image of Sainte Jeanne d'Arc that had given him so much solace.

He befriended Pierre Duval. A 24-year-old dark-haired student from Quebec City that was in his second year at Concordia. The two of them began to develop a friendship that grew stronger as the weeks went by. Pierre had never been outside Canada and the knowledge that the United States was so close, served as a constant temptation that was becoming practically an obsession. True, in America they did not speak French, but he knew English and he could serve as a translator to Michael, if the two of them would dare travel there. Of course, Pierre did not have a car, but Michael did, in a way. "You just have to ask him", referring to Father Eusebious' car, "You have nothing to lose; if you do not ask, how can he tell you no?" And Michael would argue back that he would leave the good Father without means of transportation and that would not be fair.

During his time of exile, Michael kept up with his

native country. The news was horrible. It was as if mankind did not have enough violence to satiate the universe. His countrymen continued to serve as food for the African buzzard. The killings were not restricted to the countryside; Bangui had its potholed streets covered in blood. The number of refugees fleeing the country was approaching 300,000 becoming nobodies in someone else's land. Blood diamonds, literally bloody diamonds, where used as currency for acquiring weapons. The fighting between rebels and government forces had become a charade, a theatrical piece, each act in the play resulting in the murder of tens of thousands of people, interrupted by an endless number of intermissions where peace treaties were signed between President François Bozize and the chieftain a la mode at that particular time, just to be broken within months, so that the next barbaric act could continue. The burnings of agricultural fields and food depots were starving Michael's countrymen –a cornucopia emptied of fruit and stuffed with starving carcasses.

Perhaps it was the crop of bad news, perhaps Michael's realization that although he could be a good stone carver, he would never be a great sculptor, or maybe it was just the constant harping of Pierre's suggestions about visiting New York, but eventually, by early summer Michael broke down and approached Father Eusebious about allowing him to take a short vacation and to lend him and his friend the Peugeot. Contrary to expectations, the good Father agreed without even blinking: "It is a well-deserved trip. Enjoy". With the blessing and transport secured, it was settled that later in September the two friends would take a two-week vacation.

Autoroute Bonaventure, number 10, is just a couple of minutes away from Rue Richmond. It had been decided that Pierre would spend the night with Michael and that early on the following day they would start driving towards New York. It was a beautiful morning without a cloud on the sky. The traffic was heavy, but by then, Michael had become a good driver. He was familiar with the laws of the land. After a while, the Peugeot entered the octopus that would feed the bridge that crossed the mighty Saint Laurent River, Pont Champlain. The view of the Saint-Laurent was spectacular, but Michael had to be prepared to make his exit immediately after the crossing to catch the number 15 that in turn would become USA 87 that would take them to New York. They had consulted the maps before their trip and had decided that the only way to give justice to the splendor of Manhattan was by approaching over the George Washington Bridge. So, they knew that the last few miles of the trip were going to be somewhat tricky for, instead of taking the Tappan Zee Bridge following 87 all the way to Manhattan, they would go through Paramus and then get into I-80 and follow it to I-95 to the

Washington Bridge. They had made reservations at the Royal Garden Hostel on 97th Street and Broadway, easy on the budget and just a few blocks from Central Park. The landscape that initially was hilly and rural, had turned monotonous, and the traffic was a continuous source of tension for Michael. He began to realize that perhaps he was not as good a driver as he had thought.

By six thirty in the afternoon, Michael could hardly keep his eyes open. They now were finally driving towards the George Washington Bridge. The sun was behind them and almost gone, the golden hue it had imparted a few minutes earlier had dissolved into an indefinite variation of grays that seemed to dominate all other colors. It was too dark to be day and there was too much light to be night, all had become opaque. The gates to the tollbooths had become momentarily invisible to Michael's inexperienced eyes. For an instant he saw the red lights and thought they were just the taillights of cars. He looked for the light switch to turn the car's headlights on. It was just an instant, what in the paradigm of astronomical time could be discarded as an insignificant nanosecond in the history of mankind, but during that moment, Michael failed to notice that the traffic had, in fact, stopped. Pierre had momentarily fallen asleep. When Michael realized what was happening, he stepped hard on the brake of the Peugeot, but being a thirty-something year old machine, braking was not one of its good pony tricks and by the time he hit the car in front of him, the speedometer indicated 60 kilometers. He felt bad that he was going to damage Father Eusebious beloved Peugeot. He thought that he would allow the church to deduct a substantial portion of his salary to pay for the Peugeot's repairs. And for some strange reason, he thought on that land of orange-red earth and of the wild dog with the broken leg. Then, all became dark. Night had fallen and it wasn't even seven o'clock.

25

Moses Benjamin woke up this beautiful September morning after a night of uninterrupted sleep. The air outside was saturated with the sound of bird song welcoming a lustrous sun. Lately, he had been experiencing these restful nights more often than the nights spent counting little sheep jumping over a fence. His life was normalizing. It had taken months, but thanks to an adoring and supporting wife and the olanzapine and amitriptyline medication cocktail that she kept reminding him to take every day, the vivid nightmare he had lived for so many years had been relegated to a blurry memory.

On this particular morning, Moses was having breakfast at the school cafeteria. He loved to have breakfast at home with Sharon listening to classical music on the radio and talking just about anything that popped into their heads. Sometimes they spoke about politics, at other times they discussed about a show they had seen, or a concert, just about anything they would talk about, except his experience at the mental institution. It was a taboo topic that Moses only discussed with his psychiatrist. However, on this particular day, Sharon planned to visit her cousin Miriam in New York. She needed to cover for another nurse early in the morning and then do last minute shopping before driving to Manhattan; this is why she had left earlier and why Moses would have breakfast at the school cafeteria.

The school's curriculum for this particular day dealt with the impact of pollution on the environment, but Moses' lecture was not going to cover what the program prescribed; rather, he had readied a lecture on how ontogeny recapitulates phylogeny during the development of a human being. Moses had prepared a Power Point set of slides that showed how as the embryo starts to develop, it first arranges its cells like a ripe blackberry and then, as it progresses into a mature fetus, it resembles first a worm, then a fish, and a lizard, and a monster from the black lagoon and finally, the baby that one expects, that beautiful, mucus covered, crying baby that will ruin many a night and will make parents age prematurely until he or she reaches maturity. Moses knew it was an inspiring lecture that would fascinate his students and that would motivate them to want to learn biology and other sciences.

He was in no hurry. Classes were scheduled for the late morning. After class, he had planned to visit the local Kitchen & Bath Store and surprise Sharon with a Panini press. They had talked about how many delicious sandwiches could be made with one of those presses, starting with a simple melted cheese sandwich, then a Cuban with ham and pickles, and many others from a list of "must make Panini" they had developed over the years. Upon her return from New York, she would find the present on the kitchen island. He wrote a note that he would later place on top of the box:

"For my delicious wife, who will always taste better than the best sandwich we can make in this press. Love Moses"

Sharon had arranged her day's chores so that by the time she parked in the garage on the Upper East side close to the apartment where Miriam lived, walked a block east and asked the front desk to call her cousin, it would give them plenty of time to walk the four blocks to the Hungarian restaurant they both liked so much. It would give them time to have dinner and talk, walk back towards the parking garage, and permit Sharon to arrive home back in New Jersey at a decent hour, probably around midnight, depending on the traffic. She would try not to wake Moses. She would be as quiet as a church mouse. Why a church mouse? A strange saying! Do mice in the field make too much noise? What about a house mouse? Is it noisy? Had she ever heard a mouse making noise in her home? This in fact, were the very thoughts and images going through Sharon's brain as she merged into the line that had formed before the tollbooth.

At home, Moses sat in front of the television set. A scene, if you will, shared with millions of other Americans. He surfed the channels without any particular goal in mind and settled on an old rerun of Star Trek, the one where Captain Kirk's vessel is captured by the god Apollo. He had seen it many times. He had always thought that it was a deeply philosophical episode, one that dealt with the need of gods to be adored, in a way, it dealt with loneliness. For some reason, the day had been tiring. Moses fell asleep by the third commercial break and well before Captain Kirk escapes Apollo's promise of life in paradise in exchange for the crew's worship. Kirk had chosen freedom over enslaving love. He was woken up by a sharp electronic sound. Was it Kirk's laser beam? Had the Enterprise accelerated to warp speed all of a sudden? Again, the sound. This time he was fully awake. He looked at his watch. It was nine twenty. He had slept over two hours. Now he became fully conscious. It was probably Sharon returning from New York. He ran to the door.

Moses opened the door at the same time he was saying "Hi, love. I wasn't expecting you until midnight!" But it had not been love that stood by the door, rather, there were two policemen.

"Mr. Moses Benjamin?" inquired one of them.

"Yes...?"

"Is your wife Mrs. Sharon Benjamin?"

"Yes!" His skin becoming clammy.

"We are sorry to have to inform you that your wife was involved in an accident," said the younger of the two officers.

"She died at the scene of the accident", said the older and shorter of the two. "She is at Metropolitan. Will be kept there until all the arrangements are made. Here is their number." And extended his arm and gave Moses a piece of paper with a number written on it.

It had been a day in early spring; rather, make it an early evening in early spring many years ago. The lights of the car as it made the left turn into the next row of palatial homes surrounded by semitropical gardens that isolated them from the tree lined street, illuminated for an instant –an almost infinite instant– the large owl chick, still covered with its fluffy feathered fuzz, with its large owl eyes looking straight at Moses. Perhaps it had been anthropomorphizing to elaborate, but those terrible eyes were expressing a deep angst. The chick had fallen from the nest high above, over the luscious vine that covered the ground by the sidewalk. That is why it was still alive. But after a short while, that chick must have realized it was completely alone, without food or the protection of its parents. Now, its expression could only be described as horrifying. Those staring eyes conveyed, without a single blink, the adumbrated knowledge that death was impending. Nature cannot tolerate that the hyperactive chick that jumps the nest before its feathers have matured to support flight should survive. The species must be preserved at all costs, even if it means the sacrifice of the innocent. This is what natural selection was and is all about. Moses knew, as the traffic moved with its inexorable pace, that within a few minutes, one of the neighborhood cats, too well fed to hunt for food, would simply play with the owl chick until it stopped responding. And then, the ants would star their feast. Moses had seen that owl for just a couple of seconds many years ago, but at that moment, when the officers informed him that his wife had died in a car accident, the first image that came to his brain, to the very forefront of his mind, was that owl chick.

Moses heard voices coming from the living room and for a moment wondered who was there. He did not recall inviting anyone. Then he remembered that he had left the TV on. Then, he called the hospital and told the supervisor that Sharon would not be coming to work anymore, on the account of being dead. The supervisor, sensing the utter desolation in Moses, offered to help with the arrangements for the funeral: "after all, we are more familiar with these kind of things" she had said to him, as an explanation for offering to help. And he needed all the help he could get, for he was paralyzed. He followed Jennet, the supervisor from the hospital, like a dutiful dog follows his master on the heel. They drove to Manhattan and identified the cadaver. Had he actually dared look through the glass window at that body? How could he look through a wall of glass? He had not seen Sharon. No, it had been the body of a woman. That is true, but it had not been Sharon. The Sharon he knew was a beautiful woman, full of vitality with bright eyes that were not afraid of questioning or for that matter, revealing some deep emotion. The woman over the stainless-steel table was too quiet, too immobile, too deformed. She did not look at him; she did not smile at him or welcome him. Only part of her face was there, the nose and her jaw were missing; or perhaps, were next to the right shoulder, over a small plastic tray. And where was her body? He could see that there was a body under the light gray sheets, but it was too flat, it was too short. Then, they had turned the lights off and the entire building became as dark as if he had been inside a cave on a cloud-covered night. Jennet had positively identified her. She had brought Sharon's file from the hospital and also a brush from her locker that helped with the DNA match. Yes, it had been Sharon.

The remains of Michael and his friend Pierre were transported to Montreal. Father Eusebious was distraught by Michael's death. He had written a note to Father Claude in Paris:

"Dear Claude, dear old friend:

Sometimes heaven has a way to rain on a parade, no matter that it was organized to benefit innocent children. Sometimes, we have to accept that perhaps there is no purpose to our lives. Today we buried Michael. The Church paid for the ceremony and the plot. I insisted paying for the stone. It was one he had worked on, we just had to carve a few words on it.

'Michael Nguapana:

A Child of the Lord

1980-2008'

Because that was what he was. It seems that his destiny was set from the moment he was born: A life without a realized purpose. A hope that would never become happiness. I better stop writing before I regret my own words.

Your friend."

26

For a while Moses had entertained the hope that his wife was not dead, that it all had been a mix up, and that she really, simply was away. She had flown to Norway, to Bergen. It all was a mistake. He knew she was up on the hill, under the shade of that tree, licking an ice-cream cone. It had to be. Last time she had done this to him he had found her at the top of the mountain. He had no choice but to go looking for her. He knew there was a way out of that cave —so dark, the cave. He climbed over large boulders, his fingers grabbing the rough edges of the rocks like if he were a salamander. There was a way out. All caves have an entrance and if you were inside one, that same entrance becomes an exit if one walked backwards. Yes! That's what he had to do, walk backwards. But how far to go? Well, that was going to be obvious once he found the mouth of the cave. He walked backwards, looking occasionally to make sure there was no precipice into which he could fall. But he had been lucky, he had not fallen into any crevasse and he had found the entrance, or rather the exit to that horrible cave that had served as a prison. Now all he had to do was go to Bergen. The coastline was not too far away and he knew how to swim. And if he got tired of swimming, well, he always could walk. He had done it before. It was a matter of losing the fear of the darkness, of all those phantasmagoric animals that found home at the bottom of the ocean. He would be careful not to be sucked into an underground volcano or be eaten by some gigantic fish or sea monster, but he had his folding-knife in his pocket ready to be used against whatever attacked him. On this part of the trip there were no roads to follow, no maps, no signs to indicate that Bergen was the next town. He had to guide himself by other means. He would talk with friendly octopuses or a cooperative tuna, they had been nice to him before and he was sure they would be nice to him this go around. After some time, he recognized the giant volcanic formations that announced he was getting close to Iceland and from there it was just a matter of time to drag himself against those currents that wanted to bring him back to America, back to the coast from where he had begun his journey. He was going to keep going. The water was cold and dark. There were no coral formations in these regions, just gigantic sand dunes and even bigger rock formations. He just had to keep marching. Sometimes, if the currents permitted it, he would swim. Carried by the dark waters he floated for weeks until one morning, he sensed that the sea was getting shallow and he climbed onto a rock and saw with utter happiness that he was in Bergen. But things, just like coins, have two sides to them. He had arrived at Bergen but had forgotten his wallet at home. How would he get to the top of the mountain? How doltish of him. If he had gone this far, how could this stop him from finding his wife? He found the funicular rails and began climbing the hill next to them. The people on the train cars waved at him, smiling like if they were on some sort of vacation. Idiotic. He was getting tired. Exhausted. But it was just a short distance to the top and now he could see the bannister by the edge of the cement plateau and the steps that his wife would have taken to get her ice cream cone. But she had not been there. It all seemed so unreal.

How come he did not remember walking on the ice fields of Iceland? He did not see any geysers. He did remember the distant wailing of the wolves. He thought they were the saddest sounds he had ever heard. Now, where Sharon once stood, there was a stone. It looked like a monument. It had Sharon's name on it and a date. "Happy birthday Sharon!" he thought. All was dark again.

Moses Benjamin had not found his wife in Bergen. The rocks of Norway revealed only pain. His Sharon had gone. That is what he felt when he woke up and found her side of the bed empty. Empty and cold. No wrinkles in the bed sheets. He walked to the refrigerator and found it empty. The kitchen sink and the counters were covered in dirty dishes. He felt hungry, a ravenous ache for food. He was already dressed. Although surprised to see that he was fully dressed, he could not remember when he had done so; he even had his shoes on. He left his home, walked to the corner and made a left turn and kept looking for food. The concept of entering into a restaurant or a supermarket and buying food did not enter his mind, at the moment, it was an alien concept to him. He simply wanted food because he was hungry. He was not thinking in a steak, or a succulent piece of salmon, he was simply ravenous and needed something to fill his stomach. He found what he was looking for in a brown paper bag next to a dumpster. Just what he wanted: hamburger and fries, or what was left of them. Moses kept walking until it turned into roaming. He had forgotten what it is he was looking for. When the night came, he found cover under the roof of the main entrance to an office building and sat on the floor, reclining against the granite wall until he fell asleep. For a fleeting moment he thought that he had not taken some medication he was supposed to take, but he was too tired and too sleepy to explore that thought in more depth. The following morning, olanzapine and amitriptyline had been washed off his memory banks and most certainly depleted from his blood. Moses was now free from his chemical chains. The noise of early morning traffic woke him up. He needed to urinate and was sore from lying on the hard, concrete floor. He stood up unsteadily and stretched his arms and arched his back and began walking towards the alley on the side of the building, finding a dumpster, unzipped the fly of his pants and urinated until he felt the involuntary trembling feeling that he was empty. He turned towards the main street and kept walking. This time there was no urgency, it was more like an animal roaming on the savanna, repositioning for another cycle of day and night. He passed by a building with a wide sidewalk where children were being unloaded from cars and yellow buses. It felt strangely familiar to him, but he couldn't tell why. He continued walking for most of the morning until he arrived at an expansive open area with trees and grass. Looking for the shade of one of the trees, he sat protected under the refreshing shade. Deep from within his very entrails, the face of an old man, with deep nasal folds and a short, unruly, gray beard began to take form. He was wearing a dark striped suit, deep brown and there was a familiar child next to him. "Grandpa, where are the horses?" But grand papa was not talking, he was looking at the distant horizon. Only his left hand moved slowly and methodically, reaching the outer pocket of his suit jacket. From it he extracted a small packet that he proceeded to unwrap with certain meticulousness until he found a small envelope of folded paper that contained salt. He peeled the onion of its aging dried up skin until it revealed the pink reddishness of its shiny pulp, added some salt and bit into it. "Can I have some, grandpa?" and he took a bite next to the larger bite the old man had left. Those were good days Moses thought. But whose?

Why had he been assaulted by such image? Was it a memory that belonged to him? Was it so precious that it merited its evocation at that time and place? He paced around the large tree as if pacing would help him answer the question he had just posed. But what was he doing here? What had happened? These were questions that were floating in a miasma of anxiety that seemed to be covering his entire body as if he had fallen into a sewer. Moses knew he was missing something. But what was he missing? He could not clear his mind. He looked down at his feet and realized that he had no shoes. Why? He was just adding one question on top of another, like laying bricks to build a wall.   But there was no wall.   Only questions. He had forgotten something or other.

He felt a hunger pang and his mouth was dry. With his tongue he went around and felt the stickiness of thick saliva deep in the recesses of the gums, and his teeth felt like chalk. He realized he was thirsty. He had walked for so long under and over the sea on his way to Bergen and had forgotten to drink water.   But that would have been salty water. Everybody knows one cannot quench thirst by drinking seawater. And then, it dawned on him that he had been looking for Sharon, but he had not found her in Bergen. Sharon had been lying on a metal table at the coroner's office. Oh God! Where was his Sharon that he missed so much? Everything became dark.

When Moses woke up dusk was hovering like a gentle mantle. His abdomen was aching. He walked in the direction of the city lights, crossing streets without regard to names or traffic. He was not looking to enter a restaurant, he just wanted to find the trash bin of one, some place where he could just crawl into and eat, without being disturbed. Finally, he located the back door of a Chinese restaurant and the object of his search, the large trash cans filled with refuse. The world had become a wasteful place. There had been a time when a whole family could have eaten from what now a single person was served at restaurants. The portions had gotten larger and larger as agricultural productivity had made it possible for the price of food to come down. He ate pieces of shrimp still attached to the last segment of their tails, and clumps of sticky rice and a dark gloppy stuff that he found delicious and went well with the shrimp. By the foot of one of the trashcans there was a missing piece of asphalt that was full of water, probably from the last time the restaurant had hosed down the alley. He laid belly down on the floor and drank from the pothole sating his thirst to great content. He left the Chinese restaurant and walked without aim. He began noticing that people were looking at him. He felt somewhat awkward about it, but he could not really explain why. After a while he felt the need to defecate. His bowels were rebelling against something he must have eaten. He sat around the corner, next to a large mailbox, pulled his pants down and let it all come out with great relieve. Fortunately, nobody was passing by him and he had time to pull his pants up and walk away, way before a cloud of flies landed on his excrement. He kept walking until he found a building with a recessed entrance that would make a perfect place to spend the night.

When the morning came and he woke up, it was raining and there was very little traffic and even less people walking around. Moses thought it must be the weekend. It was a gray, opaque morning, but what it did promise was that he would not go thirsty on that day with all the puddles filling with clear and clean heavenly water.

Life without striving can become a routine. Living without someone to love is akin to being a sailboat without wind, just bobbing up and down in a random yet predictable fashion. The sun goes up and one moves, and when it goes down one lays down, no different than a balloon filled with air that floats when it gets hot just to sink to the ground when night comes along. There is no horizon, no goal, no mountain to walk to or to climb. Life becomes existing, in a way it becomes the centripetal shell of a snail with no snail inhabiting it. One night, as he walked past the empty display window of a jewelry store, he saw a reflection on it staring at him. For a moment, his fight-flight reaction accelerated his heart, filling his chest with dread. His body told him to run, but his mind stopped him, daring him to look into the image that appeared to be mimicking every move he made. Moses' mind had been running on empty for quite some time and it took him a while to realize that he was peering at himself. But the image he saw he did not recognize. He had forgotten who he was, or had been, but he did not form a concept of who he was at that moment either. He had been busy chiseling away memories, becoming nothing, and yet, whom he saw reflected on that glass brought dread and confusion. He had seen a disheveled human, with long and uncombed hair, a straggly beard, sunken eyes with dark skin and crumpled, dirty clothing. Worst of all, he had not seen light in those eyes. There had not been any sparkle, no hope, no tomorrow. He ran away, crossing traffic lanes and honking cars. He ran until his legs gave away. He sat, panting, behind the cover of a bench under the shield of the plastic canopy of a bus stop and tried to recover his breath. It was then he realized he was bleeding profusely from his right foot. He must have stepped on a piece of broken glass. He was not wearing shoes and his socks had eroded away remaining only around his ankles, giving him some warmth during cool nights. As he calmed down, he began experiencing a pulsating pain. Vaguely, he seemed to recall that he had to clean and explore the wound, to make sure there were no leftover pieces of glass or other foreign bodies. He grabbed his foot and brought it up over his left knee and saw a two-inch long, deep cut on the sole of his foot, close to the big toe. He squeezed on both sides and saw a shard of green glass jutting out. He grabbed it and pulled, repeating the maneuver until he was convinced there were no further shards. A few minutes later, the bleeding stopped. He limped to a nearby garbage can and found a rag; he washed it in a puddle and tied it around his foot.

The rumbling of a bus on its first morning run woke him. The bus was almost empty. Moses became aware of a pulsating pain on his foot. He limped his way to the trashcan of a restaurant and gathered as much eatable food as he could from the sandwich wraps and leftovers that still had not been picked up by the sanitation truck. He shoved as much as he could into his pockets. Moses continued limping his way from trash bin to trash bin —a bee and his flowers— and then headed for the park. There he sat under his tree and ate until he was sated. He felt cold even though the wind was not blowing and there were no clouds to block the sun. Later on that day he felt thirsty and walked to a water tap that was used mostly for watering the lawn and drank copious amounts of water. He even surprised himself of having done so but couldn't figure out why. His foot was aching and throbbing. He washed the bandage and reapplied it around the foot. It was then that he noticed the discoloration of the skin. He went back to lay under the shade of his tree. Unaware he had gone to sleep; he was awakened by a sharp cracking pain on his rib cage. Was he dreaming? Could he do something to escape this punishment or was he the victim of his own nightmare? Reflexively, he curled into a defensive posture guarding his head from the savage blows and at the same time trying to prevent those hands from robbing him of the food he had saved in his pants' pockets. The kicking intensified. He thought he would be killed. Then in a moment of lucidity he wondered why he had not been attacked earlier. He was living like a solitary animal among a pack of professional wolf-beggars. He had broken into their territory. The image of a man reflected on the window, a wild looking ugly ogre, filthy and unkempt, mimicking his own gestures filled his mind. Then all went dark.

27

The sirens became louder and louder as the police car approached the edge of the park-like Holy Name Cemetery. Someone had reported a fight between vagrants somewhere around the southeast corner of the grounds. It had been an anonymous call from a jogger. The Jersey City Police had sent a unit to investigate. The fight would have ended by the time of their arrival. It always was the case. And if one of them was left behind wounded, it was going to be like finding a needle in a haystack –an almost dead victim among thousands of the dead. The unit drove slowly on the central avenue while both officers scanned for a possible victim. They were going to park by the rotunda and start walking on the grounds proper when one of them discovered the body of a man under a tree, about hundred and fifty feet away. It wasn't moving.

"Joe, we have an unconscious man at Holy Name. We need an ambulance pronto", one of the officers called on his radio to central. Both policemen were pretty much grossed out by the bloody mass of stinking, dirty man wearing nothing more than his underwear, his right foot swollen and red like a delicious apple. The two did not move Moses. They had learned that in school. Moving an unconscious person could make much worse an incipient spinal injury. These things were better left to the medics, and they were on their way. Twenty minutes later the flashing lights of the ambulance disturbed the garden of the dead.

"Sorry Mark, but the traffic was really heavy". Joe said this as he carefully applied a plastic collar to the neck of the beggar lying on the grass. Once the neck was secured, Joe and his trainee-assistant slid a long plastic board under Moses and lifted him onto the stretcher.

"Blood pressure is low and pulse is rapid", Joe stated as a matter of fact. "What do we need to do?"

His assistant replied, "He needs i.v. fluids right away".

"Good boy. Get on with it". Joe watched patiently as his charge cleaned the left antecubital area of his patient and inserted the intravenous line connected to the saline solution. They covered the patient with a blanket and secured him to the stretcher with the orange nylon straps.

"Good. Now let's take him to the truck and to the hospital".

The ambulance rushed Moses to the emergency department of Jersey City Medical Center. Moses was unconscious, and one would say better off this way for it spared him seeing the faces of those taking care of him as they recoiled when breathing the air near him. All were wearing facemasks, protective eye shields, gowns and latex gloves. It had become regulation after the epidemic of AIDS and hepatitis that so frequently afflicted the homeless drug users that not infrequently were brought agitated and aggressive, spitting or bleeding from open sores and wounds. At first, it had been seen as a sign of weakness, to wear gloves, but eventually, political correctness was overcome, and the old rules of preventive medicine were wisely instituted for all. No longer was there a stigma if one used gloves to touch a patient.

The first striking finding was the malnourished

aspect of the guy lying on the emergency bed. After determining that there were no external bleeding sites, the patient was taken to x-rays were a quick body scan ruled out any brain bleed. It also made apparent that there were several fractured ribs coinciding with the extensive bruising over his trunk, but no major accumulation of blood inside the chest. And of course, there was also a bad looking infected wound on the right foot, foul smelling and purulent with inflammation of the lymph nodes up to the inguinal area. Blood samples were taken for determination of all relevant parameters and also for culture to determine if the patient was suffering from a blood infection coming from the leg.

"Anybody came with him?"

"Do we know if he is allergic to any medications?"

"Is he taking any medications?"

No one had any relevant information. Moses was not carrying his billfold. Since the death of Sharon, Moses had forgotten himself. He had erased his persona; he had become an amputated leftover; but no one knew this. On this day he had become John Doe # 3 within the hospital system.

Soon he was given a sponge bath and his facial hair was shaven, his finger and toenails were trimmed. He was given an indestructible plastic band around his right wrist with a number and a computer code bar and transferred to the intensive care unit for observation and care.

The diagnosis of gangrene was apparent. He was given potent antibiotics, but it was clear that they would have to amputate the foot if the infection showed further signs of spreading. The swelling had been partially controlled with some relaxing incisions along the length of the leg below the knee, a procedure reminiscent of making cuts along the casing of an overstuffed sausage to relieve the pressure.

Moses woke up a day and a half after his admission. The pain in his leg was overpowering. The room was filled with the smell of a rotten corpse. Deep inside, he became aware that the smell he perceived originated in himself. He was filled with fear and anxiety. He was tied up to the guardrails of the bed and his right leg was elevated and covered with a bed sheet that gave the appearance of a mini airplane hangar. Breathing was also very painful. He felt his chest as if a thorny wire cage surrounded it. Every time he took some air in, he felt the needles bursting into his ribs –he remembered the attack in the park. He became agitated. The beeping sound of the cardiac monitor accelerated. A nurse came into the room and injected something into the intravenous rubber portal. Soon the pain began to subside, he was floating in a sea of white. There were wide waves and the water was just right, not to cold or hot. He could breathe the water and not drown. He could move without effort, floating from one white place to another so silently that it felt as if he was flying. There were no sounds that would inform him if there were others with him. There was no horizon, no top or bottom. So much white that he almost felt he was floating inside a cloud, like he used to see when he was a child and his parents took him on a vacation trip. The small commuter plane had been flying on clear air and low enough to see the pastures and little houses on the ground below. All of a sudden, small tufts of white powdery cloud would pass along his window, and every time the wings of the plane cut the clouds, the plane gave a jump making him feel as if he was falling, and then, the landscape beneath disappeared as if someone had painted the windowpane white and he had the distinct feeling that he was floating, just as he was floating now inside an ethereal white. What had happened to his parents? He could not remember their faces, their bodies, the way they dressed, the timber of their voices. And yet, he knew he had had parents, it was the most natural thing. In the middle of this wondering, he became aware of some pain, although he could not place exactly where was this pain coming from. He tried to speak but realized that there was a tube in his mouth. He could not bite into it for someone had placed a piece of hard plastic in between his teeth. In the middle of this fog, he became aware of voices, even though he could not listen to what they were saying. Where was he? Had some sailors rescued him as he was walking by the Faroe Islands? But then, what was he doing there? A sharp pain, like a knife on his leg, woke him up. There were two people close to him and covered in surgical gowns from head to toes. He again became aware of the rapid beeping sounds and the pain in his chest when he breathed in, and now he also became aware of a sound like a bellows that accompanied his breathing. In...pshoooos, out...pshoooos, repeating over and over without ever tiring. His world had been reduced to fog and pain and constant beeping and a rhythmical bellows pushing air in and out.

The first time Moses remembered to have emerged from the chaotic cloud in which he had been floating he was sitting on a padded blue chair and a nurse was pulling out of his mouth a spoon. He was surprised by the fact that he tasted apple compote as he pushed with his tongue from side to side before swallowing. How had he gotten to the chair? He was not surrounded by fetid odor. He became aware that he was not experiencing too much pain when breathing. More importantly, when he looked at his right leg, there was no sign of swelling, only some darkened skin extending to the mid-calf. For the first time, he looked into the eyes of the woman in front of him and heard her saying, "Well hello there! How are you feeling?"

Moses had no idea how long he had been in the hospital, although he now was fully aware that that is exactly where he was being held at the moment. After waking up in the morning when the nurse came to take his vital signs, he was asked how he was feeling and if he had any specific complaints. Then after a while, another person would come in with a tray of food that would be placed on a bedside table on wheels that was placed in front of him. The same person would then raise the reclining portion of his bed, effectively leaving him in a seating position, then, saying "have a good morning", would walk out of the room. Breakfast consisted of a small carton with 2% milk, a small container of cold chopped fruits, strawberries, blackberries and blueberries, and either scrambled eggs or pancakes. After a while, someone would come and withdraw the tray. Later in the morning, he would be helped out of bed by a male nurse that would encourage him to walk with a pair of crutches on the long corridor and then bring him back and place him in the blue chair in front of the television. Then, the narrow table on wheels became his lunch table where he would consume some apple juice, some soup, and a dish with warm vegetables and either fish or chicken. Sometime in the afternoon, he would be helped back to the bed, and a person that was not a nurse, but was not a doctor either, would change the dressings on his right leg, saying. "Much better, much better looking".   He would dose off for a short time just to be woken by someone bringing him his dinner, which looked like lunch, but also had rice or potatoes, and sometimes meatloaf.

One day, they all came along with what turned out to be a social worker and it was clear that they were planning his discharge from the hospital. He knew his wounds were not healed yet, but they were not talking about letting him go onto the street, rather a transfer to a nursing home so he would have additional time to recover. They were going over names of several nursing homes. Clearly looking for one that would take him. But why so many problems?

"Well, we have to place him where they take him." One of them said.

"Sunrise at Edgewater is mostly for people with vision disabilities or older patients with some dementia."

"What about AlarisHealth? He could do well there."

"Yeah, but they are full at this time. And he is too young for St. Ann's. Pity."

"What about Cusack's? "

"Naah. He is neither blind nor old."

"Well, that leaves you know what."

"Yeah. I was trying to avoid that one."

Moses was barely following the conversation. They were talking in hushed voices and in any event, he was not familiar with the names. As it turned out, Moses was not completely aware of the "21 day" rule. He thought he had heard someone mention it. But give or take a couple of days that rule rules the healthcare system in America. There is nothing magical with 21 days. There are no medical texts that mention this period of time as anything different or special, but our government and our health insurance companies have made it relevant. It is the sweet spot, the magical number of days that musters the most efficient reimbursement for expenses incurred on a patient. This is what our society had come to distill after a century of great strives into improving healing. Of all the healthcare advancements in the history of medicine, advances that included the practice of sterility, vaccination, anesthesia, specialized surgeries, chemotherapies, and compassion, it was the 21-days rule, the one that alerted hospitals to mobilize the troops. Too many days short of 21 and the reimbursement would not be sufficient to cover the costs incurred during the acute phase of an admission; too many days beyond 21 and the reimbursement to the hospitals would be proportionally insufficient to cover the overall care of the patient. One of the doctors was saying, almost with nostalgia, "Combating disease used to be the kingdom of doctors and nurses. Now, it has been taken over by the empire of healthcare providers."

There are many illnesses that require of healing or rehabilitation time and institutions have been set to provide for it. You will hear about it –if you have not already– when taking a loved one recovering from a medical condition that requires some extra time for further improvement. If you could have access to the thousands of these patients' charts, you would discover the almost formulaic citation: "After careful consideration and examination of the patient, it is concluded that Mr. So and So, will require physical strengthening of his legs and rehabilitation to secure a more stable walking. This process will be carried out in our in-house rehab facilities. It is estimated that it will take about three weeks". And by miracle, almost with desperation, a lot of these patients are discharged after 21 days.

"Well then, it is to Powder-Bridge Home then." Said the social worker.

Moses could not understand why he could not go home. Except, he thought, he had been living under a tree in the middle of nowhere. What was happening to him? He was sharp enough to ask himself this question, but then he realized that he had not bothered to pose that question to anyone. All this time he had found no need to talk at all. Who would he talk to, what would he say? It was as simple as that.

28

Powder-Bridge Home is a licensed nursing home, like thousands of others, founded on the principle that eventually someone needs to be extruded from some medical facility, be it a psychiatric clinic or a hospital, or a primary rehabilitation center. On paper, they fulfill all the requirements that our society has placed upon these institutions. The physical grounds need to be clean of trash and rodents; there needs to be a general waiting room area, a kind of living-room for those visiting the inmates; there needs to be a staff to care for the patients and since all of them receive some kind of medication, there is a need for a registered nurse; there must be a room with some equipment that is advertised as a physical therapy and rehabilitation facility; there is a doctors' examining and treatment room; an institutional kitchen and a general dining room, and of course there are the patients' rooms – the inmates' lodging.

Powder-Bridge is located in the industrial part of Jersey City, just a few hundred yards from the docks, in a building that once had housed a furniture store. Its parent company had bought the adjacent building and made renovations to the space so that it could house one hundred and twenty-eight inmates, two per room. The patient bedrooms were located along two corridors, united at one end by the television room, the nurses station and two rooms, one used as an office and the other made, by necessity into a conference room, but frequently used by the social worker as her own office. Along each corridor there were thirty-two rooms, sixteen on each side. Two beds were placed parallel to each other and separated by a curtain. Each room had a bathroom consisting of a sink with two side cabinets for toiletries and a large mirror between them; next to them there was a standard toilet, like a toilet one can order by catalogue or buy in any plumbing store. Behind the nurses station were three complete bathrooms with showers that were used to give patients their supervised baths, also, the medical offices, kitchen and dining room. Across from these, there was a large waiting room, and through a side double door, the administrative offices and mail room. On the other side of the waiting room was a small non-denominational chapel. The waiting room was decorated in light colors, with framed faded color photographs of landscapes of the American West. Against one of the walls, there was a large glass enclosure, about seven feet wide and three feet deep, where some live birds were kept –patients seldom looked at the birds, on the account of being too ill– for the enjoyment of anyone capable and willing to look at them hopping incessantly from dry branch to wooden perch, back and forth.

From the outside, the building was adorned with rows of white plastic colonnades extending along the façade's brick walls. Three sides were devoted to parking for staff and visitors, and the back was reserved for loading and unloading supplies, trash and other deliveries. Save for the windows at the front of the building, there were no other windows on the premises.

On a Tuesday morning two men in brown shirts with a logo he could not read came to transport Moses from Jersey City Medical Center to Powder-

Bridge nursing facility. They placed him on a stretcher covering him with a cotton blanket and securing his body with orange nylon straps. He got to see the neon lighting along the long corridors as they rolled the stretcher towards the elevator and then was blinded temporarily by a ray of sun that had escaped a dense cloud covering over the coast that promised severe thunderstorms for later in the afternoon. Without any apparent effort they slid him into the transport van, securing the stretcher unto clamps. The ride lasted a few minutes through stop and go traffic and then he heard the latch unlocking the double doors and the two guys proceeded to roll him into his new home. There was a delay, or a wait, while the admitting staff checked that all the paperwork had been completed. Then, he was taken into a room with two beds. He was transferred onto one of the beds, the other was not occupied, in fact, it was not made at all, exposing a green neoprene or plastic covered mattress.

"Hey, Joe, whoa's goin be fo lunch?"

"I doughno, you deeside."

Those were the last words Moses heard from them. Those were the only words he had heard that morning, until sometime later when a young woman walked in and introduced herself as Nancy, the social worker. She asked him if he had family, but there was no point in belaboring the fact that he was alone in the world. Sometime later in the day, a woman brought a tray for lunch and placing it on the bedside table on rollers, said, "Good morning, I brought you some lunch" and walked out. He could hear the sound of a heavy cart rolling for a few seconds, then he heard the same voice, this time more distant, repeating "Good morning, I brought you some lunch". After a while someone came and pushed the table over the bed rails and manipulated the bed controls placing him in a semi reclining position so he could eat more comfortably. "My name is Jane, can I do something else for you?", she said and then proceeded to show him how to use the bed controls. "Well, I guess it is all for now", clipped the control to the side of the guardrail and left the room.

It was a long day for Moses, who had been spoiled at the hospital, occupied with physical therapy, doctors' visits, nurses changing his wound dressings twice daily, occupational therapy sessions, visits from nutritionists, social workers. Now, he was resting in a room with one empty bed, and an imitation window. On the other hand, it was a busy day for the nursing home staff. A new admission kept everybody on their toes. The system demanded filling literally dozens of pages of documentation, Medicaid forms, insurance forms, ambulance transfer paper forms, admission forms, nurses' notes, social workers notes, rehabilitation medicine notes, assembling of a clinical history and entering all or most of the same information into the computers. And of course, the new patient had to be seen by a doctor. The doctor, more frequently than not, would send his or her physician's assistant. These notes and any orders written had to be eventually countersigned by a physician, and one was scheduled for the day after. Nursing homes ran like well-oiled machinery, in a way, like a government agency, even though they acted somewhat independently, and some were for profit institutions. Like in most of these, personnel tended to become entrenched in their routines, like trains on their tracks. All forms needed to be filled, all i's needed to be dotted, all t's needed to be crossed.

At five thirty in the afternoon, a haggard-looking guy with short, cropped hair came into Moses' room bringing the evening meal. He noticed that the lunch tray was still on the table, mumbled something, lifted it up and placed the new tray on it. "Night meal", he said in a heavy accent, and then walked away.

Moses lifted the tray top and cherry-picked some of the food and drank the apple juice and the small carton of milk. He was tired and fell asleep without washing his teeth. He woke up sometime during the night. The lights in his room were off. Someone had removed the food tray. He needed to urinate badly. He made an effort to get out of bed, but the bed rail was too high and the mechanism to disengage it was different from the one in the hospital. He just could not do it. After a while, he just could not hold it anymore and let it go. He felt the warm liquid first around his crotch, and then soaking his buttocks and back, and the back of his legs. At the time, perhaps he was dreaming he was in the park, standing in front of a tree, holding his penis and guiding the stream towards the light-gray bark that was changing color as the warm urine percolated it thoroughly, but he soon was fully awake and realized that he was all soaked in urine and the urine was getting cold all around him. The bed sheet and blanket were sticking to him in an unpleasant manner. He called the nurse, but his door was closed. He doubted anyone could hear him. The dressing covering his foot was wet. He made a point of asking someone how to manage the side rails. It was difficult to tell if it was day already. He had not yet become adjusted to his new environment, and the room had a useless fake window, with the picture of a park with trees. The sky was yellowing from the heat generated by the light that illuminated it during the daytime, but he had not yet learned this trick. His body ached of being in bed all the time, and he had a desire to get out of the bed that grew stronger by the minute, like being thirsty in the desert with the passage of time.

Day two arrived abruptly with the flip of a switch. Through the window one could see the park and the trees –branches perfectly still– and the blue-yellowing sky. The fluorescents of the room were on. The bed next to Moses was empty. Moses's bed was wet and stinking of urine. His foot was hurting. Shortly thereafter, a woman brought a food tray and placed it on the bedside table on rollers, said, "Good morning, I brought you some breakfast" and walked out. A nurse came in and took his blood pressure, pulse and temperature, and then proceeded to push the table with the breakfast close to Moses. He tried the controls of the bed and was able to lift his head to reach the food tray comfortably. There was coffee in a Styrofoam cup, a small package with artificial powdered cream, some chopped fruit compote, and a serving of scrambled eggs. He cleaned the plate and drank all the coffee.

Sometime, perhaps an hour after breakfast, a nurse assistant came and walked him to the shower room. He was limping on the account of the foot wound, and the leg cuts felt tight under the soaked gauze dressings. He was seated on a white, one-piece plastic molded chair and the nurse gave him a shower with a hose connected to the showerhead. She had been kind enough to ask him if the water temperature was okay. He felt refreshed, and for the first time, his nostrils got rid of the fetid stench of old urine. At the end, the nurse assistant cut the dressings and washed the wounds with the shower at a reduced pressure. He then gave him a set of pajamas and took him to a room with a television where there were other patients in wheelchairs already watching the Muppets on the PBS station. At around noon, two workers came and escorted all of them to the dining room for lunch. He ate a clear soup and a piece of meatloaf with rice. There had not been an opportunity to elevate his leg or place it on a chair. He felt some pain. About two hours later, someone came and took him to his room. The empty bed remained empty. He found that his bed had been cleaned and there were freshly laundered covers on it. He told the assistant he needed to go to the bathroom. He urinated but could not have a bowel movement. He was helped onto the bed. He fell asleep.

Moses woke up listening to a man saying in a heavy accent, "Night meal" after placing the tray on the narrow table. Before Moses could ask him to roll the table over to him, the man walked away. Nonetheless he was able to reach it and brought it close by, finally positioning it so that he could eat the food before it got cold. It was fried chicken and boiled chopped vegetables with a small serving of peach preserves. He was tired even though he had not done anything all day long. His leg hurt him. He realized he had forgotten to ask how to operate the side rails and made a point of remembering to ask the next person visiting him. At some point, he woke up and the room was in darkness, save for the night light in one of the electrical plugs by the wall in front of his bed. He wanted to pee. He tried again to lower the bed rails but was not able to do it. He went back to sleep and had a strange dream. He was visiting a city he had never been in, yet he knew there was a place he needed to go. When he finally got there, there were lots of people standing by the sidewalk. As he got closer to them, one said, "You finally showed up. Here, put these on" and gave him a full fireman's suit, complete with a helmet. He put it on and was given a hose from one of the fire trucks parked nearby. He put out the fire and the people from the neighborhood shook his hands thanking him profusely. Then, in this dream, he was alone again, standing in front of the still smoldering ruin. In the morning, when he was woken up by the instant daytime and the immobile park landscape, framed by the faux window, he realized he was again all soaked in urine. His leg was throbbing. He was not feeling well. Someone must have been fooling around with the thermostat in his room; he felt chilled to the bone.

"Good morning, here's your breakfast". The voice came from far away. Moses could see a large female figure placing a tray with food over the side table. This time, he did not feel capable of reaching for it. He just lay in his bed staring at the window. The trees just stood there, not a single branch moving. No birds flying or hopping from branch to branch. He vaguely recalled that it was an illuminated lithograph, but it did not make sense. Why would they have a lithograph of a park stuck over a windowpane? He liked his park better. Why did they not let him go back to his park? He had his own tree, with shade and a view to the green expanse studded with shrubs and small square stones –curious why a park would be studded with these square stones. He knew that fieldstones were irregular in size and shape; the stones in his park were angular. Why? His leg was becoming more and more painful. He would let the nurse know about it. A park with regular stones? Could it be a cemetery? Had he been sleeping in a cemetery? He had once been in a cemetery, rather, he had passed by one. He had been a child and the woman that was holding his hand said that it was full of dead people and that during the quiet nights, one could see the dead walking around. Yes, one could tell so because the tips of their bones were like little lights floating in the air. And indeed, when the following year, he walked at night by the same cemetery, he had seen the little bright lights floating in the air, zagging and zigging like bees from here to there. He had been scared, but not terrorized. These were the dead saying hello to him in a friendly manner. He remembered he had felt some sort of communion with all those people. He had felt reverence.

The door of his room opened and an obese woman with a voice like a trombone picked up the food tray and said to him as she turned away and march through the door, "You better stars liking dis food, cause you ain't gotten n'other one". She could not possibly hear what he was trying to say about his leg. When he turned, he thought he saw a bird flying to a tree branch, but it turned out to be a fly over the window panel.

Sometime later, the social worker entered the room to ask him some details about his insurance. Her nostrils flared and her facial expression could not hide the reaction she felt on breathing the air surrounding Moses bed –the sweet and blunt odor of death. She called the nurse by pressing the switch clipped to the upper corner of Moses pillow, out of his sight. When the nurse finally came, the social worker walked to the entrance of the room, where the nurse stood like a guard with her arms crossed against her chest, as if reluctant to get close to her patient. Words were exchanged. Moses could not hear what was being said. After a while, housekeeping came and changed the soiled beddings.

When lunch came, he was able to ask that they place the table close to him and that he be positioned so as to be able to eat from the food-tray.   He ate the meat loaf with its crust of caramelized ketchup but left the fibrous green beans on the plate. He also ate all of the apple compote. He was awakened by the noise someone was making in his room. He said "Pee, pee, pee!" For the first time, he was helped out of his bed and into the bathroom so he could urinate. It was then, when he noticed that his foot was swollen and almost black. He showed the foot to the nurse assistant and she said she would report it to Miss McCaughly. But Miss McCaughly was too busy to visit with Moses. The nurse's aide had told her that he had a dirty foot. McCaughly made a point of checking what was going on with Moses later on during evening rounds.

Moses opened his eyes when he felt the fluttering of bed sheets as the aide lifted the blanket on Miss McCaughly's command. He had not wet his bed – not yet– and it was easy to tell that there was a brownish ooze coming from behind Moses heel. "I better let the doctor look at it in the morning", she said to herself.   Later, by the nurses station, McCaughly sat by the telephone and dialed Dr.

Kareem's telephone. After ten rings the answering service picked up and McCaughly left the message that Dr. Kareem should examine Moses's foot in the morning.

That night, Moses dreamt of the sea. He had been there, on a cruise, he thought. He felt the delicate swaying of the ship as his body responded to a minimal change in pressure on his skin and gravity massaged him accompanied by the gentle, rhythmic, unending sound of the waves split broken by the massive bow of the vessel. Next to him, was the love of his life. But who? He had known her for so long and loved her for so long that he had lost the boundaries between them. That much he knew. The two of them were swaying to the gliding hills of passing waves, breaking in phantasmagoric pale bluish crests of foam, like if a god-like composer or painter was moving their arms unendingly.

29

Moses is rotting on his bed. His memories are erasing in his brain. It was as if his life's history had been written on sand unaware that the tide of living was rubbing off the sentences with every passing moment. Distantly, music seems to create waves of fresh spring as if some goodness is filtering its way into the palace of desolation – sediment of goodness from the storm of institutional sloughing of society. Nothing has changed and all is slightly different and all because music is crawling through the crevasses of his door. And somewhere not too far away, in the dining room, they have collected most of the inmates –residents if you will. Some are in wheelchairs, some in regular chairs, some are keeping upright, still others dangle their heads, slumped to one side, or their chins propped against their skeletal chest. Some are dressed in hospital garb and others in colorful shirts and pants, daring color combinations that would wake up from their deep slumber the corpses of Lanvin or Versace. At some point someone must have thought that dressing the old and decrepit like clowns contributes to their happiness. Saliva drools from those too weak to swallow properly –or more properly those afflicted with Parkinson's disease– trekking the deep skin folds that point downward from the corner of their lips. There are a few tables that have been put together giving the appearance of a banquet table. At one end of the large room there is a piano. Not a grand piano, a regular stand-up model donated by the children of a previous patient that might have died with perhaps a hint of dignity, or more likely, the indignity of his or her death erased by time or guilt. The piano is oriented so that the person playing it can see towards the room, thus exposing its unfinished back, the un-lacquered wooden frame, the one portion not subjected to the same beauty standards of its white and black front. Only the head of the pianist is visible to the audience: short hair, black, peppered with gray and mostly white on the sides, over her ears. She is physically of medium built, not too chubby, a woman of about 45 years of age, dressed more in the style of a flower child of the 60's than a hermaphrodite flower of the 21st century. Her face is partially obscured by dark-rimmed glasses. Her eyes are fixed on the other musician present in the room, not quite close to the piano, but more mingling with the audience. She plays without subtlety in a manner that indicates she is used to playing for those that have been auditorily challenged by advanced age or one that guides others –less musical than she– through popular songs and ballads rather than lieder and arias. The other musician is a man holding in his right hand a three-ring folder with sheet music protected in plastic slips. His left holds a microphone that he keeps close to his mouth. His face is elongated, thin but not cadaveric. He is almost five-ten in height and his squares-printed shirt is unevenly tucked into his beige cotton pants kept from falling from his lean abdomen by a pair of red suspenders. His hair is combed from left to right across a large expanse of hairless cranium –a battle lost against the genetic laws of inherited nature. But if he lost the hair battle, he has declared victory about his voice. Not an operatic quality, but a nice healthy baritone-ballad-singing voice. He is also singing with an exaggerated rhythm adopted after performing in front of many sing-along groups that need that extra push as to not disband into chaotic randomness.

"*I want to wake up in a city*

That doesn't sleep

And find I'm king of the hill

Top of the heap"

Some of their enthusiasm is contagious enough to have motivated several of the residents to sing along; each one on its own tremulous key. Old Stella, dressed in a red and yellow kaftan, partially stretched on a wheelchair, her overextended right leg pointing immobile to the piano, her left leg flexed by a contracture, face drooping on the right by an old stroke, is singing along "I waann…nt sssleep…hing hill…thhe heeaf." Others are singing too –those that still can– for music truly is embedded into the deepest core of our brains, perhaps one of the last vestiges we lose before becoming barely alive or simply dying. Most if not all used to sing or whisper the song to their sweethearts decades before. These sing-along sessions seem to make a mockery of old people were it not for the fact that in reality, deep down, it is a most decent and tender act of sharing beauty with others. Here and there, now and then, we are still able to admit that sharing kindness is necessary within the confines of a nursing home. But, just like insects on a highway, the heavy trucks roll over those too slow to move away, the traffic too fast to notice a dragonfly batting its one remaining wing over the heated asphalt, so do those that work the corridors of Power-Bridge Home. The music will stop in about an hour. The incapacitated will be rolled back to their rooms. Dinner will be served and then, night will be declared with a flip of a master switch. Moses does not feel hunger anymore. He hears voices of visitors speaking louder than it is needed, reverting to a pattern more like addressing children. "Mother, so good to have seen you. Doesn't Sammy look good? I will come by next week", he hears in the distance the voice of an old man speaking in that fake bonhomie, adding that spin of happiness and hope, as if that lilt would bring light to the darkness of those too old or infirm to be able to care for themselves.

Doctor Kareem enters Moses' room. His neck recoils for an instant at the stench. He is 48 years old, of medium height and slightly overweight. He is bald with a fringe of black hair cut short, like a monks. His brown shoes are spotless and shiny, if one could see them in the gloom of the room. He has lived a long and fractured life. A childhood in Cairo and education in strict schools, he eventually made his way to England where he got his medical degree in Liverpool. Then, discontent with being treated as a small screw in the social medicine delivery of Her Majesty's Health Care System, he emigrated to America, passing his entrance examination as a foreign medical student on his second try. After two years of postgraduate training in general medicine, no longer being able to afford accumulating debts, he became part of a medical clinic that covers medical treatment in nursing homes. He is not resentful, but his attitude and dedication has been molded more towards filling the blanks on pre-printed consult formats than with treating the patient in a holistic manner. His speech is a mixture of Middle Eastern and British accents, even if somewhat softened by the twang of New York and Jersey.

Even at this level of medical knowledge, he knows that Moses has a gangrenous infection of his foot. Lifting the sheet that hides Moses body, he discovers a swollen, discolored, oozing foot. More so, he knows that it must be treated in a hospital environment. There won't be any brownie points earned by saving the system from some expensive treatment. Leaving it untreated will surely bring a medical malpractice claim to the practice. He quickly exits the room and heads for the nurses station. He writes a brief clinical note and orders for transfer to a hospital. After consulting his watch, he realizes he is late and needs to visit another patient in a nursing home on the other side of town. He leaves in a hurry.

The morning shift is completing rounds, making sure that all patients' rooms have been visited. Following rounds, the nurses begin their tedious task of completing the patients' charts –failure to do so may result in loss of accreditation should a review by Medicare/Medicaid personnel reveal such an omission. Doctor Kareem has left Moses' chart on the left corner of the elongated countertop that constitutes the nurses station desk and working space. It will be up to the next shift to discover the chart and find that the doctor has left medical orders.

Moses is running a fever. The bed sheets are soaked in sweat and sticking to his thinning body. He has not moved in the last day and is beginning to feel pain in his lower back. It eventually will become a large bedsore. For the moment he is thinking he is running away, that he can get away from his surroundings that stick to him like oily paint onto a burlap canvas. He is partially aware of the fusty odor that invades his nostrils with each breath as inexorably as the growing tide of an oncoming tsunami. Some far remote corner of his brain reminds him of what must have been the numbing, paralyzing, putrid all-encompassing environment that one would have experienced walking on the fields a few days after the battle of Waterloo. But had he been there? No, not possible. He had not been a soldier. He did not recall enlisting in Wellington's forces and for sure he spoke no French to believe he had fought under Napoleon's standard. Yet, he was familiar with the stench of death. But from where? He thinks he is remembering something, and yet, it seems so difficult to remember details of his life. Did he have friends? Was he married? Were there any children? He believes he is awake enough to know that there is something wrong with his mind, but not well enough to open the drawers of his memories. It is as if someone had shaken his head so hard leaving his thoughts all scrambled. The fine neural filigree that constitute the trillion connections that define a human being's self-awareness fractured when Sharon's face had shattered the windshield of her car, and the bones of her body had bent and cracked after the back bumper pressed upon her spine. Now, he seemed to live submerged in a swamp where there is no air to breath and where the only way out is by being still.

By the time the social worker is notified of the transfer back to the hospital, she knows the ambulance service and the system will respond by delaying as much as possible. It will be in the morning that Moses will be taken to the promised land. He hears the voices of the EMT guys as if he were inside a long tunnel. He feels he is moving yet he is not walking. The environment passes by him, walls, then street noise, and then the inside of what seems like a gray room. He hears sirens and his body is shaken by the bumps of the road. He wakes up at the sound of voices around him. There are nurses and doctors coming and going. Beep...beep...beep. He knows he is hooked to an EKG machine. "Can you hear me?" A person with a mask and a light blue paper garment is shouting at him. "Can you hear me? If you can, blink twice". Why would he blink when he can speak? Has he not spoken? What do they want with him?

When they lift the blanket from his legs, their faces cannot hide the revulsion, the concern, the final judgment. There is nothing to be done for that leg. No amount of antibiotics will ever control the purulent rotting of the advancing infection. Pus, pus all around, and swelling with darkened dying flesh. Amputation! Says the medical jury. "Let's hope that amputating below the knee will suffice", is the final verdict from the senior orthopedic resident on call.

There is no medical history. Rather, the only clinical history comes from their hospital records of a few days before. Those were the days when the jury had declared that their mystery patient could not stay any longer at the hospital and he needed to be discharged as soon as possible to a chronic care facility. When Moses had been transferred to the Powder-Bridge Home that offered shelter but never a home. Now, the interns and residents were confronted with the early returns of their selection. The administrator was called to sign a consent form for the incapacitated patient. The documents had been completed, the "i's" had been dotted, the legal gods had been appeased.

It took the surgeon 32 minutes to amputate the leg. It was placed in a basket, wrapped in blue cotton towels with more care than Moses had received during the last several days. Antibiotics were pouring into the antecubital vein. Now all that remained to be done was to wait twenty days and transfer Moses back to the Powder-Bridge Home. No blame would be assigned. No recrimination would come upon anyone. The angels of mercy would continue to brandish their swords, fulfilling their designated chores among the infirm hidden by a mantle of loving indifference.

Moses battled with sword and knife; he wrestled with the angel like Jacob had done three thousand years before. Jacob had a dream of angels going up and down a ladder to the heavens. Jacob had been left with a limp. Moses was having a dream, one so confusing and desolate and real, that only brought confusion to his mind. It was a dream that he could not tell apart from reality, a dream where only bad things were happening, a dream that left him with only one leg. But at the time, he only felt pain in that leg. The clean hospital bedding tented tight around his body barely permitted him to get his arms under or over the sheets. The constant howling of alarms and the electronic pacing of cardiac monitors' beeping served as an orchestral accompaniment to his *missa solemnis*, more like a caricature of life, more like a Philip Glass' repetitive two tone, minimalistic composition, torture was a dreamy nightmare alternated incessantly with a horrible reality.

How long was he going to last? How much time had passed? Days and nights were obscured by intravenous sedation. At one point a young doctor came to his room and announced, in an apologetic tone that he was going to insert a nasogastric tube so that he could receive nourishment. The question of course was why not let him eat by himself? Was he not able or capable or willing to do so? But the decision had been made by the higher-ups and it fell to the young medical student to carry the order. After all, it was item twelve on his scut-list. He slobbered the tube with K&Y jelly and began pushing it into his right nostril. The initial discomfort was soon replaced by pain as the tip of the tube hit the back of his palate, then came the gagging, the feeling that he could not breath as the tube took the wrong turn and slid into his trachea causing him to cough like a drowning man, and finally the correct passage into his stomach and the constant feeling that he had to swallow. The intra-gastric feedings began in a timely fashion that respected no time of day or night and with them, Moses' strength began to increase. At times, physical therapist came and helped him out of bed, and at other times took him in a wheelchair to their dominium, where they made him hop on the parallel bars on his good leg. Even Moses could notice that he was getting better, except that as he began recovering, he also became more alert to the fact that he was missing a leg, that the pain he was experiencing on that leg, was a virtual pain that occupied the exact same space that the empty space next to his good leg. For some inexplicable reason he knew he was suffering phantom pain.

After two- and one-half weeks of antibiotics the intravenous lines were discontinued and the nasogastric tube was also pulled out of him. He began eating by mouth. The whispering of the medical group that visited him twice daily informed him that something was being planned on his behalf. Hospital food is never very good, but

Moses distinctly recalled that he had not been eating this well for a long time. He did not have salt restriction in his diet and consequently everything was tasty. The morning eggs, sometimes western style, with green peppers and onions and tomatoes were memorable. The chicken at lunch was nothing to sneeze at either. Physical therapy came for him mornings and afternoons and forced him to walk with a crutch. Little by little he was getting to be independent.

30

It was on a Tuesday morning that they came for him. This time it was not the transport system to take him to physical therapy, this time, they put him on a stretcher and rolled him down the corridor towards the elevators and down to the first floor. For a brief moment he saw the sky and then just the bare inside of a stripped ambulance. No electronic monitors, no oxygen, just the metal casing of what many years before had been a top of the line first aid service on wheels. He heard one of the attendants secure the stretcher's feet to the floor and close the door. Moses suspected that he was on the way back to wherever it was he had come from; he was on the way to hell. After some time in heavy traffic, the ambulance backed up to the unloading dock of Powder-Ridge Home. Moses did not know if they put him in the same room he had had before his leg went gangrenous. By the time he was accommodated on his bed, it was past noon. The staff did not have him for the lunch schedule. He laid in bed hoping that someone would bring him a pair of crutches, but by the time the person with the dinner cart came rolling down the corridor, they had closed physical therapy. He was semi-reclining in his bed when they brought the food tray to his room. The attendant placed it on the bedside table and got it close to Moses. There was lukewarm water to make tea, a small container with apple juice, and a main dish of mashed potatoes and what looked like meatloaf. Moses ate what he could, but the food was not very appetizing and besides it was tepid by the time it arrived. After a while, he needed to go to the bathroom, and since he did not have his crutches, he called the nurse. When someone finally came to his room, he had urinated in bed. The nurse took him to the bathroom, giving him one shoulder for support. While he finished with his needs, the nurse placed a dry sheet over the wet ones. She had no time to make an entire bed, she had other patients waiting to be seen. She entered the bathroom and extending her arm helped Moses stand up. They headed for the bed, she shuffling and him hopping along. It was going to be a long night, Moses thought as he lay on his bed and after a few seconds began to feel the wetness seeping through the bed sheet that still was holding some of the sharp edges from the laundry press.

Soon the lights went out. It was officially night. The artificial landscape installed in the make-believe window became nondescript gray. There was enough light filtering from the corridor to give the room the aura of a crypt under a full moon. But there would be no Wolf-Man howling at midnight. Only the occasional sobs of one of the inmates, only the solitary notes of a repeating musical trope "nurse...nurse..." as in a bad Phillip Glass opera. Mary Shelley and Bram Stoker had it all wrong, there are no monsters in the wee hours of the morning. Perhaps they do exist amidst the marshes and swamps of European landscapes soaked in the blood of the thousands perished in wars long forgotten, but here in America, there was no need for them, here we have created even more scary monsters that do not have an odd appearance, they have no fangs, no blood shot eyes, here we have our monsters looking innocent, mixing with other innocent looking people, even worst, in a twisted turn taken by our society, we don't persecute monsters, instead we turn against our Van Helsings, creating a shroud of silence more inviolable that the thickest ramparts of the old castles. They don't have long capes to wrap around and hide their faces, we give them uniforms and pay them salaries and encourage them to care for our weak, our elder, our very own parents.

I somehow know that not all the people that take

care of patients are bad. In fact, I know otherwise –
but from where I derive such knowledge, of which I
am so clearly convinced to be true? All is a
mystery to me, Moses thought. Yet I know that
only a few are rotten among the precious many.
The problem is that, when it comes to healthcare
workers, often, ten good ones cannot reverse what
one incompetent caregiver causes. Sometimes
during a previous life, I had compared it to a game
in which a thousand people stand in line; their task
is to pass a delicate crystal vase from one end of
the line to the other without breaking it. I am
convinced I said it in front of a class –but why could
I not remember when or where? I had said that if
the crystal vase was passed smoothly along nine
hundred and five players and the next one dropped
it unto the concrete floor shattering it into a
thousand pieces, all the care and effort given by the
previous players meant absolutely nothing. The
precious vase is lost forever.

But what turns a good person into a bad one? Oh,
I know, some can be a bad seed from the very
beginning. We tend to believe, for the sake of our
children, the goodness of our children, that there is
no bad child. Well, even if it were so, at one point
that child grows and becomes an adult. Some of
those adults enter the health services system and
assume roles that put them in direct contact with
patients. And then, somehow, the good intentions

metamorphose into monstrous acts. Don't misunderstand me, thought Moses, I am not saying they go into murderous stampedes, entering nursing homes with automatic rifles clearing the place of their putrefying load. No, no, far from that. Their actions are more insidious, less detectable, but not necessarily less deadly. Take this as an example: Tomorrow, nurse Sharesse will, under instructions written at the hospital before they transferred me, remove the dressing from my leg stump. She has done it many times –removing a taped bandage– and will continue to do so for many more years after I am gone. What is so hard about removing a bandage? You may ask. Just wait, sit tight and watch.

There are moments in each one of us when one pauses and wonders about the paths we have been walking all along. And in stopping, we take hold of a little respite to perhaps wonder as to where we are heading. In such moments a person may dare examine possibilities of failures, of dreams never accomplished, of promises made and never kept. During such moments, we must be thoroughly honest with our selves, to the point of being cruel, if need be. It happens to most of us. As to when it happens, well, there is no telling. It may be totally unexpected: when we are confronted with an infinitely beautiful landscape, or during a moment of solitude, or during illness. It can happen when we are young and have time to remedy, to make corrections to our course, or it can happen at the end of our life's, when it is too late to make amends, when the only option left is regret and sadness after we see our life's as if we were watching a psychedelic film where there are not only images, but sounds and aromas, and emotions to be experienced again in an instantaneous, hyper warped speed that leaves us with an almost eternal aftertaste that does not linger in our mouths, but deep in our chests, in our brains, in our souls.

I pressed the calling button and no one has come! "Nurse...nurse! I have to urinate." I don't want to do it in my bed. Perhaps I can hop to the toilet. Where are my crutches? I know they brought them with me from the hospital. "Nurse!" No one is coming. Oh God, I really need to pee. I will try to get to the toilet.

A decision to be made and to be carried out. Like "let there be light and there was light". Except I am no God. It is morning. I can see the park through the window. I have a tremendous headache. There is a bandage around my head. I am soiled. The bed is a mess.

"Good morning. Breakfast". A man dressed in a

grayish, greenish uniform, perhaps two sizes larger than he needs, walks in bringing a tray. He places it on the narrow side table and hands me a paper. He says is the lunch menu. My vision is blurred. Did I use eyeglasses? I don't know anything of myself. It is as if someone erased my past. Clearly, I am an adult. I am not a child, and even if I were a child, I would be able to remember something. I have no linear memory of my life. I must have lived a life. The tray has scrambled eggs, coffee and powdered milk in an envelope, a sealed container of orange juice, a slice of white bread toasted and now dry; I eat some.

Now that I am more alert, I become aware that my leg is hurting as well. Time has been studied for decades if not centuries. Some say it is the fourth dimension. We measure time as something ethereal that happens between two events. It can be the tick-tock of the clock, or the oscillations of atoms. Now I measure time as the space between pulsing bouts of pain. And I visualize time travel as the oscillation of painful pulses between my head and my stump. *I am turning into a philosopher.* Nurse Sharesse enters and looks at me with an expressionless face. "I am going to change your dressings". She walks out of the room and returns after seven hundred and twenty-three pulsations have elapsed pushing a cart that bangs on the wall in front of the foot-end of my bed. On the stainless-steel surface there is a paper towel with scissors, clamps, gauze and tapes of various kinds. On the side there is a plastic bag with a biohazard sign stamped on it.

"We gets to give yours a bath after this", she says as she begins to uncoil the wrap from the head wound. The gauze over the scrape on the back of my head is stuck to the scalp, but she removes it with a single sharp movement. "Ouch!" I grin. I look at the gauze she just removed and notice that there is a piece of scalp attached to it. A sharp, constant pain supplants the dull headache, as if I was being burned with a hot rod. "Yous better take care of that heads of yours", nurse Sharesse says in a marked accent that I cannot place exactly. She now turns her attention to my leg bandage. She proceeds to work on it with the same jerky movements she displayed on my head wound. The pain I felt on my head is nothing compared with what I feel when she rips that scab from the edges of the wound. Blood begins to drip. She places some four-by-four pieces of gauze over the bleeding wound and reapplies tape. It feels too tight. How will the story end? I know at least what is coming next, which is more than most of you know about your own lives. In mine, sometime in the future, perhaps tomorrow or in two or three days, a nurse will come to remove the bandages and things will not look good. Skin was not made to be ripped away by an alienated nurse. Wounds need to be dressed properly and undressed delicately –too much to ask in this environment. A sealing clot is formed that conforms to every nook and cranny in contact with it, making a complex, corrugated surface, that when becomes dry, is difficult to separate without denuding the surface. In fact, careless removal of a bandage can form an ulcer and careless placement of a bandage can contaminate a wound, turning the healing serum into a purulent paradise of decaying tissues. This is what I see in my future. Soon they will bring lunch or dinner. I tend to forget.

It took three days for anyone to come and change the dressings covering my stump and my head. This time it was not nurse Sharesse. She has been busy with the patient that was brought yesterday to share the room with me. I have not been able to see him well and I don't have access to his clinical chart. I gather that he is a very old person, quite weak and with great difficulty in breathing. The mucus secretions in the back of his throat are abundant and very musical. The last two nights I spent counting how many gurgling breaths it took before he coughed the plug away. I miss the silence of the night interrupted by a water drip from the bathroom, or the incessant chat of nurses walking down the corridor always managing to bypass my door when I call for help to go to the bathroom. It is now official: I am a bed wetter, so now they don't even bother to come and help me, or to change the bed sheets. No, that is a task that awaits the morning staff. I am in charge of soiling the bed and stewing in it for hours on end. Last night I had an episode of loose stools and did not have time to hop to the toilet. I am afraid to find out what is happening to my wounds.

The nurse used some saline solution to soften the scabs attached to the gauze. She finally did it. It did not hurt too much. She applied some sap onto them and covered them again with bandages. I could not help to notice that she seemed worried when she left me. She was too nice.

The person sharing my room is not doing too well. They brought a suctioning pump so that the nurses can aspirate the secretions from the back of his throat, but so far, it has been done very few times. For me, when night comes, the cacophony of gurgling mucus illuminates darkness. However, lately, I have been concerned about a new thing entering my world. Once in a while I detect the distinct smell of rotting. I hope that it comes from my neighbor, and I fear that it is coming from me. Also, with all that wetness constantly surrounding me, my lower back is beginning to itch. I try not to scratch, but sometimes I just cannot help it.

Doctor Kareem comes to visit me. A nurse removes the dressings from my head and leg. He looks at them with the aid of a penlight. He tells me that I am not healing well, that I have an infection. He is going to order some antibiotics and wound care. It is not a long visit, but at least he came. At least the nurse spoke with him about my wounds. At least she cared.

31

I am experiencing another of those moments when I wonder about the paths I have been walking all along. It is a thought that occurred to me several days ago and has not let me relax for an instant. You know, one is walking on a path clearly marked as "To Water Fountain", the next thing we become aware of is that we are standing in front of a taxi stand next to a hospital. What happened to the water fountain? Were we not walking on such a path? Well, that poses a problem for me.

I have been very somnolent on the account of the infections that are eating my leg and my scalp. To that add the antibiotics that the doctor ordered for the infection and that effectively managed to exterminate most of the good bacteria I had in my intestines and now I have been afflicted with this uncontrollable diarrhea. But I am perhaps distracting you with unimportant details. Ah yes, I was talking about wondering about the paths we have walked during our lives. Perhaps it is a prelude, an anteroom to the feeling I have had lately, that my days may be counted. I know; we all have our days counted. We all live and we all die. An old story. But for you who are reading this book, dying is something that is not at the forefront of your mind, at the very forefront of your nose. You are not surrounded by the fastidious odor of decay —even worse, your own decay. But I, I can smell myself and I am rotting. Most of the nurses here appear to be blind and deaf to me. It is like watching cows crossing over a sand-covered field. They are herbivorous, their only interest lies in grassy fields, and they don't care for sand. I am sand to a cow. I am now so weak that I cannot turn myself in bed. It is up to the nurses and their assistant aides to turn me. The doctor ordered that I should be turned every two hours so that the wound on my lower back–bedsore– does not get worse. I suppose you thought the whole business was going to end with the wounds on my head and leg, but like the saying goes: when it rains it pours. With the running of my intestines I got really weak. I lost the strength to hop to the bathroom. I became completely dependent on the nurses. God knows I called them, I pushed that button, I howled their name when they passed by my room's door, but to no avail. I became the howling patient, the one every ward has disturbing the peace, the lonely wolf left behind by the pack, the one present every time you visit your parent at a nursing home and your ear gets habituated to it so that you can talk in that happy, smiling voice about trivialities. But the nurses have their rhythm and their tasks, and if it is not an emergency, they are not going to deviate from their routines. So, it was left to me to stew in my own excrement. With all that humidity, the skin on my lower back began to get irritated. At first, it was itchy, then it began to peel. Then a crust formed and it got infected. The crust became larger and larger. When one of the nurses finally looked to see why I was scratching my back, she discovered that some of the bones of my back were exposed. She called the doctor and when he came, he ordered that they put me on a doughnut ring and that they turn me every two hours –which was the original order to begin with before I began to develop the bedsore on my lower back. Do you see the circularity? Do you see that all is connected? That when it comes to taking care of those in need, actions or, lack thereof, have consequences? Sure, now it is me and you don't care. But tomorrow it can be your wife, or your sister, or your grandfather, and then you will care, but you will be complaining to a hardened system. These nursing homes developed their callouses on people like me. By the time you care, you will be facing the walls of Jericho and you will be missing the trumpets to bring them down, your voice alone will not suffice.

But I digress. I know, I was talking about getting lost on a life's path. I was wondering what kind of person was I. But to do so one has to know oneself. In other words, there must be images, memories, engrams of things and events one once lived. But I cannot remember too much. I vaguely remember an old man holding me by the hand and walking towards a shady tree. But why? What was he doing, who was he? The smell of onion comes to my mind. But of what consequence can that be?

We all have lived our life's. I am no child. Thus, I must have lived a life. Did I have friends?

"Nurse! Nurse! Someone please!" I think I soiled the bed again, but I am not sure. They put a curtain around my bed and when someone enters, they are dressed in a yellow paper gown and wear gloves. I think that it is so cumbersome for them that they try to avoid coming to visit me –like if before I began to rot, they visited me!

Anyway, I was thinking about having had friends. Perhaps when I was a kid I dressed up as a pirate and me and someone else went to a party. But it has been so long that it is a blur. I remember going up a hill. It was a green hill. At one point, we had to go through a low and narrow tunnel. I know I was scared. We would come out on the other side of the hill and kept going up until we could see the city extending all along the horizon. And there was wind. Yes, a soft, refreshing wind. Yes, there we were, but who is we?

I must have gone to school. I can almost see from inside my own eyes the blackboard and the teacher writing something on it. I was seated in the third row. I raise my hand. I know the answer. Yes, I know the answer! But what was the question? I remember the voice of the teacher, his prominent nose and the loose skin under his chin. I remember the unraveled threads on the right side of his white collar, and the unevenness of the heels of his shoes, as if he favored his left leg. I even remember that when he was by himself, he would grind his teeth softly, more like a habit rather than a sign of tension. I remember all these things, but I cannot see his face or my face.

I cannot possibly be an idiot. There are too many events going on inside my head and yet, as soon as I am about to zero in on one of them, it vanishes or it becomes nebulous. It loses its attributes as if I were looking through a windowpane fogged up by the vapor from my own breath that is blocking my eyes from seeing details. I see the forest, but I miss the birds seated on the tree branches. Like the other day, I remembered that I used to ride on the back of a pickup truck. It was a Dodge, green. I can feel the warm wind slapping my face when I lean to the side to see how far we are from arriving. I smell the dust from the road raised by the turbulence of the tires. The sun is intense, but not yet burning. It must be still early in the morning. I am a child, barely a teenager. I am wearing an explorer cork hat with a strap under my chin. We are driving on a dirt road with tall grasses on both sides. But who is driving? Where are we going? We must be going somewhere. No one goes nowhere. There must be a destination, a purpose. It is a weekend. So, I must be going to school during weekdays. I had some friends. There were some classmates. Yes, classmates; both boys and girls. I can't remember their names; I don't see their faces. It is as if with every piece of skin I lose, stuck to the bed sheets, there is a portion of my memories that is lost as well –and today I lost a big chunk. Even I could notice the reaction on the nurse's face when she finally, after many hours, came to turn me on my right side. Now I am watching the window with its artificial landscape: trees with green branches, on a sunny day, totally immobile. There are no birds flying, no insects crawling. There is no noise coming from these woods. Once in a while, there is a flicker. First, I thought it was due to some passing clouds, but then I realized it is the ballast in the fluorescent lights trans illuminating the poster. Society has now placed me and, by extrapolation, tens of thousands others, on our right side, to ventilate our rotting bedsores and to contemplate the passage of time by counting the flicks of fluorescent lights. In the meantime, a housefly walks defiantly across the wooded landscape, bringing all to ridiculous proportions.

I was wondering whether I had been, or rather, whether I am a good or a bad person. Did I live my life well? Did I hurt someone? Did I help someone? I know I must have had friends. But you see, to know the answers to these questions, one must have memories, and at the moment I am kind of short on that department. Does it matter? I mean, to know if I have done right or wrong? Clearly, I am going to die, and not that far from now. So, does it matter if I remember? And here come to my mind – am I crazy that I can remember these ancient words?– that in the Torah, God tells Moses to "*Speak to the sons of Israel, and say to them, that they shall make themselves fringes on the corners of their garments throughout their generations, and they shall put on the corner fringe a blue thread. You will have these tassels to look at so you will remember all the commandments of the Lord.*" In other words, remembering is important. Memories are important, even if when one dies, all memories turn into nothing. Yet, here I am alive and without memories. How can it be possible? And yet, I happen to know that the blue die required in staining one of the eight fringes, is derived from the *Hexaplex trunculus*, a snail that inhabits the rocks of the Mediterranean coast. Somehow, I know that it was the most coveted color of ancient times. And don't even ask me how I happen to know that depending on whether it is exposed to sunlight, it can turn from purple to blue. It is that blue that is demanded by God. And what is the reason given? It is to remind the Israelites about God's commandments. The emphases on "remind". And here I am, looking at a plastic imitation window with no memories to remember.

I live in the present, you may say, and my present is not very likeable. Yesterday, the nurse took another large piece of me on the bandages from my leg. I can now see the bone beginning to show up by the edge. They think I don't see, that I don't know, but that piece of hard bright straw is the bone of my leg. A life, in some ways, is like a traveler walking on a path up the mountain that occasionally stops and turns to contemplate how far he has traveled, or to look at the landscape from whence he came from. For most of you, that landscape is vast and as old as you are, but for me, that landscape is the room around me. It turns itself dark at the command of a switch and when it is morning, all is the same. All smells to the same mixture of rot, and wet carpet that never seems to dry up and bed sheets soiled by human sweat and urine and feces, and the purulent sputum that eventually comes out during coughing seizures.

Does it matter what I did to others and for others or what they did in return if these events are cloaked in a cloud of infinite fuzziness? Here is where that saying about the tree that falls down in the forest with no witness around achieves its full significance. Does it make a sound? Physicists will tell you that it does. That it is a physical event that involves energy expenditure and consequently has a given set of repercussions. But I am not a physicist, that much I know. Perhaps I am a philosopher, or even more accurately, I am a person. A person dying in a nursing home, and from here I can't hear the noise that my tree makes as it falls, and neither can anyone hear my own fall. My current home is a way station where people are placed for convenience to be taken care of during the transition between having been and not being. The problem is that most of the personnel that work in these institutions have learned to cheat death. They have moved the clock ahead so that we, in society's eyes, are dead when still living.

I began to bleed from the sore on my back. Perhaps a small artery was eroded by the rub of the bed sheet. It will be a matter of hours now before I don't even remember that, in fact, I have forgotten all about my life. How many times can a life be lived so that the scribe will record it accurately on the parchment of history? There cannot be any smudges. All that occurs happens. All is recorded in the universe with the precision of a diamond scalpel and the speed of light. Nothing can be lost and yet, here I am, taking perhaps my last breath and still wondering if I ever loved or was loved, if I ever played when I was a child. Was it all just a waste? Then, it will be a matter of procedure. The system will take over as if the beast is awakened by an inmate's death. Cerberus, eager and protective, will have its Hades' gates wide open. Efficiency will shine. The bed rails will be raised and a sheet placed like a tent over them to obliterate any signs that a human lies forever recumbent under them. The doctor, or his designee, will come and get from the nurse the time of death. But death almost never happens at that time. That is when the cadaver is discovered by some roaming personnel. And even then, death might have occurred sometime before. No witness to this tree falling. And as in the jungle, the space vacated by the tree will be soon filled with another one; here in the nursing home, after a quick detergent pass by the cleaning personnel, someone else will be given the opportunity to look at that artificial transparency of a park hour after hour, and perhaps one day, they may even get to imagine birds flying and playing coquettishly around the green leafy branches aided by the wind.

THE END